BASS

AND THE

LADY

BASS

AND THE

LADY

BY

KEN FARMER
&
BUCK STIENKE

BOOK #5 IN THE NATIONS SERIES
THE BASS REEVES SAGA

Cover by K. R. Farmer & Adriana Girolami

THE AUTHORS

Ken Farmer – After proudly serving his country as a US Marine, Ken attended Stephen F. Austin State University on a full football scholarship, receiving his Bachelors Degree in Business and Speech & Drama. Ken quickly discovered his love for acting when he starred as a cowboy in a Dairy Queen commercial when he was raising registered Beefmaster cattle and Quarter Horses at his ranch in East Texas. Ken has over 41 years as a professional actor, with memorable roles *Silverado, Friday Night Lights, The Newton Boys* and *Uncommon Valor*. He was the spokesman for Wolf Brand Chili for eight years. Ken was a professional and celebrity Team Penner for over twenty years—twice penning at the National Finals—and participated in the Ben Johnson Pro-Celebrity Rodeos until Ben's death in '96. Ken now lives near Gainesville, TX, where he continues to write novels.

Ken wrote a screenplay back in the '80s, *The Tumbleweed Wagon*. He and his writing partner, Buck Stienke adapted it to a historical fiction western, *THE NATIONS*—a Finalist for the Elmer Kelton Award. They released the sequel, *HAUNTED FALLS*—winner of the Laramie Award for Best Action Western, 2013—in June of 2013. *HELL HOLE* was the third in the Bass Reeves saga written by Ken alone.

Buck and Ken have completed thirteen novels to date together including the westerns.

Buck Stienke - Captain – Fighter Pilot - United States Air Force, has an extensive background in military aviation and weaponry. A graduate of the Air Force Academy, Buck was a member of the undefeated Rugby team and was on the Dean's List. After leaving the Air Force, Buck was a pilot for Delta Airlines for over twenty-five years. He has vast knowledge of weapons, tactics and survival techniques. Buck is the owner of Lone Star Shooting Supply, Gainesville, TX. As a successful actor, writer and businessman, Buck lives in Gainesville with his wife, Carolyn. Buck was Executive Producer for the award winning film, *Rockabilly Baby*.

ISBN-13: - 978-0-9971290-0-7 - Paper
ISBN-10: - 0-9971290-0-X
ISBN-13: - 978-0-9971290-1-4 - E
ISBN-10: - 0-9971290-1-8

Timber Creek Press
Imprint of Timber Creek Productions, LLC
312 N. Commerce St.
Gainesville, Texas

ACKNOWLEDGMENT

The authors gratefully acknowledges T.C. Miller, Brad Dennison and Doran Ingrham for their invaluable help in proofing and editing this novel.And a special thanks to Art T. Burton for his tireless efforts in researching Bass Reeves.

Published by: Timber Creek Press
timbercreekpresss@yahoo.com
www.timbercreekpress.net
Twitter: @pagact
Facebook Book Page:
www.facebook.com/TimberCreekPress
214-533-4964

DEDICATION

ACROSS the RED is dedicated to all writers of the Western Genre. With special notice to Louis L'Amour, Zane Grey and Edgar Rice Burroughs.

First printing - December 22, 2015

HISTORICAL FICTION WESTERN
THE NATIONS by Ken Farmer and Buck Stienke
HAUNTED FALLS by Ken Farmer and Buck Stienke
HELL HOLE by Ken Farmer
ACROSS the RED by Ken Farmer and Buck Stienke
DEVIL'S CANYON by Buck Stienke

SY/FY
LEGEND of AURORA by Ken Farmer & Buck Stienke
AURORA: INVASION by Ken Farmer & Buck Stienke

Coming Soon

MILITARY ACTION/TECHNO
BLACKSTAR MOUNTAIN - by T.C. MILLER
HISTORICAL FICTION WESTERN
LADY with a BADGE by Ken Farmer

HISTORICAL FICTION ROMANCE
THE TEMPLAR TRILOGY
MYSTERIOUS TEMPLAR by Adriana Girolami
THE CRIMSON AMULET by Adriana Girolami
TEMPLAR REDEMPTION by Adriana Girolami

TIMBER CREEK PRESS

CHAPTER ONE

WILD HORSE CREEK
CHOCKTAW NATION

"I'd keep my hands wrapped around that cup…unless you want to make that the last Arbuckle you ever drink," said the voice from the shadows at the edge of the campfire light.

The giant, dark-visaged man seated on a log near the ring of rocks surrounding the fire stiffened. The steam rose up from the tin cup into the cold night air as his right hand moved slightly down the side.

A shot rang out from the shadowy figure. "Unh, uhh. Not smart."

The cup spun out of the man's hand, splashing hot coffee over his bearded face, legs and arms. Some of the stout trail brew landed in the fire where it sizzled on a burning log.

"Ow, ow, ow, Gawd dammit!...Jesus Christ!" The man looked at his right hand which now only had four fingers. He glared over at the figure. "Who the hell are you?"

"F. M. Miller...Deputy United States Marshal and I got paper on you...Bosco 'Mad Dog' Walters. For larceny of horses, rape, arson, attempted murder and murder...You've been a bad boy."

The figure with long dark brown hair hanging out from a wide-brimmed, flat-topped black Stetson stepped into the firelight—a .38-40 Colt Peacemaker, with ivory grips, in each hand. "Stand up and turn this way...I'd be real slow about it, now."

The six-four, slightly paunchy man got to his feet, holding his right hand and moaning. "My trigger fanger's gone! You done shot it off! God damned law dog!"

"Don't think you're in a real good position to go to callin' names right now...slick nickel. Be a real shame to lose another one...or an ear."

He looked up as the six foot tall figure stepped nearer where more light illuminated under the big hat.

"You wouldn't do that, wou..." He looked closer at the flickering shadows under the wide brim. "A woman?...I got took down by a split-tail? Son of a green bitch!" He turned his head and spit into the fire. "I thought yer voice sounded kindly funny fer a man."

"It doesn't matter whether I stand or squat to pee...I'm wearing a Deputy United States Marshal's badge...and that trumps just about everything else I know...So, looks like I've taken this pot." She reached into the slash pocket of the long dark brown oiled-canvas coat, pulled out a set of steel shackles and pitched them at the groaning man's feet. "Put those on...now. I know you've had experience in doing that."

"I cain't...My fanger."

"I'd be for figuring out a way or you're going to lose your right ear...You got five seconds. Two...three..."

"Hey, hey, what happened to one?"

"Four..." Her steel-gray eyes flashed.

"Alright, alright!" Mad Dog reached down with his blood covered left hand, picked up the shackles, slipped one half over his maimed right and closed the shank. He braced it on his leg, put his left through and managed to snap it shut with his right wrist. "There, satisfied?...Now, you gonna do somethin' 'bout this 'fore I bleed to death."

"Don't know...might save Judge Parker's court some money, if you were to bleed out...I'll still collect the re-ward and the two dollars for serving the warrant...in any case."

"Aw come on...You cain't...I'll be good. Honest Injun...Uh, what do I call you?"

"Marshal will do just fine." There was a trace of forged steel in her voice as she pulled the flap of her coat back that served as

3

a rain slicker and a cold weather outer covering and replaced her left pistol in its cross draw holster.

The law officer stepped closer and pulled out a blue bandana. "Drop to your knees an' hold your hands way out in front."

The docile outlaw did as he was told. She stuck out one end of the large wild rag.

"Grab the end with your left hand." She started wrapping the cotton cloth around what was left of his index finger, and then around his hand and stuffed the end under the wrap. "Now don't move it around much and it might stay on until we get to McAlister.

"Marshal Cantrell is anxious to have a little word with you," said the dashing brunette with just a hint of a smile that showed her even white teeth.

ARBUCKLE MOUNTAINS

Deputy US Marshal Jack McGann—accompanied by his big white wolf-dog, Son—worked his red and white Overo paint down the steep slope along the side of Turner Falls. An eight-point buck was draped across the horse's rump—tied on by the long saddle strings behind the cantle—as they headed back toward the cabin.

A cottontail jumped up right under Chief's front feet. He shied hard to the right, stumbled and flipped over—head first.

BASS AND THE LADY

Jack was thrown forward in front of the tumbling horse and caught his leg under the saddle as the gelding went over. There was a sickening snap and McGann cried out in pain.

"Aaaah!"

The horse scrambled to his feet, the deer still tied on, but it had shifted to the left. Chief was further frightened by the antlers of the buck banging against his left flank and headed on down the mountain and toward the security of the barn. Son trotted back over to Jack as he was writhing in pain.

"Son of a bitch!" He tried to sit up and got high enough to see his lower left leg was bent at an unnatural angle to the right. "Aw, damn!…Go git Angie, Son. Go!"

The big animal spun around and charged down the hill, running around the larger gray boulders that outcropped and jumping over the smaller ones as he made a beeline to his home a half-mile away.

Angie McGann, Jack's wife, and her uncle, Winchester Ashalatubbi—who was not only the shaman of the Chickasaw Nation, but also a trained medical doctor—were sitting on the porch having coffee. They looked up as Chief thundered into the clearing and stopped in front of the big red barn. Son ran in right behind him, jumped the white slat fence around the yard of the cabin and stopped at the bottom of the steps leading up to the porch. He spun around in a circle and barked twice.

"Uh, oh," Angie and Winchester said simultaneously.

"Saints preserve us...something's happened to Jack." She jumped up, handed her twenty month old daughter to her uncle. "You watch after Baby Sarah...I'll follow Son. He'll lead me to me husband."

"Child, it would be best if I go. If he's unable to move, you'll never be able to get him back here and if he's badly hurt...at least I can treat him." He handed the baby back to his niece, stepped inside and grabbed his black valise that he carried his medical supplies in. Winchester seated his black, tall uncreased crown hat and snatched up Angie's Irish grandfather's shillelagh. "Got a feeling he may be up past the falls...Need to use this as a climbing stick."

"*Anompoli Lawa*, it's always wise ye are."

Angie often referred to the shaman with his Chickasaw name which meant, 'He Who Talks to Many'.

"Just common sense, my dear, just common sense...and it looks like it was a good thing I chose today to come by and check on Baby Sarah."

"Aye, that it is."

The native Chickasaw followed the big white wolf-dog up past the roaring falls and halfway up the hill. "You could slow down a bit Son, not used to climbing around these mountains anymore." The faithful animal stopped and looked back over his shoulder for a moment, and then moved on.

"Winchester! Over here."

6

He looked up the slope nearly twenty yards past Son and saw Jack, propped up on his elbow and waving his other arm in the tall grass. The dog reached his master and licked his face.

"Alright...that's enough Son." The stocky, mustachioed man laid back down.

"Well, I'm glad you weren't any further from the house than this, Jack. Where're you hurt?" Winchester asked as he reached him.

"Broke leg."

The doctor looked down at his left leg underneath his right. "Oh, my goodness, Jack. Right you are." He moved the top leg off to the side a little, got out his scissors and cut his jeans up from the bottom. "Well...at least it's not a compound fracture, but both the tibia and fibula are broken and will have to be put back in place."

"Wonderful, how lucky can I get?"

"But, I'm going to have to splint it before we try to get you back to the cabin."

"What do you mean, 'try'?"

"You're going to have to put your arm over my shoulder and hobble down to the trail by the falls...That's assuming we don't both fall...and that would not be a good thing."

"See your point," said Jack.

"Let me have your Bowie...I've got to cut some sticks for the splint."

Jack pulled his a razor-sharp knife from his belt sheath and handed it to the older man.

"Be right back." He reached into his bag an dug out a small green bottle. "Here, take a couple of pulls of this…it'll help deaden the pain."

He took the bottle from the white-haired shaman. "Laudanum?"

"Yep."

"Hate this stuff."

"Beats the alternative."

"What's that?"

"The pain you're going to experience when I set that leg."

"Cain't wait." He twisted off the cap and turned the pharmaceutical bottle up. "Gag."

"Another."

He did it again and made another wry face. "Why don't you just thump me in the head with that shillelagh?"

"I can do that too." *Anompoli Lawa* walked toward some willows growing near Honey Creek.

After he had trimmed the handful of three foot long branches, he cut the rest of Jack's jeans off at the knee and ripped the tough denim cloth into strips.

He handed him a piece of one of the sticks big around as his finger. "Here, bite down on this…Even with the Laudanum, this is going to hurt a mite." Winchester grabbed the back of Jack's boot and the top of his foot. "Look! What's that over there?"

"Huh," Jack mumbled with the stick in his mouth and looked off toward the creek.

The doctor gave his leg a sharp jerk.

A rumbling sound came from deep in Jack's throat as the ends of the thick willow stick fell from the corners of his mouth. He arched his back, fell back heavily, spit out what was left of the branch and huffed loudly three times. "Jesus, Mary and Joseph!...You tricked me!"

"Let's call it a distraction." Ashalatubbi started placing the splints evenly around Jack's lower leg.

They hobbled into the yard at the cabin, Jack with his left arm around Winchester's shoulder and the black shillelagh in the right.

"Woman of the house," McGann shouted with somewhat of a slur.

Angie opened the front door and stepped out on the porch.

"Saints be praised, ye found him." She stepped down and assisted Winchester getting him up the four steps.

"He has a badly broken leg. I set it...but I'm going to have to check it and put a cast on it. He's lucky the bone didn't break the skin...won't have to worry much about infection."

"I gotta g...go unsaddle ol' Chief. He's got a buck deer ridin' on the b...baaaack...Hee-hee-hee."

"He's already unsaddled, husband of mine...and I'll be dressin' the deer when we're done with ye." Angie turned to her uncle. "It's splifficated, he is."

"The Laudanum...Had to give him a pretty stout dose before I set his leg. He still bit completely through a half-inch piece of willow branch."

"We'll be having to send a telegram to the Judge. He was supposed to meet Bass in Fort Smith early next week for their next assignment."

"Your husband won't be going anywhere for four or five months."

FORT SMITH, ARKANSAS
JUDGE PARKER'S CHAMBERS

"Enter," boomed Judge Parker from his big cherry-wood desk when he heard the solid knock at the door.

"Mornin' yer honor." A huge black man with close-cropped hair and jug ears stepped into the office. His prominent mustache showed a touch of gray mixed in and partially covered his broad grin.

"Morning, Bass. Have a seat."

He hung his black Boss of the Plains hat on the Judge's hall tree next to the door and strode over to one of the wing-backed burgundy chairs in front of the desk and sat down.

"Bass, got a telegram the other day from, Angie..."

The big lawman shot to his feet. "Jack alright?"

"Well, that's the thing...No. He apparently took a tumble on his horse coming back from deer hunting. Broke his left leg below the knee. *Anompoli Lawa* happened to be at the cabin checking in on the baby. He got him home, set the leg and put it in a cast. The upshot is, Jack is out of commission for the next four to five months."

"Lordy, lordy, and we got us a stack of warrants to serve." Bass shook his head and sat back down.

"I got somebody to ride with you until McGann comes back. Hell of a hand with a gun and damn good on a horse...I'm told."

"'Nybody I know?"

"I don't think so...Deputy Marshal F. M. Miller from over at McAlester."

"Nope, don't know him."

Parker looked up at Bass over the top of his Pince-nez reading glasses with a wry grin.

There was a light rap on the door.

MCINTOSH COUNTY
CREEK NATION

"Put yer knee on his neck, Coop." Clifford 'Bull' Carter held the red-hot running iron between two green willow sticks and quickly turned the Rafter M brand into the Diamond M.

11

The stench of burning hair and flesh wafted through their nostrils as the smoke curled up in the cool morning air. The three hundred pound Hereford-Longhorn bull calf bellowed in pain until the barrel-chested, sandy-haired cowboy finished with his artwork—then bellowed again when the waddie split his scrotum with his jack knife, grabbed the testicles with his teeth, severed the cords and pitched the mountain oysters in a nearby bucket to fry up for supper. "Let 'im loose."

Coop looked at the third cowboy holding the legs down and nodded. Rail-thin Adicus "Stretch" Carter slipped the pigging string off the yearling's legs at the same time his brother lifted his knee from his neck. The steer scrambled to his feet and ran bawling back to the herd.

The oldest of the Carter clan laid the cinch ring back in the fire. "How many's that make now?"

Cooper Carter, the short, stocky middle brother, pulled out his tally book and a stubby pencil from his shirt pocket, licked the tip and made a mark. He counted the number on the page. "That makes twenty-seven steers and sixteen heifers, Bull."

"That ought to be purtnear enough to hang all you Carters."

The three rustlers spun around at the sound of the voice to see a man step out of a copse of cedar trees with a sawed-off double barreled scattergun leveled in their direction. There was a crescent and star Deputy United States Marshal's badge pinned to his vest.

"Gol dang it, Marshal Finch. Them was our critters that wandered over on old man Martin's place. We was jest markin' what was our'n."

Lank Finch chuckled at Cliff. "Not accordin' to Martin...an' the fact that there ain't no mature breedin' stock atall on yer place...Done checked...Kindly makes that sack have a hole in it, now...Don't it?"

"Air you callin' me a liar?"

"Well, I ain't in the habit of callin' folks liars...but in yer case...I'll be makin' an exception."

Cliff turned to Coop. "What'd he say?"

"He said he was callin' you a liar."

"You wouldn't say that if'n you didn't have that widowmaker pointed at my belly," Bull hissed.

"Meby so, meby not. We'll never know..." He glanced around the camp. "Where's that backward brother of your'n...How do you say it? Bar-zillai?"

"Yeah it is kindly hard to say them Bible names, but Ma liked it...We jest call him Biscuit...an' it's funny you should ask, Marshal...He's up in that big oak tree right over yonder..." He pointed off to Finch's left. "Got his Winchester trained on yer head...Now, granted, the boy is a mite slow...but he kin shoot the balls off'n a squirrel at fifty yards."

Lank didn't look around. "Uh, huh, an' I got some swamp land over in the Palo Duro Canyon fer sale, too."

13

A shot rang out and the short pistol grip Greener spun out of the marshal's hand.

"Son of a bitch!" Lank shook his hand to get the feeling back in it...and then he looked where the shot came from.

Barzillai 'Biscuit' Carter, the slightly retarded and youngest of the brothers, sat twenty feet up in the big oak, straddling a thick limb where it stuck out from the trunk. He held a Henry rifle against his shoulder with a big grin spread across his freckled face as he giggled.

"Now, what was it you was gonna make an exception to, Marshal?...I seem to fergit," Cliff taunted Finch.

Lank looked off at Barzillai again. "Danged if I kin remember...at the moment."

Bull snapped his fingers. "Oh, yeah, I got it...You wuz callin' me a liar...whilst you was pointin' that boom stick at me...'Pears as though I'm the tall hog at the trough now...don't it?"

"Yer holdin' the ace."

"But, tell you what...Me bein' a fair an' square individual...unlike some folks I know...gonna give you a chanct." Carter unbuckled his gunbelt and pitched it to Stretch. "You got a opportunity to whup me, jest knuckles and skulls...You win, we'll all four go in to the hoosegow with you, all peaceable like...I win, we go our merry way."

"What about me?"

Cliff chuckled. "You? You won't be goin' nowhere, Marshal...ever."

Coop and Stretch guffawed and Finch could hear the young one up in the tree giggling again. He looked the bear of a man in front of him straight in the eye.

"So, if'n I win...you intend to shoot me?"

"Nah...Now, that wouldn't be fair." Carter scratched the dark stubble on his chin. "Ya see, when I whup a man...why they usually jest wind up dyin'...right then an' there from bein' all busted up inside...Don'tcha see?" He held up his fists which resembled hams on the end of his arms.

Bull Carter stood well over six feet and weighed in the vicinity of two hundred and fifty pounds—a real giant of a man for his time.

"I still got no feelin' in my right hand."

"Well, Marshal, that jest breaks my heart...but that ain't really my problem...Now is it?" Clifford lowered his head and charged the one hundred and seventy pound marshal like a mad bull.

Finch waited until Carter was almost to him before he stepped to his left, pivoted and chopped the big man behind the ear as he went past with his good hand.

Cliff plowed face first into the dirt, lay there for a short moment—crawled to his hands and knees, shook his head and spit out a mouthful of dirt and grass. "Good lick, Marshal, but now you done gone an' made me mad." He got to his feet and slung a devastating backhand before he even turned around.

Lank sensed as well as saw it coming when the big man clenched his right fist just as he straightened up. He turned, ducked and almost got out of the way. The giant club-like hand glanced off the top of his head, knocking his hat flying and staggering him.

Carter roared and bull-rushed again, but with his feet a little wider this time.

The marshal, seeing that sidestepping wouldn't work again, dove at the pounding feet and rolled when he hit the ground. The big waddie's momentum took him over the spinning body and, once again, he kissed the ground with his face.

"Come on, Cliff, quit yer playin'," extolled Stretch.

This time, before he could get to his feet, Lank kicked him on the side of his head, knocking him around. He tried to kick him again, but the big man blocked his leg, grabbed the toe of his boot and flipped him back over to the ground.

"Yeah!" yelled Coop.

Barzillai giggled.

Lank scrambled backward away as fast as he could—it wasn't fast enough. Carter lunged over, grabbed him by the front of his wool vest and jerked him upright like a rag doll.

He wrapped both his thick arms around the marshal, pinning his hands to his side and started to squeeze as he lifted him completely off the ground.

"Ahhhhhhhh," Finch managed to get out as the awesome strength of the big man completely shut off his ability to take a breath. His eyes bugged out as he opened his mouth, but no sound came—he had no more air.

With the last of his strength, the marshal wrapped his right foot behind Carter and raked the back of his leg with his big rowel rock-crusher type spurs tearing through the coarse denim.

"God damn you," Clifford cried out.

Finch did it again, just like raking the shoulder of a bucking bronc for more action. Carter threw the smaller man aside and backed up, favoring his left leg. He rubbed the back of his thigh and his hand came away covered in blood.

He grinned and moved toward the marshal again, but this time slow and cautious. "I'm fixin' to pound you to a pulp."

"Come on, then…You've been sayin' that."

"Git 'im, brother," yelled Cooper.

Barzillai just giggled.

Lank kept shaking his right hand and flexing his fingers as he circled. Bull swung a right haymaker at the marshal's side, who danced back and flicked a left to Carter's face, smashing his nose. Blood spurted as the big man backed up.

"That ain't fair, you gotta stand still."

"Guess I musta missed that in the rule book on knuckles and skull fightin'."

Finch stepped in and popped Bull twice in the face with his left, and then swung his right elbow across his jaw—Carter went to his knees and spit a tooth to the ground.

Lank moved in again to throw a left hook. Bull—still on his knees—connected with the marshal's open left side with a wicked short right cross, stunning him.

Bent over, holding his ribs and trying to get his breath, Finch moved to get out of reach of the seething giant, but Coop threw a piece of limb from the firewood pile, spinning under his feet. Lank tripped, lost his balance long enough for Bull to catch up to him and hit him with a right and then a left to the side of his face, snapping his head over and another right to his ribs again.

The marshal toppled to his side—and didn't move. Carter kicked and stomped on him several times for good measure. There was no reaction.

"Want me to plug 'im, Bull?" asked Stretch.

"Nah, looky there, see them bubbles in the blood comin' out his mouth?"

"So?"

"I busted up his lungs, busted 'em real good…he'll be dead by sundown…'Sides, I give my word I wouldn't shoot 'im." Carter belly-laughed.

"Biscuit, climb down from there an' git the horses. Stretch, you grab the bucket an' we'll have us a mess of calf fries tonight. Coop, you git his guns, an' then go find his horse…We'll take the cattle over to Derdeen Creek bottom and put 'em with the others…an' head over toward Oak-ta-ha.

"What about him?" asked Coop.

"Leave him fer the bear and wolves. They'll be drawn by the blood comin' out of his nose and mouth…Now let's mount up."

Bull walked over to a giggling Biscuit holding the reins to their horses and stepped up on his big blood bay gelding.

"Couldn't find no marshal's horse, Bull, musta hid him out somewheres…Kin Biscuit have some stick candy, now?" asked an expectant Barzillai.

Cliff reached back into his saddle bags and pulled out a brown paper sack, opened it and held it out. His brother reached in and took one stick of peppermint.

"Thankee, thankee kindly." He nodded, giggled and started sucking noisily on it.

The sun cast long late afternoon shadows across the clearing where what was left of the branding fire had one tiny tendril of smoke slowly drifting up from the last of the hickory limbs.

The body of Deputy US Marshal Lank Finch stirred ever so slightly and moaned. His one good eye in his bruised and swollen face, flickered and finally opened halfway.

"Well, Marshal…been wonderin' if you dead."

Lank tried to focus on the sound and directed his blurred vision to a man in black. He was wearing a tall uncreased crown, black hat and sitting cross-legged directly in front of his face. "If'n you came to fight, yer gonna have to give me…me a headstart…Kinda stove-up…May have to git better to die." He wheezed out some foamy blood.

"Me see."

"Who're you?"

"Efv Catë…Red Dog, Creek Lighthorse. Christian name, Pleasant Underwood."

"Well…that's a relief…Thought you might be another rustler…I wuz gonna have to whup."

"Look other way to Red Dog, Marshal."

"Was goin' purty good till the big bastard…hit me."

"Uh-huh…Can sit up?"

"Not today." His one eye blinked. "Think ribs're busted on both sides."

"Uhhh, no good."

"Oughta see it…from this side." He groaned again.

Red Dog got to his feet, removed his broadcloth jacket, rolled it up and placed it under Finch's head. "Efv Catë make grass bed, stoke fire, fix broth. Then go get shaman. He help…you no move."

"Don't…don't have to say that twice. You mind gittin' my horse? He's…"

"Already got him. Him hobbled over on some grass. Saddle over under tree." He pointed with his head. "What called?"

"Finch…Lank Finch."

"Uhh, like tiny bird."

"Yeah…somethin' like that."

"Who you fight?"

"Bull Carter…Caught him an' his brothers…" He moaned low. "…alterin' brands."

"Me see cinch ring in ashes of fire…Carter bad man…likes kill with hands."

"Now you tell…me."

***

CHAPTER TWO

FORT SMITH, ARKANSAS
JUDGE PARKER'S CHAMBERS

The door swung open and a tall attractive woman stepped in. "You asked to see me, Judge?…Oh, didn't mean to interrupt."

"No, no, it's fine. Come on in, Fiona."

Bass got to his feet as she stepped into the room and hung her hat on the tree by the door. Her dark wavy hair hung loose, tied only by a turquoise embedded strip of latigo at the base of her slender neck.

Reeves noticed the twin ivory-handled Peacemakers she wore strapped around her slim hips—in cross-draw.

"Bass, this is Fiona May Miller…Deputy Marshal F. M. Miller…Fiona…Bass Reeves."

Her steel-gray eyes twinkled as she walked quickly over to the chairs with her hand out and a big smile. "Marshal Reeves, I've heard so much about you. I'm very happy to finally meet the indomitable marshal...You are a legend and an inspiration, sir."

An embarrassed and dumbstruck Bass stuck out his hand. "Uh, yes, Ma'am...uh, Marshal...Uh, thank you fer yer...uh, kind words." He shot a quick glance at a grinning Parker. "It's, uh, a pleasure to meet you, too."

She pumped his hand twice, and then let go.

"That's a real grip you got there, uh, Ma'am."

Fiona nodded. "When I saw the size of your hand, I figured I needed to give you a real firm one...or I might not get my hand back...'Course, since we wear the same badge, it pays to create respect from the get-go. Right?"

"Yes, Ma'am...Miz Miller. You got that right...I'd say we only git one chanct to make a good first impression."

"Call me Fiona, please...Ma'am was my mama."

It was his turn to nod. "Folks...friend and foe alike, mostly just call me Bass." He grinned a big toothy smile. "Well, sometimes the malefactors have other names for me...usually not too complimentary."

"I've heard that, too." She chuckled. "You should hear some of the things the riffraff and ne'er-do-wells call me...but they don't make a habit of it...If you know what I mean." Her eyes twinkled again.

Bass appraised her favorably and nodded his head.

"Please sit down, if you would." Judge Parker indicated the chairs in front of his desk.

Bass waited until Fiona sat, then he took his seat, still looking a mite uncomfortable.

Parker smiled one of his rare smiles. "Bass, you look like your collar is a little tight."

He tugged at his cravat. "Uh, no sir…Just a tad lost fer words right now. Ain't never worked with a woman afore…Not sure what my Nellie Jennie is goin' to say."

Fiona giggled, and then looked Bass straight in the eye. "Tell her not to worry, Marshal, I take my job as seriously as I've heard you do…I'm not just a woman…I'm a Deputy United States Marshal…and by the way, I've never worked with a man of color before either."

Now it was Bass' turn to chuckle. "Good point, Fiona. I think we be gittin' along jest fine. I trust you know how to use those irons on yer hips there?"

"Oh, I get by, Marshal." She smiled, showing her even white teeth. "I get by."

"Which hand, right or left?"

"Yes."

"Yeah, me too." He grinned. "You kin call me Bass…we might marshal each other to death."

Parker cleared his throat and they both looked over at the big bearded man. "If you all are through getting acquainted…Bass

BASS AND THE LADY

I'm afraid I have some more bad news...Your eldest son, Bennie, caught his wife with another man last week. He shot and killed her and is now on the run...The marshal left a warrant with me for him. I'm going to send it over to Bud Ledbetter in Muskogee...I just wanted you to know."

Fiona looked over at Bass. He showed no emotion at all, but she did notice a slight twitching of his jaw muscles and his already dark eyes had taken on the look of obsidian.

Reeves locked eyes with the Judge. "No, sir. Not Bud's job...It's mine. Bennie is my son...It's my responsibility to bring him in." He leaned over and held out his hand for the warrant.

"Are you sure, Bass? You don't have to do this. I'm told he's hiding out in the Shawnee Hills. I'm sure Marshal Ledbetter..." He looked at Reeves slowly shaking his head. Parker nodded and placed the document in his hand.

MCINTOSH COUNTY
CREEK NATION

Red Dog rode into the clearing with another older man in similar garb—black three-piece suit, blue striped collar less shirt and black tall uncreased crown hat with the traditional Creek multicolored wide hat band. The Lighthorse stepped off his buckskin and took the reins to the white-haired man's bay while he untied a black leather satchel from the saddle.

25

Underwood hitched both horses to a tree limb, loosened their cinches and they walked over to the dying fire.

Lank blinked his one good eye but made no move to get up.

"Took you long enough...you go by way of Tulsa?"

"At least he can talk...that is good sign," said the older man.

"Lank Finch, this is Doctor Alexander Harjo our medicine maker and shaman...also goes by Talof Harjo or Crazy Bear," said Pleasant.

The marshal groaned. "Crazy Bear?...Cain't say I'm too happy to hear that name."

"How so? Crazy Bear is much revered Creek name. I kept part for my Christian name...Harjo."

"That mean bear?"

"No, mean crazy or joker. All same...Why you not happy to hear name?"

"Fought one once."

"Injun?"

"No, bear...He was crazy. Kept runnin' in circles an' then...then would run at me."

"You kill?" asked Pleasant.

"Naw, put six rounds in him, pissed him off and he left...One tough son of a bit...ch." Lank groaned again.

"Look like you do much fightin'. You like fight?"

"Not really...but sometimes it beats a bullet."

Alexander handed his hat to Red Dog. "Build up fire. Need make compresses."

Underwood nodded and walked off to gather more firewood as the medicine man knelt down, unbuttoned the marshal's vest and store bought shirt, and then eased the suspenders off his shoulders.

"Ah-ah-ah."

Harjo studied the sides of his chest—both were black from his armpits to the top of his hips. He slowly and carefully ran his fingertips along the ribs.

"Ahhh, Jesus Doc, feels like you're doin that with yer foot."

"No, that already been done. Can see heel mark on left side."

"Ummm…Not surprised. Thought he was tryin' to stomp out a grass fire."

The elder man leaned over and held his right ear to Lank's chest in the center. "Breathe big."

"Cain't."

"Breathe much as can, then." He listened for a few moments, moved his ear to another location and listened again. The shaman moved several more times and finally set back up. "Uhhh, got good news and got bad news."

"What's the bad news?"

"Several ribs broken both sides, much bruising."

"An' the good?"

"Not go in lungs…But, you no can move for a week…they could yet. I make poultice…You no laugh, cough and never no sneeze…Bring much pain."

"Yeah, wadn't figurin' on it…What about the blood comin' from my mouth? Thought it was my tongue, but there's more."

"Bruise chest, stop soon." The old man got to his feet and turned to Red Dog building up the fire. "Got bone meal in bag, *Efv Catë*, make him more broth. I get what needful for the poultice." He fished out a wooden bowl and a small leather pouch from his saddlebags, turned and headed toward nearby Grass Creek.

After Lank drank what broth he could, *Talof Harjo* returned to camp. He sat cross-legged close to the fire, sprinkled some powder from the small leather pouch into his wooden bowl on top of what he had gathered down at the creek. Picking up a stick that was by his foot, he stirred the mixture, added a bit of hot water from a pot and stirred some more.

"Ready now. *Efv Catë*, bring deerskin from saddlebag." He started smearing the black goop on Finch's ribs in thick layers with his fingers.

"My God, Doc, what is that stuff?…Smells like somethin' dead."

"Not dead…yet. But if *torwv hvtke* not be still, maybe soon be."

"What's *tor-v hv-tke*?"

"White eyes."

"Oh."

BASS AND THE LADY

The medicine maker placed the soft deerskin over his chest, covering all of the poultice.

"I think I know why that black mud stuff works," said the marshal as he wrinkled up his nose.

"How so?" asked Red Dog.

"It smells so bad you have to hurry up and heal over just out of self defense."

"That one way," said Harjo. "Now we have some coffee."

"What about me?"

"No, you sleep now...Send Red Dog into town for more supplies tomorrow."

CHECOTAH
CREEK NATION

Bass and Fiona jog trotted their horses down the middle of Front street in the small agricultural community. She held the lead rope to a star-faced dark sorrel with a disgruntled man in the saddle—hands shackled to the saddle horn. Banners were displayed across the street and on many of the store fronts signifying a county fair was going on.

"What kinda name is Fiona...you don't mind me askin'?"

She glanced at Bass out of the corner of her eye. "Gaelic."

"Beg pardon?"

"Old Irish...Means 'white' or 'fair'."

He shook his head and smiled. "Well, that works. Jack's wife is Irish...You'll like her."

"Looking forward to meeting her and Jack one day." Fiona looked around as they slowed their horses to a walk down the street. "This is where you took down the Larson gang and captured Ben Larson, isn't it?"

Bass just nodded and glanced around. "Growed a mite."

"Glad Sheriff Waters back at Cowlington was able to take those whiskey peddlers off our hands."

He nodded again. "He owed me a favor anyhoo...had already scheduled a trip up to Sallisaw to put some other nabobs on the train to Fort Smith...Said Marshal Black was to meet him there. Now if'n we kin just drop off this yahoo, we kin git on 'bout our rat killin'."

"How many more warrants do we have not counting the one on your..."

"Two," Bass cut her off.

She remained silent for awhile knowing the big man was still sensitive about the subject of his son.

He glanced over at Chick's Mercantile as the memories of one of the most violent gun battles he had in his career flooded his mind. Four men dead—Wes Larson, Kell Brophy, Johnny Hawkins, Comanche Bob—and Jack wounded, all in less than two minutes. "Right there's where Wes Larson died." He pointed to the front of the store.

"My, my." Fiona tried to picture the fight.

They drew rein in front of the Blue Bird Cafe.

"How's about somethin' besides trail chow?"

"Thought you'd never ask." She had a big grin on her face.

As they tied up to the hitching rail and loosened their mounts girths, a red-haired young man around twenty in a dark green bowler and a light gray vest with a Deputy City Marshal's badge penned on the front, stepped out of the restaurant.

"Marshal Reeves!" The young law officer stuck out his hand.

Bass had a puzzled look on his face. "Howdo...I know you?"

He whipped off his hat. "Yessir, I'm Bradley Porter...Brad fer short...I seen the fight ya'll had with the Larsons!...You give me your boot heel with the bullet from Ben Larson in it...Still got it!" He grinned proudly. "You're the reason I decided to go into law enforcement."

Bass looked at his shiny brass badge, grinned and shook the boy's hand again. "Well dog my cat, son...You've changed some." He appraised the strapping young man up and down.

"Yessir, been most twelve years."

"Huh, guess it has at that...Oh, this here's Deputy Marshal F. M. Miller." He nodded his head toward Fiona.

"Wow...a woman marshal?"

She smiled as she shook his hand. "So they tell me."

He glanced at the twin cross draw Colts strapped around her hips and then at the black lindsey-woolsey vest with a crescent and star Deputy US Marshal badge with IT in the center penned to the front. The buttoned vest accentuated her small waist and the form-fitting black canvas pants with the riding leather seat and inner leg inserts left no doubt she was a woman.

She had removed her long dark brown oilskin top coat and rolled it up behind her cantle with her soogan. Her white button-up shirt was remarkably clean—considering the three days they had spent on the trail—and her bright gray silk neck scarf seemed to match her eyes.

"The food still good in the Blue Bird?"

"Oh, yessir, Marshal. Miss Fanny sets a table you won't soon forget."

"That's good…Kindly tired of trail chow."

"Are you complainin' about my cooking, Bass Reeves?"

He shot her a grin. "No, M…uh, Fiona, it's jest we're a bit limited with what we kin carry. Don'tcha see?…Been hankerin' fer a mess of fried chicken, cut corn, smashed taters 'n sawmill gravy with a big jug of fresh buttermilk."

"Mmmm…well, that does sound good, doesn't it?"

Brad had a big smile on his face. "I do believe that's her special for the day…I'm sure Miss Fanny will be happy to see you again."

Brad, you mind seein' to our prisoner here?" He pitched him the key to the shackles, and then pulled the executed warrant from his coat pocket. "One Buford Pauley, wanted for three counts of larceny of horses, one of armed robbery an' two of whiskey peddling…they's a two hundred dollar re-ward on him."

"Oh, yessir, seen the dodger on 'im just the other day…And we just happen to have a vacancy." He stepped over to the man's horse, unlocked his cuffs from the saddlehorn and dragged the recalcitrant outlaw from the saddle.

"Hey, don't I git nothin' to eat?"

"You'll eat when I say you can." There was a touch of steel in the young lawman's voice.

Bass looked back over his shoulder and nodded. "You'll do…Brad, you'll do." He swung the door open and stepped aside. "After you, Ma'am."

"What have I told you about calling me, Ma'am?"

"Uh, yessum, uh, Fiona." He winked at Bradley.

She swatted him across the chest with the back of her hand. "I saw that."

MCINTOSH COUNTY
CREEK NATION

Red Dog stoked the fire and added a couple of hickory branches broken into short lengths. He set the coffee pot on a flat rock close to the blaze. "Arbuckle ready soon."

Link stirred and moaned low. "Unnn…Think I hurt more today than I did yesterday."

The medicine maker strode into the camp with a large handful of leaves and strips of peeled bark. "You drink tea, Crazy Bear make, feel better soon." He put the vegetation in a

33

pan and poured some water from his canteen on top and set it next to the fire.

"You mean them leaves and bark will make me better?" wheezed out Lank.

"No, not say make better...say make feel better. This white willow bark...make pain go hide...Only time and *Chihoa-bia-chee* make better."

"*Chihoa-bia-chee*?"

"Great Spirit."

"Ah...Well, whatever you say...Kin I have some of that coffee this mornin'?"

Crazy Bear nodded. "Then have tea."

"Good. Kin Red Dog bring some meat? I'm hungry enough to eat a folded tarp...Needful for somethin' 'sides yer bone broth."

"No. What go in must come out...No good. Red meat come out slow...hard. Strain much...Be bad as sneeze."

"Oh, believe I understand...You got a point."

"Red Dog will bring makin's for soup. Very good."

"Ya'll don't eat dog, do you?"

"Paugh! Comanche eat dog. Mvskoke Creek eat boar, deer, bison, turkey, squirrel, rabbit and fish...never dog or snake."

"That's good to know...what kin I eat?"

"Corn...We believe as long as Indian can eat and drink *osafki*, he will not go dead...I make *osafki* for you."

BASS AND THE LADY

CHECOTAH
CREEK NATION

Bass and Fiona headed down the boardwalk toward the Blue Bird Cafe from the Perryman Hotel where they spent the night. They passed a large vacant lot festooned with red and white banners and a big booth with a number of Winchesters lying on a counter. A sign underneath read:

CHECOTAH TURKEY SHOOT.

"Oh, let's stop. Are you any good with a Winchester?"

"I get by," responded Bass.

She pulled him over to the counter by his elbow. "How much to enter?" She asked the rotund man behind the counter with a big black cigar between his jaw teeth.

"Fifty cents, Ma'am, fer the two hundred yard target…Three shots. All bullseyes git a breakfast fer two at the Blue Bird."

She laid two quarters on the counter, picked up a Winchester and handed it to Bass. "Here you go Marshal. Give it a go."

"Wait a minute," said the barker. He looked at the badge on his vest and then at his dark eyes. "You wouldn't be Bass Reeves, would you?"

He glanced over at Fiona and then back. "I would."

He reached over and took the rifle from his hands. "Uh, sorry Marshal. Heard about you…They say you never miss. Cain't let you shoot. Wouldn't be fair to the others."

She looked back at him and grinned. "You get by, my foot."

Bass just shrugged.

Fiona turned to the barker. "How about me? You already grabbed my fifty cents."

He took the cigar out of his mouth and grinned. "Well shore, lady. Just cain't let Marshal Bass Reeves shoot...His reputation precedes him." He handed her the Winchester and three rounds. "Have at it."

She took the .44-40 cartridges and slipped them past the loading gate, looked down the range at three six inch white saucers propped up on a row of oat straw bales, stuck a wet finger up into the air and nodded.

In one smooth motion, she levered a round in the chamber, brought the rifle to her shoulder and fired the three rounds as fast as she could work the lever. The three plates shattered almost at the same time.

The cigar fell from the man's mouth as his jaw went slack. "Good God in Heaven," he whispered.

Fiona handed him the rifle and held out her hand for the breakfast tickets. He grinned, shook his head and forked them over. "Ain't never in my life seen the like...Who'd a thunk."

She nodded her head, took the tickets, grabbed Reeves' arm and headed toward the Blue Bird. "Breakfast is on me, Marshal."

He looked at her with some degree of admiration. "Yer purty handy with that long gun."

Her gray eyes twinkled. "Oh, I get by."

The Blue Bird Cafe was permeated with the mouthwatering smells of bacon frying, pancakes, buttermilk biscuits and fresh coffee as they finished their breakfast.

Bass took a sip of his third cup of the black brew. "You be *Missus* F. M. Miller...what does yer husband do?"

"I'm a widow." She paused and stared out the front window a moment. "We owned a store in Tahlequah...Miller's Merchantile...My husband was Frank Miller...he was half Cherokee...His mother's mother had come over *Nunna daul Tsuny...*"

"The trail where they cried," interrupted Bass.

She nodded. "They left from their home in east Tennessee known as Great Tellico...I think it's called Tellico Plains today. The word Tahlequah is for a type of red-topped wild grain that grew back there...Anyway, one day, almost two years ago now, an outlaw on the scout came in and robbed us...As he was leaving with all our cash, he stopped at the door, turned around and shot Frank in the heart...in cold blood...right...right in front of me." She took a breath. "He said, 'Hate half-breeds,' spat on the floor, went out the door, mounted his horse and rode out of town...pretty as you please."

"I'm powerful sorry, Fiona...Know who he was?"

"I found out later when I was at the sheriff's office going through his wanted posters and saw a sketch of his face...he had made no effort at hiding it plus he had what looked like a knife scar from his left ear to the point of his chin…He was a full blood Cherokee named Cal Mankiller…An apt name, don't you agree?"

Bass nodded and got a wry smile. He reached in his coat, pulled out the two remaining warrants and handed them to her. She looked at the first, shuffled it underneath, stared at the second for a moment and looked back up—her eyes took on a glint of steel.

"This is why I became a law officer. I've been hunting this trash since I became a deputy. I swore I would get him…but I have to do it legal. I'm no vigilante or bounty hunter…but God as my witness…I will see the man dead." She looked hard at Bass' eyes. "We catch up to him…He's mine," she hissed.

An Indian entered the cafe, looked around, spotted Bass and walked over. "Deputy Porter said might find Marshal Reeves here…me Creek Lighthorse Pleasant Underwood."

Bass got to his feet, glanced at the brass shield penned to his vest that simply read, *Indian Police* along with a bow and arrow, and stuck out his hand. "Bass Reeves…an' this here's Marshal Miller."

Red Dog removed his hat and nodded. "Ma'am."

"Wouldn't call her 'Ma'am'…she might hurtcha." Bass grinned. "Goes by Fiona er F.M."

Pleasant almost smiled and nodded again. "Fi-o-na."

"Pleasant."

"Me also go by Red Dog."

"Have a sit…. Efv Catë." Bass pointed to a chair. "Coffee?"
He shook his head. "You speak *Mvskoke*."

"Some."

"If he says 'some' or 'I get by', you may rest assured he probably knows all there is to know about it," said Fiona.

Bass arched an eyebrow at her.

Red Dog nodded. "Pickin' up supplies for Nokose Harjo. Got hurt marshal down near Grass Creek."

"I know Crazy Bear…Good medicine maker," said Bass.

"Shot?" asked Fiona.

He shook his head. "Him hurt inside…break ribs. Catch *kolowa* waddie Bull Carter changin' brands on cattle. Him much bad man. Them fight…Marshal lose. You come."

"*Kolowa* waddie?" Fiona was puzzled.

"Large hairy rustler," replied Bass as he got to his feet.

GRASS CREEK
MCINTOSH COUNTY

Red Dog led Bass and Fiona into the clearing near the creek. They dismounted, tied up and walked over to the fire—Crazy Bear's back was to them. He had propped the marshal up with his saddle as a support so he could breathe better and was handing him a cup of willow tea.

"Bring supplies and Marshal Bass Reeves, Nokose Harjo."

The old medicine maker turned around. "*Shee-ah*, Marshal Reeves, is good to see you again."

"*Shee-ah*, Crazy Bear, it has been too long. The moon has slept many times."

The grasped each other's forearms and shoulder as was the Creek custom.

"Who do you have here?" Bass leaned around the old Indian. He stepped aside to reveal the injured marshal. "Name is…"

"Lank!" Fiona blurted, stepped quickly over to him and knelt down.

"Sis! What are you doin' here?"

She leaned over to hug him.

"Ah, ah, easy now…Kinda stove up."

Fiona kissed him on the cheek and held his left hand in both of hers.

"Sis?" Bass' eyes went wide. "This marshal is yer brother?"

She turned her head and nodded. "Landford Finch, I couldn't say that when I was little, so I called him Lank…My maiden name is 'Finch'."

"Thought you were workin' with Marshal Cantrell over to McAlister."

She turned back to her brother. "I was, but the Judge assigned me to Bass here until his regular partner is back on his feet."

"Jack git shot agin?"

Bass grinned and shook his head. "Nope, broke leg. Has to stay to the house fer four er five months...got saddled with yer sister here."

"Saddled? Now you listen here, Bass Reeves..." Her eyes flashed as she stood up and backhanded him across the chest.

He smiled and held up both of his huge hands. "Jest joshin' Fiona. Anybody kin shoot like you, I wanna keep on the good side of."

"That is a gurandamnteeyou fact. Fiona kin shoot circles around me and I ain't no slacker...She's got a special eye...and damn quick with them Colts, too."

"I kin believe that." Bass squatted down. "Now, you want to tell us about it?"

"...and that was about the size of it. Reckon I bit off more'n I could chew...but didn't see as I had 'ny choice in the matter at the time."

"Bull Carter most usually leaves them he fights dead," said Red Dog.

"Reckon he thought I wuz agonna die...Some of that blood that wuz a comin' out of my mouth come from the hole in my tongue. I bit it when he hit me upside the head...mayhaps I fooled him."

He started to chuckle, caught himself and glanced over at Nokose Harjo who shook his head. "Crazy Bear said I wasn't to laugh, cough, an' fer damn sure don't sneeze."

The old Indian nodded. "Or eat meat."

"Yeah, that too."

"Why not eat meat?…Oh…never mind." Fiona blushed.

Bass looked over at her. "Well, Marshal, looks like we're needful of takin' a bit of deviation 'fore we's head to the Shawnee Hills…Whilst the trail's still hot."

She nodded in agreement. "Be real easy to follow a herd of cattle."

"I 'spect when we find them cows…we'll find the Carter's close by."

"Be sure to take a caution, Bull usually has the baby of the family up in a tree some place er other. Boy's a mite slow in the head, but he kin shoot…If'n you'll hand me a piece of paper an' a pencil, I'll write out their names fer ya."

"Not necessary…Jest tell us…I 'member most ever'thin' I see er hear…'sides cain't read nohow."

Lank got a puzzled expression. "Cain't read?…How is it you serve warrants?"

"Have somebody tell me the names on the paper whilst I look at it…an' I 'member. A name is like a picture er a hoof print to me…ain't no two alike."

"Never make a mistake?"

Bass shook his head. "Not yet an' I reckon I've served most over two thousand warrants since I started marshalin'."

Fiona nodded. "I can attest to that. He can pull the right one out of the stack in his coat pocket every time."

Finch grinned. "Well alright…They's Clifford 'Bull' Carter, he's the oldest and big as a bear. Then come Cooper…he's kindly short, stocky and keeps the tallybook. The next is Adicus 'Stretch' Carter…boy kin take a bath in a gun barrel. And finally the one that's a tad slow, Barzillai Carter…They call him Biscuit. Likes stick candy."

"Barzillai…That's from the Bible, ain't it?"

"Thought you couldn't read?"

"Cain't, but my reg'ler partner, Jack, he's ever and anon reading from it, er Shakespeare, er a feller named Keats…I listen real good. Jim Cracker stories…Well, I mind we better head on out. I 'spect they won't think they's 'nybody on their tail so soon."

Fiona nodded, knelt back down and kissed her brother on the forehead and stood back up.

"Oh, Marshal, watch his left…he chops up with it. Like gittin' kicked by a mule. He starts with it low by his leg."

"Had a turn with knuckles an' skulls a time er two…ain't no pilgrim, but much obliged fer the ad-vice."

"By the way, got a warrant in my coat under my head."

Bass nodded to Fiona who knelt down, eased the coat out from under her brother's head and extracted the warrant. She rolled the coat back up, plumped it a little, slipped it back under his head and handed the folded paper to Reeves. They both turned and walked toward their horses.

"Marshal Reeves."

Bass stopped and looked back at Red Dog.

"Brands be fresh. Find runnin' iron in fire."

He pitched the discolored cinch ring to the marshal. Bass snatched it from the air and looked at it before put it in his coat pocket. He headed on, with long strides, toward his horse, Blaze. Fiona blew Lank another kiss and followed after him.

"You kin stay with yer brother till I git back, if'n you like," Bass said as she caught up with him.

"Not a chance. Who's going to watch your back?"

Bass nodded, stuck his foot in the stirrup and swung easily up into the saddle. "I done learnt all about tryin' to argue with a woman...They's two ways...an' neither one works."

***

CHAPTER THREE

MUSCOGEE COUNTY
CREEK NATION

Bass chuckled. "Follerin' a slew of cattle is fair easy," he said as he and Fiona jog trotted along the well-marked trail.

"How many are in a slew?"

He glanced at her. "Well, in this 'un…purtnear a hunderd, I 'spect."

"How many are steers and how many are heifers?"

He laughed out loud. "Ain't quite as good as Jack would have me be."

"How's that?"

"He used to say I could track a fish up a river…Haw!"

Fiona appraised the big black man riding alongside. "I'm surprised you can't."

He reined up his gray stallion and shifted his saddle back to centerline. Removing his black Boss of the Plains hat, he wiped his brow with a faded red bandana. "Kin tell you one thang." He pointed at the multitude of tracks.

"And that would be?"

"They's all young stock, judgin' from the size of their hooves and they's four men on horseback afollerin' 'long."

She stared at the ground and nodded. "But I only see three sets of horse tracks."

"One pulled off back a couple of miles an' is parallelin' the trail, not carrin' much weight. 'Spect as it's the shanny one, Biscuit…He's runnin' lookout, either that er his horse is a bit snuffy."

"Snuffy?"

"Spirited…Might spook the cattle. But, I 'spect the first…Runnin' lookout."

"You can tell all that just by looking at the tracks?"

He wrinkled his forhead. "Shore…Cain't you?"

"No."

"Well, now this is gittin' to be a tad interestin'." He looked around.

"What?"

"Do you know where you are, Fiona?"

"Of course…with you."

"No, I mean, we've crossed into the Cherokee Nation." Bass paused a moment and pulled out his worn rosewood pipe, filled it. He struck a match on the butt plate of his Winchester sticking up out of its boot and lit it. After a long draw, he exhaled a blue cloud of maple syrup flavored smoke over his head and nodded.

"What is it?"

"Lighthorse don't go from their home nation into 'nother...got no jurisdiction. Injun'll figure it's a waste of time. Onlyest time they will is if'n they's deputized as a posseman by a US Marshal."

"And?"

"The Carters know that. So they been rustlin' cattle er horses in one nation and take 'em to 'nother...Don'tcha see?"

DERDENE CREEK
MUSCOGEE COUNTY
CHEROKEE NATION

"Coop, pour me another cup of coffee." Bull handed his tin cup toward his brother.

"Is yor leg broke?"

"Naw, but yer's might be you don't git me my coffee. I'm still a mite sore. That marshal could hit, plus them scabs on the back of my legs is pullin' some." He tongued the hole where his left eye tooth had been.

"Want me to git you a sugar tit whilst I'm up?"

"I ain't too sore to knock you into next week...you don't watch yer lip."

"I'll git the damn Arbuckle..." Stretch got to his feet. "...rather than listen to the pair of ya rattlin' on at the mouth like a coupla tittybabies."

He walked the short distance over to the campfire and picked up the coffee pot with one of his folded over leather gloves and filled Bull's graniteware cup.

Their camp was at the edge of the tree line at the bottom of a hill. It bordered a large fertile grassy meadow that was formed when Derdene Creek cut through a loop and the channel moved to the north. The headwaters flowed out of the Cookson Hills that were the western extension of the Boston Mountains of Arkansas to the east.

Between the camp and the creek were over a hundred head of mostly two year old cattle the Carters had rustled over the past two months, contentedly grazing on the lush grass.

As Stretch set the pot back on the flat rock next to the fire, a large black man in greasy buckskins with Apache style knee-high moccasins, stepped out of the woods. He had three gray and one fox squirrel hanging from the wide belt around his waist—behind a big bone-handled Bowie knife. He carried a long barreled .38-40 Winchester in the crook of his arm.

"How do...You fellers got'ny coffee to spare? Trade you a couple of squirrels fer a cup.

"Reckon that'd be a fair trade. Make some good stew…Out huntin' air ye?" asked Bull.

He grinned a big toothy grin. "Oh, 'spect you might say that."

The hunter slipped the tails of two of the grays out from under his belt and handed them to Stretch who pitched them to Coop.

"Help yerself, they's a cup over yonder on top of the pannier," said Adicus.

The man picked up the cup, pulled the faded red bandana from around his neck and used it as a hot pad as he poured the coffee. He sat down on a pine log they had dragged up, propped his rifle next to his right leg and took a sip.

"Ummm, ummm, that's fine…Mighty fine." He glanced out at the cattle, some of which were laying down, chewing their cud. "Got some good lookin' stock there. Notice some of the long heifers er springin', but don't see no bull…Jest git 'em, did you?" He took another sip.

Bull squinted his eyes at the man. "You be kindly nosey fer a hunter, ain'tcha?"

"Jest makin' conversation, is all."

"What'd you say yer name was?" asked Coop.

"Didn't."

"Well?" Stretch added.

"Oh, some folks call me one thang…an' some folks call me 'nother."

"What do they call you...mostly?" asked Bull.

He grinned sipped his coffee and finally said, "Well, I 'spect, by an' large, it's usually jest...Bass." He paused and looked up from his cup with a wry grin. "Bass Reeves...Deputy United States Marshal...Bass Reeves."

Bull guffawed. "So you be Bass Reeves you say?"

He just smiled bigger and nodded.

"An' you ain't really out a huntin', air ye?" Bull said sarcastically looking at the squirrels laying beside Coop.

"Oh, no, I got them squirrels fair 'n square...They noticed it wuz me a huntin' an' they jest jumped down from their tree an' fell over dead...right there in front of me."

"Haw, he's funny, ain't he, Bull?"

Clifford Carter got to his feet. "Yeah, Stretch, real funny. He oughta be on the Chataqua circuit er in a minstrel."

Coop slapped his thigh. "Yeah, that's it. A minstrel show...least he wouldn't have to put on any blackface."

"Now that's a fact, a guarandamnteeyou fact...but, then agin, he might need some blackface after I'm done with him...I ain't stomped the hell out of a darky in a long time." He stepped toward the marshal.

Bass laid his hand next to his rifle.

"Uh, uh, wouldn't do that, nigger. Got my little brother over there in that red oak with his Henry pointed right at yer haid." He pointed off to the left.

50

"Oh, I know…See'd him 'fore I walked into yer camp." Bass slowly got to his feet. "But, see, here's the thang…they's another deputy marshal behind that big hickory over yonder…" He pointed to the opposite side of the camp to the right. "…with a Winchester pointed right at Barzillai. Now, if'n the shot don't kill him…an' it probably will, the fall'll finish him off."

"How is it you know his name?" asked Cooper.

Bass reached inside his beaded buckskin parfleche, pulled out a folded piece of paper and waved it—grinning all the while. "Got a warrant fer the bunch of you…fer rustlin'." He took the fire-mottled cinch ring from the pouch with his other hand and held it up. "Peers you left yer brandin' iron back in McIntosh County in yer firepit."

"How d'you know that wuz us?" asked Stretch.

Bass chuckled. "Well, fer one thang, I followed yer tracks…An' fer two, the marshal you left fer dead there by Grass Creek tol' me…Oh, an' by the way, reckon we gotta add attempted murder of a Federal officer to this here warrant. That, along with the rustlin'charges…jest might git ya'll a hemp necktie."

ARBUCKLE MOUNTAINS
MCGANN HOME

Jack sat on the porch in a slat-backed rocker with his dog, Son, lying beside the chair snoozing. The infirmed marshal had a

51

long skinny peach limb he had trimmed and was steady working down inside the plaster cast on his left leg trying to scratch an irritating itch on the back side.

"Dadgummit!" He smacked a porch post in front of him with the switch, breaking it in two. Son jumped up from his nap, looked at the post, and then at Jack.

Angie opened the screen door. "And what would it be that's botherin' ye, Husband?...Did ye drink all of ye tea?"

He looked up. "Got an itch on the back of my leg that's drivin' me crazy...Jest cain't git to it...and yes, I drank all my tea."

She stepped back inside, allowing the screen door to bang shut. In a couple of seconds she came back out with a small three-legged stool and a fly swatter. "Prop ye foot up on me stool."

Jack wrinkled his brow. "Say what?"

"Just be doing what I'm telling ye."

He took both hands and lifted his leg—heavy as it was with the plaster cast from the knee down—and set his foot on top of the stool. Angie leaned over and stuck the long wire handle of fly swatter down inside the cast, just behind his knee and slowly worked it up and down.

Jack leaned his head back. "Ahhh...that feels so good, darlin'...What would I do without you?"

She giggled. "Figure out how to do it ye own self...eventually. They say necessity is the mother of invention."

"I know, jest wish this leg would hurry up and heal over…Bass needs me."

"The judge said that lady marshal can stand toe to toe with most any man. He figured she would have to if she rode with Bass Reeves."

"Lady marshal…My hind foot! Whoever heard of such a thang?"

Angie popped him behind the head with the fly swatter.

DERDENE CREEK
MUSCOGEE COUNTY
CHEROKEE NATION

"So you fixin' to take us in, air ye?" asked a somewhat contentious Bull.

"Yep, got paper on you. Law says I have to…But tell you what. Hear tell you like to bust knuckles an skulls."

Carter's eyes brightened and he cocked his head. "Nothin' I'd ruther do…Ain't busted up a nigger in quite a spell…You offerin' somethin'?"

"Make you the same deal you give Marshal Finch." Bass grinned, unbuckled his belt and dropped his knife to the ground. "Undo yer gunbelt an' drop it…yer brothers too."

Bull looked over at the big hickory as he and his brothers undid their belts, too. "What 'bout the other marshal?"

53

"Come on out F.M." He looked over at the oak. "You kin come down too, Biscuit."

"You got'ny stick candy?" came the voice from up in the tree.

"'Spect as we might could do that...Come on down, now." A pair of oversized old black Jefferson brogans showed out of the foliage, followed by a set of skinny legs sticking out of ragged bottom brown canvas pants. The retarded teenager hung down, holding on to the thick branch—his Henry looped over his shoulder by a leather thong—and then let go and dropped to the ground.

He had a big grin on his freckled face as he walked toward the others.

Fiona stepped out from behind her tree, her Winchester pointed in the direction of the Carters from her hip in her right hand and one of her Colts in the left.

Bull glanced her way. "A woman! We dropped our guns fer a God damned woman? Jesus Christ." He stomped around in a tight circle, stopped and glared at Bass. "So what's it gonna be, nigger?"

Reeves slipped the buckskin shirt over his head and was down to his union top. "You whup me, ya'll go free...I whup you, you sign a written confession an' go in with us peaceable...Suit you?"

"What about her? What's to keep her from shootin' me when I stomp a mud hole in yer black ass?"

54

"You have my word…Just have your brothers lie down on the ground away from their guns," Fiona said.

"How do I know I kin trust a woman."

She smiled. "Well, it's either that or I shoot you where you stand right now for resisting arrest…Your choice."

Carter frowned, nodded at the others and they did as directed. She holstered her pistol, sat down on a log, uncocked her Winchester, and then laid it on the ground.

"What about my stick candy?" an almost in tears Barzillai whined.

"You got some in yer saddlebags?" Bass asked Bull.

He nodded and pointed to a set leaning against a saddle. Reeves walked over, lifted the flap and pulled out a small brown paper sack and took out a six inch piece of peppermint candy. He stepped over to where Biscuit was lying, propped up on his elbows, handed it to him and tousled his unkempt red hair.

"Thankee…Thankee very kindly." His close-set almond-shaped eyes looked up at the big man in rapt gratitude as he stuck the red and white stick in his mouth and started sucking on it.

Bull pushed up his sleeves and started to circle the big marshal. "What's the rules?"

Bass never moved from where he stood. "Ain't'ny."

Bull remembered the lesson learned from Marshal Finch—don't charge the other man. He stepped in closer, feet spread and both of his massive hands hanging clenched at his side. Carter looked right, over at his brothers as Bass still hadn't moved. "This ain't gonna take long, boys."

Using the look as a feint, he quickly shuffled his left foot, raised his right hand, and then snapped his left fist from down low at the marshal's jaw in a hooking uppercut. Bass merely leaned back, allowing the ham-like appendage to whistle past, and then like a striking cottonmouth, countered with two quick openhanded slaps to each side of Bull's head—centering on his ears.

Carter staggered back a step, grabbed his ears and shook his head like a wounded bear. He closed his eyes as if in pain, and then suddenly lashed out with his foot, catching Bass on the side of the knee, spinning him around and down to the ground on all fours. Bull charged just as he started to get to his feet.

He drove his two hundred and fifty pounds into Bass' chest, knocking the wind out of him and sending the marshal to his back. Carter dove on top, wrapped his left arm around the back of Reeves' neck, pulled his face up into his armpit and started driving his right fist into his midsection.

Bass yelled out and with superhuman strength, hurled the heavier man off his chest and to the side. He spun to his knees and drove his own massive right fist into the middle of Bull's face. Blood exploded in all directions from his smashed nose.

Carter staggered to his feet only to be hit again, this time in the solar plexus, doubling him over. Bass pummeled the right side of his face with a left hook, and then connected with the middle of Bull's forehead with a right roundhouse that sounded like a rifle shot, straightening him back vertically—his eyes rolled up into the back of his head. The big man toppled over on his back—out cold.

Bass rose slowly to his feet, favoring his right knee. He looked over at Fiona and nodded. She got to her feet, walked over to one of the Carter's saddles, pulled three braided rawhide piggin' strings from it and proceeded to tie the hands of the clan.

"Don't tie Barzillai," said Bass. "But, pitch me yer shackles fer bigun here."

She nodded that she understood as she looked over to see Biscuit sitting up, very confused with tears running down his face and holding his stick candy with both hands. Fiona retrieved a set of steel cuffs from behind her belt and flipped them to Bass.

Bull had set up and was shaking his head, blood still streaming from his nose when Reeves snapped the shackles around his wrists. "Grab one of them lariat ropes and we'll daisy chain the three elders together."

He walked over to Barzillai and helped him to his feet. He knelt down so he could look the boy straight in his round face.

Biscuit looked over at his brothers and then back at Bass. He sniffed. "What's gonna happen to me?…Will I git hung er put away in a nut house like Bull tol' me on account of I'm dumb an' ain't right in the haid?" The tears began to flow heavier as he tried to catch his breath.

Bass wrapped his arms around the frail boy and held him tight. "Naw, boy, you ain't gonna git hung...an' yer jest different, that's all." He paused. "Biscuit, is they anybody to home...a mama er yer daddy?"

He nodded. "My mama an' daddy is both daid...My granny is at the house, an' Aint Mamie...she be colored like you...She does the washin' an such an' blisters my hiney when I mess up."

He choked back more tears. "Bull, he taken care of me most of the time...an' give me stick candy, but sometimes he wuz powerful mean to me...He'd kick me an' call me stupid."

"Well, he won't be mean to you no more." He leaned back and held the boy at arm's length. "Tell you what. We have to take yer brothers into town to the marshal's office...We'll stop and git you a big sack of stick candy at the mercantile an' then take you to yer granny's...how that be? You like peppermint doncha?"

He sniffled again and nodded. "Like root beer an' butterscotch some too."

Bass hugged him again and then got to his feet. "You mind gettin' their horses?"

Biscuit nodded and ran off to where their mounts were picketed.

BASS AND THE LADY

Fiona had been hanging back until Bass finished talking to Barzillai and then walked up. "That was a nice thing you just did."

"Wadn't none of it his fault. He don't need to go to no asylum...they'd just make a slave out of 'im...an' I know what that's like...Won't see that done to nobody...'specially a innocent child...long as I draw a breath." His voice got husky as his eyes began to fill.

She turned away for a moment to allow Bass to gather himself and then turned back. "How was it possible that you could throw that man mountain off of your chest like he was nothing? I thought you were done for when he got on top of you."

Bass wiped the corner of his eye and smiled a little. "Well to be honest, I did too when he wrapped his arm around my neck...But, he stunk so bad, I thought I was gonna suffocate an' well, reckon I just panicked...Had to git me some air...I'd wager he ain't bathed in the last year...meby two."

She shook her head and grinned. "Remind me to stay up wind of him on the way into town."

"Don't 'spect I'll have to be remindin' you...He'll water yer eyes you git close enough."

CHECOTAH
CREEK NATION

"Ahem," Bass coughed loudly as he and Fiona reined up in front of the Marshal's office.

"Hot damn o'mighty!" Deputy Porter jumped up from his chair where he had been leaned back against the wall napping with his hat pulled down over his eyes. "Marshal Reeves! Sorry, didn't see ya'll ride up...Guess I was restin' my eyes."

Bass chuckled. "Uh, huh...Well, here you go, Bradley, some more nabobs fer ya...the Carter clan."

"Well, bless my soul, both the Marshal and Sheriff Childs over to Eufala, been tryin' to catch that bunch of waddies since I signed on."

"Here's the warrants on 'em."

Deputy Porter took the papers and scanned them. He looked back up at Bass. "Ain't they four of 'em? A young one named Bar...somethin'?"

"Barzillai...He wadn't on the warrant. Took him to his granma's. Don't even shave yet."

Brad looked down at the warrants again, back up at the big marshal, and then at Fiona. She smiled and nodded.

"Do need you to send a wagon out to Grass Creek...Fiona's brother, Marshal Finch is purty banged up. Alexander Harjo, the Creek medicine maker and Red Dog is tendin' to him."

"Lank is yer brother?" He looked over at Marshal Miller in amazement.

60

"He is that…at least that's what our mama told us."

Brad slapped his thigh. "Well, ding dang, learn somethin' new ever day. Wouldn't a guessed in a million years."

"I'd wait another day er so…Bull liked to kilt 'im."

"If he fought that bear, he is lucky to be alive." He looked at Carter with his battered and bruised face—his left eye was swollen completely shut. "Finch do that to 'im?"

"Marshal Reeves," said Fiona.

He snapped his head back to Bass. "You fought Bull too?"

"Lank softened 'im up a mite fer me."

"You should have seen it," Fiona added with a grin.

"Wooboy, wish I had of…Musta been somethin' to behold."

Bass, looking a bit uncomfortable, backed his gray up and reined him toward the hotel. "Gonna clean up some an' git a bite…Be headin' out to the Shawnee Hills of a mornin'." He clucked and the stallion trotted on down the street.

Brad called after him. "Goin' after another lowlife outlaw on the scout?"

Bass didn't turn or respond. Fiona looked hard at Brad, shook her head and squeezed her horse after Reeves.

Deputy Porter had a puzzled look on his face for a moment, and then turned to the Carters. "All right, you ne'er-do-wells git down an' don't do nothin' dumb." He rested his hand on the butt of his walnut-gripped Peacemaker.

Bull stepped off his bay gelding. "Ain't got nothin' to worry about, Deputy, give my word to Marshal Reeves we wouldn't give no trouble."

Brad shook his head. "This is liable to be one hellova day 'fore it's over."

BLUE BIRD CAFE
CHECOTAH

Bass and Fiona were finishing their breakfast of fried eggs, bacon, grits, biscuits and gravy plus coffee as Brad and another man approached the table.

"Mornin', Bradley, who's yer friend?"

"Mornin' Marshal Reeves, meet Marshal Jim Boy Holatte."

Bass got to his feet and looked eye-to-eye with the tall full-blood middle-aged Creek lawman. "Pleased to meetcha, this here's Marshal F.M Miller." He nodded his head at Fiona.

Marshal Holatte whipped off his tall black uncreased John B. that covered his dark hair with a white streak above his right eye. "Mornin' Ma'am, heard tell of you from Marshal Cantrell over to McAlister...You've got quite a reputation."

She smiled. "Oh, I wouldn't believe everything Carlton says."

"Never known the marshal to steer me wrong yet...Says you're right salty with those side irons...both of 'em."

"Oh, I get by."

Bass snapped a glance at her, grinned and shook his head.

"Did I miss somethin'?" asked Brad.

"Just a private joke," commented Bass. "Interestin' white streak you got there, Marshal...Scar?"

"Knife fight...Cherokee named Cal Mankiller, last year..."

Fiona shot to her feet. "Did you kill him?"

He shook his head. "Busted his head up some with the barrel of my Remington and locked him up. Had warrants on him."

"Where is he now?" she asked, her steel-gray eyes flashing.

"Wish I knew...Escaped 'fore I could transport him to Fort Smith. Killed my night deputy and tried to burn my jail down. By the time we got the fire put out...he was long gone. Heard he headed down Texas way...Got an interest in him?"

Her jaw muscles clenched. "You could say that."

"Well, hope you catch up to 'im...take a caution, though. He's a snaky SOB."

"I know."

Holatte turned back to Bass. "Really happy to finally meet you Marshal. I was out of town, deliverin' a prisoner when you were in the other day. Porter here told me 'bout your big gunfight with the Larsons...'fore I hired on here. It's legend 'round these here parts."

Reeves ducked his head a little. "Well you know what they say about facts and legends."

"But in this case, even the legend don't tell it all…I seen it…I's there," stated Brad with a sharp nod to his head for emphasis.

"Well, anyhoo, is there anythin' I can do to help you with, Marshal?" asked Jim Boy.

"'Spect not…jest get the Carters to Fort Smith fer me. Ain't no sense in botherin' Sheriff Childs over to Eufala…they's Federal warrants on 'em. 'Fraid the Judge has jurisdiction."

Marshal Holatte nodded. "I'd say…Who're you goin' after in the Shawnee's?…Don't mind my askin'."

"My son."

***

CHAPTER FOUR

SHAWNEE HILLS
ATOKA COUNTY
CHOCKTAW NATION

Bass and Fiona had followed the Missouri-Kansas-Texas Railroad right of way from Checotah down until it crossed Coal Creek. They then followed the creek along the edge of the Shawnee Hills to the small town of Barnett next to Grubb Mountain.

"If you'd like a root beer, I'm buyin'," said Fiona as she eyed the only general store in town.

"That sounds passable...Go good with a sour dill pickle."

"A pickle?" Now I've heard just about every combination of foods, but root beer and a pickle is a new one on me. How in the world did you ever get started on that?"

The big man chuckled. "Aw, Jack an' me was atrailin' some miscreants one time an' went through a little place they called Slap Out and stopped at the local store sorta like this'un an' all theys had to go with the root beer was a pickle…Had a big barrel of 'em. Don't put it down till you tried it…Mebe with a cracker, if'n theys got'ny."

"Ugg…Why did they call it Slap Out?"

He laughed out loud this time. "The storekeep said they named it that on account they's always slap out of most ever thang."

They dismounted at the wood water trough and let their mounts drink while they loosened their cinches. When they'd had enough, they led them over to the hitching rail to the side, looped their lead ropes around it and loosely tied a single pull slip knot.

Bass opened the white gingerbread screen door and stepped aside.

"Don't say it," she cautioned and wagged her finger at him.

"Say what…Ma'am?" He grinned as he was almost able to lean back far enough to dodge her backhand across his chest.

She shook her head and mumbled as she stepped into the interior. "All the people in the world I have to be hooked up with…I get Bass 'Wiseacre' Reeves."

"Some folks is just lucky, that's all." He followed her inside and let his eyes adjust to the dim light.

BASS AND THE LADY

The screen door slammed shut behind them with a bang as the coil spring pulled it closed.

"Ya'll come in, folks call me Lulabell. We ain't got it, you don't need it. That's our motto...an' don't let the damn door slam next time," said the dowdy heavyset middle-aged woman behind the counter. She looked down at the end at a sleeping orange tabby. "You'll wake Jethro...Now, what can I help you with?"

"Believe we'll have a root beer," Fiona said.

"Slap out."

Bass and Fiona glanced at each other and burst out laughing.

"What's funny about bein' slap out of root beer?"

"Long story. What other kind of phosphates do you have?" asked Miller.

"Sarsaparilla, lemon, strawberry..."

"That sounds good. Where they at?" inquired Bass.

"Over yonder in that wooden case. Ice man come today, so they'll be right cold."

They stepped over to the square cooler made of one and a half inch thick cypress and a fitted top like a butter churn. Bass lifted the lid by the brass handle and looked down into the bottles nestled on a pile of chopped ice—there was half of a twenty-five pound block left at one end with a iron-handled ice pick lying on top.

"What's that one that looks dark red?" asked Fiona.

"Oh, that's a new one. Called cherry creme soda. Haven't tried it myself, but folks seem to like it. They say it has egg whites and vanilla in it...can't imagine."

Bass grabbed one and wiped the moisture off with his bandana—it had a blue Boudreaux's Cherry Creme Soda label painted on the side.

"Hand me one too. Love trying new things."

He handed that one to Fiona, got another for himself and dried it off too. They looked at the metal top on the bottle that was crimped all around the edge.

"Uh, where's the wire?" Bass looked it over.

"Oh, it's somethin' else new. Called a crown top. Got a little do-hicky over here to open it with. Let me have 'em."

They set the bottles on the counter, she took a wooden handled tool that had a metal triangle opening at one end. Lulabell slipped the open end over the cap and lifted up—there was a slight hiss as it came off. She handed the first one to Fiona, and then the second to Bass.

He picked up the blue painted crown-shaped tin cap and studied it for a moment. "Don't this beat all...even got cork on the bottom. Whole bunch better that them ceramic tops with the wire through 'em bangin' into yer nose."

Fiona glanced at him out of the corner of her eye. "Most people turn it to the side." She pitched a dime on the counter.

"'Cept when they's in a hurry." He turned the bottle up and took a healthy drink. His eyes got wide as he looked at the bottle, and then at Lulabell. "Great jumpin' pollywogs! This is like drinkin' a desert."

Fiona took a sip. "Oh, my goodness. It's perfectly decadent."

"Purty rich, too...Believe a pickle'll go good with this." He lifted the top to the pickle barrel and fished out a large one. "Want one?"

Fiona rolled her eyes. "Might as well. Can't dance."

Bass frowned. "What's dancin' got to do with it?"

"I meant this soda pop is so good, you could serve it at a barn dance."

"Oh."

Lulabell glanced at their badges, and then looked up. "Don't suppose you be Bass Reeves?"

He took another sip and a bite of pickle. "Reckon I am today. This here's Marshal F. M. Miller."

"Huh, never seen a woman marshal afore."

"Well, can't say that anymore after today, can you?" Fiona commented.

"'Spect not...You on somebody's trail, are you?"

"Colored man, in his twenties..."

"Bennie somethin' or other?" she interruped Bass.

A look of sadness flicked over his face, and then was gone. "Yessum."

He was in here a week or so ago with a real hard case...Tom Story."

"The gunfighter?" blurted Fiona.

She nodded. "So I'm told. Hear he likes horse racin' plus bein a horse thief, too...He was orderin' the negra around like he was his personal servant. Could tell right off they wasn't gee-hawin'."

"They say where they wuz goin'?"

Lulabell looked up at the big marshal and the stern visage on his countenance. "Not particular, Marshal Reeves, just that they was headed to Texas. Sold 'em some trail supplies. He made the colored tote the two gunny sacks outside."

"You happen to see what they were riding?" asked Fiona.

She nodded. "The negra was on a spavined bay, but Story rode a nice tall red roan geldin'...Stole, I 'spect. They also had a pack mule...he looked pore as a church mouse."

Bass nodded. "Not much chanct of trackin' 'em now. Been a couple of rain storms."

Miller looked over at Bass. "I'd say let's ride over to Frink, it's only ten miles or so, we can catch the KATY down to Denison. Not much sense in pushing our horses that far anyway...Maybe pick up their trail there."

A smile finally broke his dark face. "Now that's the second best thang you've said today."

She wrinkled her brow. "What was the first?"

He turned and headed to the door. "That you wuz payin' fer the sodeepops...an' the pickle."

She followed him and caught the screen door before it slammed shut. "I didn't say anything about paying for the pickle."

MKT TRAIN

Bass and Fiona rode facing each other in the third passenger car of the train heading to Texas from Sedalia, Missouri. The KATY—as it was known because of its stock designation of K-T—was the first railroad to enter Texas from the north in 1875.

"I wish you'd quit fretting, we only had to wait one day for the train and if we had of trailed our horses to Denison it would have taken a week...not to say anything about wearing them out."

The tracks cut right through what was called the Cross Timbers—a peculiar forest growth that was from five to thirty miles wide and extended from the Arkansas River 400 miles southwest to the Brazos in Texas.

Bass stared out the window at the passing trees. "I know...Patience ain't one of my strong suits. They's gonna have a good week head start on us. Don't have any idee which way they went after they crossed the Red."

"Guess we'll have to do some good old-fashioned law work."

71

"An' that would be?"

"Ask questions…Didn't Lulabell say something about Story being a horse thief, too?"

"She did."

"You got some blank John Doe's?"

"I do."

"If you were a horse thief…where would be the most likely area you'd go for the best horseflesh in Texas."

"That's easy…Cooke County…uh, Gainesville. They got some of the finest breedin' stock in the country there…We broke up a big rustlin' ring a few months back…the Red River gang."

"Any of them get away?"

"Nope, all dead, but one an' he got a date with the hangman."

"So that leaves it somewhat open, wouldn't you say?"

"You might have a point there Miz Miller…Ma'am."

She stuck her finger in his chest. "You're trading on thin ice there, Mister Reeves."

He grinned.

"You enjoy deviling my goat, don't you?"

"Now would I do somethin' like that?"

"Yes." She paused for a moment and looked out her own window. "Thinking like a horse thief, I believe I'd go where the horses are." Fiona looked over at Bass. "Don't you?"

72

He nodded. "Uh, huh, arrested a bank robber one time an' when I was puttin' the shackles on 'im, I asked how's come he robbed banks."

"What did he say?"

He shook his head and grinned. "On account that's where the money was."

DEXTER HOTEL
DELAWARE BEND
COOKE COUNTY, TEXAS

A tall, somewhat slim man with pale blue eyes in a black three-piece broadcloth suit with a dark red cravat and a black flat-brimmed hat, tapped the bell on the registration counter of the wooden two-story hotel at the edge of one of the three most notorious spots in North America.

Dexter, Texas shared that *honor* with Leadville, Colorado and Tombstone, Ariz. It was widely known throughout the southwest as an outlaw hangout.

Standing behind the thirty-five year old man with dirty blond hair, was a twenty something colored man in a brown sack cloth coat and light tan canvas pants, holding a carpet bag and two tow sacks, tied together.

A thin, balding clerk in a white collarless shirt with black arm garters stepped out of the office at the sound of the bell. "Yessir, kin I help ye? Name's Basil."

"Need a room...Basil." His voice had a raspy sound to it, somewhat like a hissing snake.

The clerk looked the two men over. "Jest one?"

"Yeah, just one...The nigger'll sleep on the floor."

"How long?"

"Start with a week. How much is that?"

"Five dollars...in advance." He looked at their dust-covered clothes, not missing the stag-handled Colt strapped low on his hip under his coat. "Six, if you want the cleanin' services."

He looked down at his coat, brushed it with his hand and sent a cloud of red dust flying. "Probably wouldn't hurt...either that or I can start plantin' corn in it."

The clerk guffawed. "That's a good one, yessirrebob, a good one." He spun the registration book around, opened on a partially filled page and handed him the ink well with a pen sticking out. "Just put yer John Hancock on that line there." He pointed. "You do write?"

The cold blue eyes snapped up and froze the middle-aged clerk for a moment.

"Of course you do...What about the darkie?"

Again the eyes flashed at him.

"Right." He turned around and took a key off the hook board behind him. "Room Thirteen."

"I don't think so." He didn't look up from the registry.

The clerk gulped. "Oh, yessir, of course...My mistake." He turned around again and reached for another key.

74

"End of the hall, on the back near the outside stairs."

He hesitated, removed another one and laid it on top of the open-faced book. "Room Twenty…Will that be alright?"

"I'll let you know." He pitched a five-dollar gold piece and a Morgan silver dollar on the counter, grabbed the key, turned and nodded to the colored man.

"There's a bath across the hall from that room…We got all the modern conveniences…Just let me know if you need anything."

There was no response as they mounted the stairs. The clerk turned the book back around and read the name softly, "Tom Story…Good God in heaven." He glanced back up to see them disappear around the landing. Basil suddenly realized he had broken out in a sweat.

KATY DEPOT
DENISON, TEXAS

The two deputy marshals stepped down the four metal steps from the passenger car to the station platform that ran along the back side of the depot.

"Bass!"

They turned to see Bodie Hickman striding along the bricked area between the tracks and the depot. He wove his way through other passengers disembarking and white-jacketed porters pushing four-wheel flat carts gathering up luggage.

"Hey, pardner, good to see you." He looked over at Fiona and doffed his hat. "An' I reckon this is the lady marshal you was tellin' me about." He stuck out his hand. "How do, Ma'a...uh..." He shot a quick glance at Bass. "Uh...Marshal Miller, I'm Texas Ranger Bodie Hickman."

She also glanced at Bass and elbowed him in the side. "Just what did you tell him...Marshal?" She turned back to Bodie. "Fiona will do fine, Ranger." She grabbed his hand and pumped it twice.

Bass shrugged his wide shoulders. "Nothin'...Honest John."

"Uh, huh...So this is who you were sending that telegram to back in Frink?"

"It wuz. Bodie usually knows most of what's goin' on in this neck of the woods...Who's comin' er goin'."

"That's true...mostly. 'Cept this time, ain't heard of no Tom Story in north Texas. Could be he ain't been here long enough fer the word to git around...an' could be he's layin' low...or could be he's passed on through."

Reeves nodded. "Yep, could be 'ny of 'em...We jest gotta start shakin' the trees an' see what falls."

"Agreed...let's go over to the Harvey House and git a bite. Annabel is already over there savin' us a table an' visitin' with some of her old friends."

"Annabel?" asked Fiona.

"My bride...She's from Alabama. We been married most nine months...She's big as a house."

"Excuse me?"

"Pregnant. Due in a couple of weeks."

"Oh! I thought you meant…"

"Fat? Annabel? Haw. There's ain't enough fat on her to render out a candle. Why, before she got with child, I could put my hands completely around her waist." He held up both hands and spread his fingers.

Fiona grinned. "I'm looking forward to meeting her." She glanced over at Bass. "We need to see to our horses first."

"Not necessary." He looked around and saw the same yard master that was here the last time he and Jack came through stepping out of the depot wearing the official MKT uniform for station employees—blue lindsey-woolsey coat with brass buttons all the way down the front and matching hat. He waved and the man walked over.

"Why it's Marshal Reeves. Good to see you again. How can I help you?"

Bass pressed two silver dollars in the man's hand. "Would you an' yer hostler see to our horses an' bags? We're gonna git a bite."

"Of course, just describe the horses to me."

"Mine's a big dapple gray Saddlebred stallion and her's is a black Palouse geldin' with a white blanket on its rump an' our bags is right here." He pointed to the two carpet bags and two Winchesters at his feet.

He nodded. "Shouldn't be hard to find. I'll tie 'em up outside the restaurant."

"Well, when's the next train west to Gainesville?"

The yard master pulled his gold watch from the small pocket on the front of his jacket. "The Paris to Witchita Falls is one hour and twenty-seven minutes...If she's on time."

"Jest load our horses and bags on it...we'll take the rifles. Water 'em first...you don't mind?"

"No, sir. We'll handle that." He looked at Fiona and touched the stiff short leather brim of his flat-topped hat.

"Much obliged." Bass nodded, picked up their Winchesters, turned and they walked toward the Harvey House.

The yard master looked at the two new Morgan silver dollars in his hand and shook his head. "Only Bass Reeves."

HARVEY HOUSE RESTAURANT

"...and this here is Deputy Marshal F. M. Miller." Bodie presented the tall attractive brunette to his wife.

"Just call me Fiona, Annabel. It's so nice to meet you. I have kin folk from Alabama. Used to visit when I was in my teens."

"Well, I do declare. Whereabouts?"

"Prattville."

"Oh, my goodness, that's right outside Montgomery...where I'm from."

"Really?...What was your maiden name?"

"Holcomb."

"Your daddy a doctor in Montgomery?"

"Why, yes."

"My uncle, Thaddius Finch, has been to him for his gout."

"Well, bless your heart. We're probably kin somewhere down the line." The blond beauty hooked Fiona's arm and walked toward an empty table with four glasses of ice tea already set on it.

Bodie grinned and looked at Bass. "Reckon we better follow 'em, don't you?"

"'Spect they wouldn't know the difference."

"I mind that's right."

They followed the ladies and got there just in time to pull out their chairs for them.

Annabel turned. "Why thank you, honey, that's so sweet. I forgot we left ya'll standin' over there."

He smiled and kissed her cheek. "I know."

"I took the liberty of orderin' for everybody, I hope ya'll don't mind. Today's special is pot roast with butter beans." She turned to Fiona. "I worked here under contract to Mister Harvey for my required two years." She looked around and smiled. "Still know most of the girls...We lived upstairs in the dormitory."

"I had heard that being a Harvey Girl was like attending a finishing school," said Fiona.

"Oh, yes, indeed. It truly is…And it was right here I met my darlin' husband." She squeezed his hand. "And Marshal Reeves too…Oh, where's Marshal McGann?"

"Busted his leg a couple of weeks ago. Gonna be homebound fer a while…Drivin' his wife crazy as two rats in a rain barrel, I 'spect."

"Oh, bless his heart. I'll have to send him and Angie a note."

"Where ya'll stayin' Bass?" asked Bodie.

"Well, we wuz hopin' Miss Faye had some rooms."

"Actually, she does, I do believe…Knowin' you, I 'spect you got a plan."

"Been cogitatin' on that some. Gonna have to go undercover again."

"Is that why you haven't been shaving? You're growing a beard?"

He looked at Fiona and nodded. "Bass Reeves is kindly known around these parts after that little set to we had with the Red River gang, so I'm creatin' a little disguise…They say white folks cain't tell us apart." He grinned. "Meby git a job at the feed store er someplace."

"What about me?"

He cocked his head and scratched the half-inch growth on his chin, and then looked up. "Don't suppose you happen to sing, does you?"

BASS AND THE LADY

"Why yes, I do. I was the choir director at the Tahlequah Baptist Church before…well, before I became a marshal…Why?"

"Jest thinkin' the best place to find out information 'bout what's goin' on around the county is at the Painted Lady in Gainesville."

Fiona cocked her head and wrinkled her brow. "What's the Painted Lady?"

"A saloon."

DEXTER HOTEL

Tom Story ran the black Bakelite comb through his still damp hair as stared at himself in the mirror atop the Eastlake-style sideboard. He sprinkled a few drops of bayberry hair tonic on his hands, rubbed it into his scalp, screwed the metal cap back on the small bottle, and then combed it again.

The second time, his slightly unkempt mop stayed in place. *Better…gotta get me a haircut afore the week's out.* He lifted the flap on his carpet bag and took out a clean, starched white cotton shirt and slipped it on, leaving the collar up. After shaking the trail dust off his red cravat, he tied it jauntily under his Adam's apple and flipped the collar down.

The young black man watched his every move from the wooden chair he sat in. "We gonna go out for dinner, Mister Tom? I be gittin' powerful hungry."

The gunfighter looked at him with a cold stare. "Ain't no we, boy...I'm not the one with a wanted dodger out on me. You need to let that nappy hair grow out some more an' finish growin' that mustache.

"Gonna drop by the local saloon and see if I can separate some of the hayseeds from their drinkin' money. Just sit tight...I'll bring you a ham sandwich or somethin'."

"Yessir, Mister Tom." If he was disappointed, he didn't let it show.

"Why don't you take a bath while I'm gone...You're gettin' a tad ripe...and take my suit and other shirt down to...Basil, to be cleaned."

Tom pulled his tobacco-colored galluses up onto his shoulders and then donned a brocade vest of a black paisley satin material over them. He reached into his bag once more and brought out a pair of hand-tooled black leather cuffs—each about four inches long. He slipped them past his hands, over the extra loose material in his shirt sleeves and tightened the laces. Last, he strapped on his Colt around his slim hips.

He took one more look in the mirror and headed for the door.

SUGAR HILL SALOON

Before the railroad bypassed Dexter—and went though Woodbine—the combination store and bar on the dirt main street would have been packed elbow-to-elbow. The obligatory painting of the reclining nude Fatima was almost seven feet long and trimmed in a Carved Rococo frame gilded with 24 carat gold leaf.

The fifty foot bar top was custom made when the town was booming with a bright future. The brass rails on the side and bottom came all the way from Saint Louis.

Tom pushed his way past the swinging doors to see a dozen men standing at the bar and ten or more seated at tables scattered around the sawdust floor. The room smelled like stale beer, tobacco smoke, whiskey and cheap perfume. *My kinda place.*

A smile came to his face as a twenty-year old sporting girl glanced his way and got to her feet. She tried her best to look alluring and met him halfway across the floor.

"Looking for a good time, Mister?"

"Possibly...How's the whiskey in here?"

"Watered down, but it'll get you where you want to go." She winked and batted her eyes. "I'd suggest the Old McBrayer, it's a Kentucky sour mash. The owner, Ed Steine, don't mess with it much as he likes to drink it too."

"Get us a bottle and a couple of glasses."

The auburn-haired winked. "Have a seat, honey...My name's Stephanie." She pointed at an open table.

Story eyed the men in the bar, looking for a familiar face—there were none. *Good. Startin' with a clean slate...easy pickin's.*

He sat down with his back to the wall with a clear view of the bar and doorway. He watched the bartender pull out a clear bottle of amber liquid—with Old McBrayer on the lable—from beneath the counter. The man set it and two shot glasses on the bar top.

Stephanie sashayed back with the whiskey, her full skirt flouncing just above her calves. She was attractive, by the standards of the day, with naturally wavy shoulder-length auburn hair and green eyes. Her makeup was too heavy, but all the girls of the line tried hard to look perfect in the dim light and smoke.

After they each downed two drinks, a man about five-ten and medium build standing at the bar turned and walked to the table. By his attire, he could have been a shopkeeper, although his string tie was slightly off-kilter. He nodded to the woman. "Evenin', Miss Stephanie...Who's your new friend? Don't believe I've seen you in here before, mister."

The gunfighter's jaw tightened slightly as he locked eyes with the man.

"Hello, Frank. This here is Tom...his first time in Dexter. Ain't that right, sweetie?"

"Could say that…What business is it of yours? You the law?"

Frank broke into a laugh. "Naw, Tom, I was just gonna see if you wanted to try your hand at a little poker."

Story's face softened and he even managed a slight grin. "Hell, thought everybody round these parts done gave up on cards." He looked around the room. "Ya'll ain't even got a faro dealer here."

"Used to…Got a mite too slow, I reckon, and they moved to Silver City over to Gainesville."

"Do tell?" Tom reached into his vest pocket and pulled out a fairly new pack of red-backed Bicycle brand playing cards. He tossed them on the table in front of Frank. "Take a load off. My cards or yours…You deal."

He pulled out a chair and sat opposite Stephanie and stuck out his hand. "Frank Pierce…Nice to meetcha."

Tom took it and shook it firmly. "Likewise, I'm sure." He looked over at the woman. "Steph, could you bring my new friend a clean glass?"

"Gladly." She slid back and headed for the bar.

"Five stud…nothin' wild? That suit ya?"

"Dealer calls the game…Table stakes?" Tom slipped a slim wallet from the inside of his vest. He took out five dollars and laid it down on the stained green felt-top table.

"Table stakes it is." Frank fished out a five from his shirt and laid it in front of him.

Each player anted—Frank opened the cardboard flap and dumped the deck into his hands. His motions showed him to be more than a rookie, but not a slick master of the game as he shuffled the cards and pushed them back over to Tom to cut. Story just waved his hand in refusal and Frank dealt out two cards—the first down, the second up and they bet. Pierce dealt out three more cards face up—they bet after each card...

The bourbon bottle was half empty when a man dressed in working cowboy duds passed through the swinging doors. A single action .44-40 rode high on his right hip. He pushed his sweat-stained tan hat back on his head as he approached the end of the bar. "Hey, Ed...how 'bout a beer for a workin' man?"

"Comin' at ya." Steine drew a heavy glass mug full and swept the foam head off with the back of his hand. With practiced precision, he placed it on the inside rail of the bartop and gave it a shove. The beer slid down the slick polished surface and came to a rest three inches from the end.

The cowboy hefted the mug, nodded his appreciation to the owner and took a long drink—swallowd twice and wheezed, "Damn that's good."

Frank Pierce laid his cards face down on the table. "Jack!...join us for a hand?"

The cowboy recognized the man seated across the noisy barroom. He nodded and made his way across the sawdust floor.

BASS AND THE LADY

"Tom, say howdy to a good friend of mine. Jack Long from out New Mexico way."

The wiry cowboy stuck out his hand. "Pleasure...Just got back from the Nations and was about to dry up and blow away."

"Cain't let that happen. Nice to meetcha, Jack...You play?"

He nodded as he shook hands with the gunfighter. "From time to time...when I got a little jingle in my pockets."

"Have a seat." Tom motioned to an open chair. "Bourbon drinker?"

"If you're in a buyin' mood."

"Why not? Frank's down twenty already...You could say it's on him tonight." He grinned.

Frank held up both hands. "Hey, hey, hey! Night ain't over...Luck could turn any minute."

"Always a possibility." Story fished a long black cheroot from his vest, grabbed a match from a glass container on the table, stuck it with his thumbnail and lit the cigar.

Jack slid into his barrel-back chair and bellied up to the table. "What's the game, gents?"

A half-hour later, four young ranch hands from a place south of Delaware Bend sauntered in. The barroom was getting more crowded after the sun went down. The Derby-decked piano player with red sleeve garters sat down and pounded out a series of songs popular on the vaudeville circuit.

Two of the cowboys went straight to the bar and chatted up the bar girls who had wandered in at six. The others looked around for a card game to join and approached the only player they knew.

The twenty-year old with a pockmarked face and bowler hat spoke up, "Evenin' Frank…Anybody join in?"

He looked the pair over and glanced at Tom. The gunfighter nodded once and took a sip of his whiskey.

"Sure thing, Johnny boy…You and Earl pull up a chair."

The men sat down across from Tom while Frank made the introductions.

Tom slid out three dollars in the pot. "I see your dollar and raise you two."

Jack turned his cards face down. "Fold…Cain't beat what you got showin'."

Frank matched his bet and turned over his hole card. "Two pair…aces and queens."

"Not bad…but three eights takes the pot, I'm afraid."

Another hour went by with each man winning a hand or two. They had switched to five card draw. Stephanie brought over a fresh bottle of Old McBrayer. The pot rose until there was forty-five dollars in it—more than a month's pay for most cowboys.

BASS AND THE LADY

Johnny Cochran chewed on his stubby unlit cigar. He stared at his hand—a full house, kings over sevens. He spit into the brass cuspidor near the table.

"Cards, gentlemen?" Tom was dealing again.

"Two." Frank laid down a four and a five of clubs and was dealt a pair of nines.

Jack watched for a change of expression. There was none. He tossed away a six of clubs. "One." He was happy when he picked up the ten of diamonds, but worked hard not to show it.

Johnny looked into the eyes of the other four players, looking for some kind of tell. "I'm good."

Earl shook his head. A pair of jacks was all he held. "Three, you don't mind." Two fours and an ace were dealt to him.

"Dealer takes one." He threw down a three of diamonds and picked up a six of spades. His face registered no emotion whatsoever. "Your bid, Jack,."

The cowboy slid out three dollars from his pile and turned to Johnny.

"I'll see your three…and raise two." He flipped a five dollar gold piece on top of the growing pile.

Everyone looked at Earl. Five dollars was four day's wages and he didn't feel all that lucky with only two pair. He put in three singles and two silver dollars. "Five dollars to you, Tom."

"That it is." He laid a crisp bill on the pile.

"Call." Frank tossed in a five dollar gold piece. "Nines over ladies." A grin spread across his face.

Jack looked on. "Dammit…Three tens." He tossed his cards in the discard pile.

"Full house too, boys." Johnny grinned and tossed down his kings and sevens.

Earl sank back in his chair, almost dead broke and disgusted. "Two pair…figured ya'll wuz bluffin'."

"Not hardly." Tom's blue eyes were cold as ice. He laid down a six of spades, followed by a seven, eight, nine, and a ten. "Straight flush…spades." He reached out to pull in his winnings.

Johnny pulled an eight inch Bowie knife from his belt and stuck in down in the center of the pile, narrowly missing Tom's hand. "Not so fast, you cheatin' son of a bitch! Saw you dealin' off the bottom of the deck!"

Tom sat back—his right hand slipped off the table as he eyes narrowed and his jaw took a set. "Son…I beat you fair and square. That's just the whiskey talkin'. I suggest you take back what you said…you might live to see sunrise."

"I ain't skeered of you…card shark bastard!" The boy sprang to his feet and went for the gun on his right hip. He had barely cleared leather when a shot rang out.

The table splintered beneath the green felt, sending one of the silver dollars flying. A bullet caught young Johnny under the chin and exited the top of his head, taking his dark green bowler with it.

BASS AND THE LADY

Stephanie screamed. Johnny Cochran sank to the floor like a marionette with its strings cut.

The barroom fell silent as a tomb.

Tom cut his eyes to Earl. "You got anything to say, boy?"

He shook his head vigorously. "No sir! I didn't see no cheating. Honest."

"Didn't think so...Why don't you and your other friends drag that dumb bastard out before he starts to stink?"

"Sure, mister...Whatever you say." He nervously pushed away from the table and waved his two pals over. They grabbed the body by the wrists and dragged him out, leaving two boot heel trails in the sawdust.

Tom watched the crowd for anyone who might be a threat. Most of the other patrons started talking low among themselves. He turned to Frank. "Ya'll got a town marshal here?"

He chuckled. "Naw. Even the county sheriff and the Rangers give this place a wide birth. You won't have any trouble. Everybody saw the kid drew first...Hell, you gave 'im a chance to walk away."

"Always best thing to do with sore losers."

Jack leaned in. "Damnation. I never even seen you draw!"

"That's 'cause I didn't." Tom reached out and pulled the knife from the pile of bills and pulled the pot to him.

"You didn't draw?" Frank's face was etched with a question mark.

Tom shook his head, straightened out the bills and separated the coins. "Got me a swivel holster...Can shoot right through the bottom." A slight smile came to his face.

Frank shook his head. "I'll be a bald-face monkey. Never heard tell of such...Say...What'd you say your last name was again?"

The gunfighter smiled. "Didn't." He looked over at Stephanie and slipped a five dollar gold piece between her ample breasts and winked. "That's for later. The name's Story...Tom Story."

The girl's mouth fell open. "*The* Tom Story?"

He had a wry smile. "Never met another one."

***

CHAPTER FIVE

GAINESVILLE, TEXAS
SKEANS BOARDING HOUSE

Faye Skeans, the dark-blond, attractive middle-aged owner of the boarding house, walked into the parlor from the kitchen carrying a tray with five short-stemmed brandy snifters and a cut-glass decanter. She set the tray on a round coffee table in front of a wing-back saddle-leather couch, picked up the decanter and poured a half-inch of dark liquid in each glass.

"This is some of my special dewberry brandy I make...my grandma's recipe," Faye said.

"Oh, and it's absolutely just to die for," added Annabel.

"Cheers." Faye held up her glass in toast.

"Cheers and good fortune," said Bodie.

Fiona nodded and smiled. "We shall need it, I fear."

They all lifted their glasses and took a sip.

"My, this is good," said Fiona. "Reminds me a little of that new drink we had at Barnett in the Chocktaw Nation...called cherry creme soda...but with a bit of a bite."

"Yep, and this bite'll take a chunk out, if you ain't careful."

"Moderation in all things, Bodie, moderation in all things," chimed in Faye. She looked at Fiona's long shiny raven-colored thick single braid draped over her left shoulder. "You have beautiful hair, my dear. I suspect it's devastating when it's down and styled...Are you part Indian?"

She shook her head. "No, ma'am, my mother was Italian and my father was Irish...I took after mama's side of the family...except for getting papa's height. He was over six feet four."

"My goodness. You must have gotten your singing ability from her side also. You have a truly lovely voice," she said, referring to some of the songs they had sung to Faye's accompaniment on the piano after dinner and before the brandy.

Fiona blushed.

"Well, that's somethin' I ain't seen before," commented Bass.

"What's that?" asked Bodie.

"Marshal Miller gittin' embarrassed."

"I'm not used to getting compliments, Mister Reeves."

"I done complimented you on yer shootin', didn't I?"

"I suppose you did...in a round about sort of way."

94

BASS AND THE LADY

"How was that?" asked Annabel.

"He said that anybody could shoot like I could...he wanted to stay on the good side of."

Annabel giggled. "Well, Marshal Reeves, that was fairly close to being a compliment...for a man, I would say...Bless your little heart."

"What did he do now?" came a gravely voice from the door to the foyer.

They all turned as Faye's long time suitor, Tom Sullivant, his daughter Francis Ann and her husband, inactive Texas Ranger Walt Durbin walked in.

"Well, looky here, looky here...it's Bass Reeves."

"Walt, how in tarnation are you?" He shook the lanky horseman's hand. "And Miss, er guess I should say Miz Francis..." Bass glanced down at her slightly rounded, normally flat as a pancake stomach. "Reckon it's purty obvious...Congratulations."

"Rangers don't mess around. We git the job done in a hurry."

Annabel playfully swatted Bodie behind the head. "You watch yourself, mister."

"Yessum." He rubbed the back of his head. "Guess I should make the introductions."

"That would be the polite thing to do...Sugar," his wife said, tapping her foot.

After all the greetings were finished, everyone took a seat. Faye brought in more glasses and another bottle of her brandy.

"Say, is Bill still around? Ain't heard from him since Jack an' I left," Bass commented.

Bodie chuckled. "Oh, yeah. He got transferred to work out of the Paris office. Comes to see Miss Millie quite reg'lar...Do believe he's got the sweets on her. Gonna have to tie kerosene rags around the boy's ankles to keep the sugar ants off."

"Bodie Hickman!" chastised Annabel.

"Just kiddin'."

"He's a good man to have coverin' yer backside."

"Who's Bill?" asked Fiona.

"Brushy Bill Roberts...he's a marshal too. Helped us out takin' down the Red River gang...Got his own self wounded, but it healed up an' haired over purty quick," answered Bass.

"Oh, I've heard Marshal Cantrell talk about him...Good hand with a side arm," said Fiona.

"Bass, you want to fill everybody in on what you and Marshal Miller are doin' in our fair city?"

"I 'spect that I should, Bodie." He glanced over at Fiona. "I'll start at the beginnin'..."

"...and Tom, I's thinkin', what with ya'll bein' in the high dollar horse bidness, need to be akeepin' a extry good eye out fer this Story feller." Bass finished bringing everyone up to date thirty minutes later. "Don't have much to go on, 'ceptin' he's fair tall an' has light brown er sandy hair an' they say he's slicker'n a greased baby's butt...uh, beggin' yer pardon, ladies...backside, and he's got a colored with him."

Sullivant got to his feet with his snifter of brandy in his hand, paced slowly across the room in the direction of the fireplace and turned around. "You said, he's partial to horse racin'?"

"What we were told," offered Fiona.

Tom drained the last of his brandy and set the glass on the mantle. "Knowin' your eye for horses, Bass...what're you ridin' these days?"

"Got me a big gray Saddlebred."

"Mare, geldin' or stud?"

"Stud."

Tom looked at Francis and Walt. They both grinned and nodded. "Can he run?"

"Ain't never been been...Say, I see where yer agoin'...We hold a big horse race. Spread the word around...See as we kin draw him out."

"That's our thinkin'." He glanced at his daughter and Walt again. "Don't see any sense in you workin' at the feed store, you kin work out at our ranch and stay purty much outta sight till you're ready. We can say we bought a new stallion and just got him in."

"And Fiona, I'm almost as tall as you are and I have a number of dresses that it doesn't look like I'm going to be able to fit in for a while." Francis Ann looked down at her belly and smiled. "They should work fine for saloon singing outfits with a little dressing up."

"Oh, oh!" Annabel exclaimed. "I just remembered...I still have my cotillion dress in a trunk upstairs. Debutante cotillions?...When young ladies turn eighteen, are rather big social events back home in Alabama...I believe we can add some lace around the bottom to make up for your height. It would be absolutely stunnin' on you, Fiona, with your black hair and all...It's a deep red satin."

"Oh, my." She waved her hand in front of her face. "I'm getting flustered again. Ya'll are just too kind."

Bass grinned. "Told you they wuz good folks...Miz Faye never even said 'nythang 'bout me bein' colored when I stayed here afore."

Faye jumped to her feet and feigned surprise. "You are?...Mercy me, I never noticed...I may need my salts."

Bass roared with his big laugh. "Reckon we'll just have to git you some new eye glasses, too."

They all joined in the fun.

"Now, I just have to get some songs to learn. I don't think Southern Baptist gospels will go over very well in a saloon."

"Just a minute, Fiona." Faye walked over to the bench in front of her piano, lifted the lid and took out a stack of sheet music. "I have *Red River Valley*, *Shenandoah*, *Streets of*

Laredo, A Bird in a Gilded Cage, Camptown Races and a brand new one, *Daisy Bell.*"

"*Daisy Bell*? How does that go?" asked Fiona.

Faye sat down at her upright, set the music up, lifted the key cover and began to play and sing,

'There is a flower within my heart
Daisy, Daisy
Planted one day by a glancing dart
Planted by Daisy Bell
Whether she loves me or loves me not
Sometimes it's hard to tell
Yet I am longing to share the lot
Of beautiful Daisy Bell
Daisy, Daisy, give me your answer, do
I'm half crazy all for the love of you
It won't be a stylish marriage
I can't afford the carriage
But you'd look sweet upon the seat
Of a bicycle built for two'."

"Oh, how fun…That should be easy to learn. I can see doing that with a parasol…twirling it over my shoulder. I think I know the others fairly well."

SUGAR HILL SALOON

Frank turned to Stephanie. "Say, pretty lady...How's about you give us men a little breathin' space? We got some business to talk about."

She looked at Tom.

He nodded. "Ain't plannin' on goin' anywhere, darlin'. Go ahead on and powder your nose or sumthin'." He winked and patted her on the rear.

"I'll be right over there when you need me." She pointed at a chair near the piano player. "Just wave."

"Of course."

Frank watched her walk away. "Nice looking hunk of woman, there."

Story grinned. "Yep...What's on your mind?"

Pierce looked around and then back at Tom. "Well, sir, it's like this...My cousins, Tom, Jim and Pink Lee, used to run the, uh...horse business 'round these parts. Made a lot of money, they did."

"You don't say?"

"I do say. Problem was, Federal marshals and Texas Rangers got a couple of men inside the operation and shut 'em down...permanent like. Pink an' Jim got themselves kilt over to Lindsay on a bank deal and Tom, well...he ain't likely to ever see the outside of a jailhouse. Jury convicted him of...swear to God, git this...twenty-two counts of murder and throwed in a few counts of rustlin'...sentenced to hang."

Story took a sip of his whiskey. "Seems I 'member readin' something 'bout that...million dollars in the local bank and whole passel of law dogs waitin' for 'em...Didn't they use a Gatlin Gun?"

"That was what they called it, alright...Local sheriff was in on the deal and got shot in his own jail by his fiancée."

Tom grinned and glanced over at Stephanie. "Hell hath no fury...What's this have to do with me?"

Frank downed his shot and poured another. "I'm putting together a new group to uh...sorta pick up where they left off...My cousins got sidetracked by that damn bank and thought that Gatlin Gun would make it a cake walk...We know how that turned out."

He pointed at his cowboy friend sitting beside him. "My padnah, Jack Long here, was number two in Jessie Evan's gang, a well-known rustling outfit out in New Mexico that Billy the Kid rode with...till they started stealing from John Tunstall and Billy switched sides."

"Smart move not going up against him. I hear tell he was real fast."

Jack nodded. "Ain't like I was skeered of him all by himself or nothin'...That bunch he rode with would as soon dry gulch or back-shoot a man...I'd woulda taken him on mano-a-mano if ol' Pat Garrett hadn't shot him in the dark."

"I'm sure you would." Tom gulped down the last of his glass and poured himself another. He looked around the bar.

"You gentlemen are lookin' for a man who can handle himself if things get dicey…am I right?"

Frank sat back. "Well, reckon that's cuttin' to the meat of it. We all heard of your reputation with a gun…" He chuckled. "…even before your little demonstration here tonight."

"What's my split?"

Pierce leaned back in and placed his elbows on the table. "Twenty-five percent."

Tom's pale blue eyes grew narrow and cold. "Thirty-five."

Frank looked over at Jack. He nodded almost imperceptibly. Pierce stuck out his hand. "I do believe we have a deal."

Story grasped it firmly. "So, when's the next job?"

Frank smiled. "Purty soon…Ranch down a little south of here, got the best breedin' stock in north Texas, the Rafter S…Got a buyer fer a couple of bred mares."

"Just what'n hell is 'purtysoon?'"

"'Bout a week. Gotta scout it out first an' find out where they's keepin the mares…It's a big place an' they tend to move 'em around some."

"What about in the meantime?…I'll get a little bored just sittin' here around takin' you boy's money at the poker table." He had a wry smile.

Frank and Jack exchanged glances.

"Well, there is an army payroll for Fort Sill, comin' north on the Gulf an' Colorado outta Dallas day after tomorrow. They offload it across the Red in Marietta, to the Stubblefield stage fer the trip."

"And you know this how, Frank?" asked Tom.

He grinned. "Got a third cousin, once removed, works at the depot in Marietta. Always knows when they schedule a payroll on account he has to arrange fer the stage to be there on time."

"Is everybody around here kin to everybody else?"

"Purtnear," Frank replied.

"So, just why haven't ya'll hit it before?"

"Well, like I said, been gittin' ginned up," replied Jack. "Jest been Frank'n me...till now."

"How many guards?"

Frank and Jack exchanged glances again.

"My cousin says jest the messenger on the stage and one outrider. Usually not room inside on account of passengers headin' to Healdton an' points west...Don't change teams till Snake Creek Station south of Fort Sill."

"Paper money or gold?"

"Cash...That much gold'd be too heavy to carry plus the soldiers would have to convert it to paper to spend it anywheres outside the sutlers," said Frank.

"Well, I do know a little somethin' 'bout the Chickasaw country. There's a creek called Walnut Bayou between Marietta and Healdton the stage will have to cross...it's a little over three feet deep at the ford...Pretty wooded on both sides."

Frank nodded. "We'll head thataway of the mornin'...Give us time to git set up on the west side of the creek 'fore the stage gits there."

"Sounds good."

RAFTER S RANCH
COOKE COUNTY

"That's a fine lookin' animal, Bass, fine lookin'. Just look at that shoulder structure...has to be smooth at the trot." They watched Blaze prance about the corral in the midmorning sun—both had their arms over the top rail.

"He is that, Walt. He can road trot all day...Rockin' chair lope, too...But the best thang 'bout him is his heart. They ain't no quit nowheres...It's not that he cain't be beat...he won't be beat."

The big gray stallion jumped up in the air, flipped his tail high, farted, hit the ground, rolled back over his heels and charged toward the other side of the pen.

Walt hesitated, scuffed the ground with his boot and finally turned toward Bass. "You really goin' after Bennie? Yer own boy?"

He demeanor darkened. To Bass Reeves, duty was not the first thing—it was the only thing. "Got to...have a warrant on 'im...The law is the law." He watched his horse frolic some more. "If'n we, as lawmen, start playin' favorites...well, we's jest as well turn this country over to the anarchists an' go back to livin' in caves…He's my son, my own flesh an' blood, so's I gotta bear some responsibilities fer his behavior…I failed him somewheres." Bass' jaw tightened. "It's my job an' nobody else's to bring him in…Some other marshal might kill him, if'n he's armed…or git kilt."

"An' you?"

"He won't shoot me."

Walt looked at him hard. "You shore?…"

"You boys got Blaze settled in?"

They turned to see Francis and Fiona walking up to the corral from the house.

"'Spect so. Think he had a belly full of train ridin' fer a spell," said Bass.

"I know Diablo did." Fiona glanced over at an adjacent trap where her Appaloosa was also playing and getting acquainted with several of the ranch's geldings. She turned to Francis Ann. "I do appreciate ya'll keeping him out here."

The tall redhead nodded. "He didn't need to be spending all day at Clark's Livery. Easy way for a horse used to being out to founder."

"Ya'll pick some outfits for Fiona?" asked Walt.

The girls exchanged looks and grins.

"So lucky that Fran's clothes fit…even the corset and bustle. She had a nice day dress I can wear into the Painted Lady to apply for the job.

"Believe I can help with that," said Tom Sullivant as he walked up to join the group.

"The owner, Timothy McPherson, is a card playin' friend of mine. I'll escort you in an' we can say you're a cousin from...uh, New Orleans, how's that?"

"That will be fine, Tom, I'm sure, but I do need to learn those songs Faye showed me last night."

"I'll get the buggy hitched up right after we have some lunch. Sing Loo'll have it ready in a short."

"It's not fried chicken is it, Daddy?"

He chuckled. "Nope, pork chops, fresh purple-hull crowders, fried squash, cornbread and tomato-cucumber salad...Oh, and buttermilk pie for desert."

"What's wrong with fried chicken?" asked Fiona.

"With soy sauce batter?" answered Francis Ann.

"Oh."

"But, his buttermilk pie will make you jump up and howl at the moon...My favorite," offered Bass.

The sound of Sing Loo ringing the triangle-shaped gong on the front porch of the house caught everyone's attention.

"'Pears at though it's ready," said Walt.

"Ya'll er waitin' on me, yer abackin' up," Bass added over his shoulder as his long legs strode toward the house.

"I thought you said that about Angie McGann's sweet potato-pecan pie."

"That too, Fiona, that too," he shouted back.

BASS AND THE LADY

DEXTER HOTEL
DELAWARE BEND

Tom slipped into a pair of well-worn canvas pants, a boiled cotton chambray shirt and a dark gray linsey-woolsey vest. He looked nothing like his dapper self from the previous evening. He flipped a silver dollar to Bennie Reeves. "Here you go, boy. This oughta keep you fed till I get back."

"Thankee kindly, Mister Tom. Where you be agoin' so early of a mornin'?"

"That ain't none of your concern. What I need for you to do is to ride into Gainesville and get yourself a job."

"What kinda job?...I mostly done farm work back to home."

"No matter. What I need you to do is get hired on at the Painted Lady Saloon down there. Washin' dishes, sweepin' floors, shinin' shoes, swampin'...whatever. Don't use your real name..."

"On account of I'm wanted?"

Story nodded. "Yeah...Tell 'em your name is...let's see, Willie Spencer...from, uh, Monroe, Louisiana. Think you can remember that?"

"Yessir. I can do that."

"I'll be back in a couple of days. In the meantime, keep your eyes and ears open. Folks won't pay no mind to a colored just doin' his job. I need to know what's goin' on without asking a bunch of nosy questions...Got it?"

Bennie shoved the coin in his pants and nodded.

CHICKASAW NATION

Three riders crossed over the Red River at the Horseshoe Bend ford with the slow moving waters barely coming up to their horse's bellies. The lead man slipped his boots back into the stirrups as his mount climbed up the sandy embankment. He turned and looked over his shoulder at his traveling companions, the brim of his hat shielding his blue eyes from the early morning sun. He chuckled.

"Ya'll still look a little hung over from last night's poker game...Man's gotta learn to pace himself."

"Easy to say...You were winning."

"Hell's bells, Frank. You act like I took your last sawbuck or somethin'...Now those two young cowboys...I really salt and peppered them."

Jack laughed. "One of 'em is pushing up daisies right 'bout now. And you...you won the pot and then took that young filly to bed like it wadn't no more than a howdy do."

Tom grinned and turned back to the direction they were riding—almost due west. "Yep. Sometime you get the bear, and sometimes..." He reined up. "Know something, Frank? You never said how much money was in that military payroll."

Pierce slapped his poppers on the sorrel gelding's neck, urged him to a trot and eased up alongside Story—about halfway up the long, shallow sixty yard high embankment. He smiled. "Oh, five thousand...give or take."

Tom let out a low whistle. "Well, my, my...certainly am glad I made your acquaintance. What the hell we doin' sittin' here jawin'? Time's a wastin."

SIVELLS BEND
CHICKASAW NATION

Jack poured the last of the morning coffee over the embers of the dying campfire near the banks of the Red River where it looped north into the Nation—known as Sivells Bend. Tendrils of smoke and steam curled up in the south breeze as he smacked the side of the graniteware pot to dislodge the last of the stubborn grounds.

Frank looked over at Tom who was cutting a thick slice of bacon in his plate with a belt knife. "What time is it getting to be?"

He set the plate down on a small rock beside the fire and pulled a silver pocket watch from his vest. "Nigh on to eight o'clock...Got plenty of time. Finish your breakfast." He picked up a forkful of pork and beans.

"Sure you know where the stage road is from here?"

"I do. Just a couple of miles north of a little town called Pike...'Bout four miles west. We'll cross the creek here and come back to the ford from the west."

Jack looked up from stowing the coffee pot in his saddle bags. "Not leaving tracks showing which direction we come from?"

"That's the general idea. Gotta be smarter than the average law dog if we want to keep them off our tail." Tom grinned.

PAINTED LADY SALOON
GAINESVILLE, TEXAS

Bennie opened the right side of the nine foot half-frosted glass double doors to the ornate restaurant and saloon at 311 North Commerce Street and glanced around. He pulled his battered slouch hat from his head and held it in front of him as he stepped inside.

It wasn't quite noon, but patrons were already filing in for lunch. A black slate placard on a three-legged easel just inside the door displayed the special for the day in white chalk. *Buffalo Meat Loaf, Cream Peas, Buttered Squash and Cornbread - 60¢.*

Bennie fingered the silver dollar in the pocket of his worn canvas pants as his mouth watered. He looked around for someone to help him.

The combination restaurant and saloon was large for the day, fifty feet wide and ninety feet deep—twenty feet of the west end was used for the kitchen and dressing room for performers. Along the south side was a forty foot ornate hand-carved bar from San Francisco, with a fifteen foot gilded, beveled mirror in the center of the back bar.

The far right corner held the twenty foot wide stage with its upright piano. There were velvet purple stage curtains pulled to the sides and a painted canvas backdrop depicting many local business advertisements. To the left was a large vertical gaming wheel just beside the stairway to the Chickasaw Parlor House upstairs.

There were thirty tables placed in an orderly fashion across the floor, twenty were four foot diameter, with four bow chairs and ten were rectangular with six chairs. All had eating utensils wrapped in white linen napkins in front of each chair.

Just to Bennie's left at the main entry, was an elaborate raised shoeshine stand with a large wooden padded chair and shoe pedestals in front. Above the heavy chair on the wall was a sign:

SHOESHINE - 10¢ BOOTS - 15¢

One of the daytime waitresses, a twenty year old attractive sandy-haired girl—with her hair up on top of her head and wearing a white ruffled front blouse with a light gray ankle length skirt—approached Bennie.

"Good morning, may I help you."

"Uh, yes, Ma'am, er miss, I'd 'preciate talkin' to the owner, if he has a minute or two."

"Lookin' for work?"

"Yessum."

She pointed to a far table over in front of the stage where two men and a beautiful woman with long dark hair styled in ring curls sat in conversation. She was dressed in a dark green day dress with a fitted bodice and a small forward-sitting Goorin Brothers hat.

"That's him over yonder, the dashing one with the sliver temples...He's interviewing a new singer...His name's Timothy McPherson...Would you like something to eat while you wait?"

"Yessum, shore would."

"You'll have to eat in the kitchen...That all right?"

Bennie ducked his head and nodded.

"Follow me." She turned her head slightly. "I'll see that the cook gives you an extra slice of meat loaf...It's really good." She smiled at the shy young man.

"I'd be thankin' you."

"What's your name?"

"Be...uh, Willie...uh...Willie Spencer, Ma'am. I be from uh...Mon-roe, Louisiana."

"My, you're a long way from home...oh, and my name's Betty Lou."

"Yessum, Miss Betty Lou...seems thataway sometimes."

"So, Miss Marston..."

"Just call me Starla, please, Mister McPherson."

He smiled. "Well, in that case, you can call me Tim...What brings you all the way up here from New Orleans...Starla?"

She batted her eyes. "I just had to get away from that dreadful heat and humidity." She waved her black lace fan in front of her face as she looked around—her eyes finally coming to rest on the stairway. "You have a lovely place here...I suppose that's a..."

"Uh...Yes, that's the Chickasaw Parlor House upstairs." He quickly changed the subject. "You don't sing that new music they're calling jass, do you?"

"Oh, no...I sing contemporary. That's another reason I decided to come north...it seems that every street corner down there in the French Quarter has a brass band of coloreds playing that type of music. Now I occasionally like some Dixieland or Victor Bechet's ragtime...heavy on the piano. You do have a piano player?"

"Of course, Jake Oliver...a colored man...comes in at four. He has magic fingers."

"Oh, wonderful." Fiona turned to Tom. "You were so right, Tom, dear, about this place. Thank you so much for inviting me up." She patted his hand.

"Where are you staying?" asked Tim.

"At Miss Faye's. My sweet cousin said I had a place out at the ranch, but I thought it would be too far to come in every day to perform...and the boarding house is only a few blocks away."

Tim nodded. "Good thinking, it's a nice place...when would you like to start?"

"I'm ready this evening. I brought my sheet music."

"Well that might be a problem."

"Oh?"

"See, Jake doesn't read music."

"But, how…"

"By ear, if he hears it, he can play it. You just have to hum a few bars."

Fiona smiled. "Of course…I know someone else who does something similar."

"Excuse me, Mister McPherson."

"Yes, Betty Lou, what is it?"

"There's a colored boy in the kitchen…he's here lookin' for a job. I know you mentioned we needed to add a swamper and someone to run the shoeshine stand…I told the cook to feed him. He looked like he could use a meal."

"Good idea…I'll talk with him in a moment." He turned back to Fiona. "Why don't you start tomorrow, Starla. I'll have the local printer do up some posters for the window and to spread around town…**Starla Marston at The Painted Lady, direct from New Orleans.**" He swept his hand in front of him like he was depicting a marque.

Fiona blushed. "I'm sure that would be fine." She moved to get up and both Tim and Tom jumped to their feet to assist her.

"My, my, such wonderful manners." She batted her eyes again at McPherson.

He took her hand and lightly kissed it. "Until tomorrow, lovely lady. I so look forward to it."

Fiona tilted her head in his direction, and then turned to Tom. "Shall we go, cousin dear?"

They headed to the doors at the front when Tom stopped and turned back to Tim.

"Say, almost forgot. I'm sponsorin' a horse race in a couple weeks, mind if I put a poster in your window, too?"

"Absolutely. Where's it going to be?"

"Out to the fair grounds on the west side of town."

"Sounds good to me...bring it in any time."

"You mind if the participants sign up here? I can add that to the posters."

"Certainly, the bartender, Rube can handle that."

Tom nodded and they continued on to the door.

"Goodness, that's some lady. I must be doing something right," he mumbled and grinned as he made his way through the tables to the kitchen door at the back.

***

CHAPTER SIX

WALNUT BAYOU

The towering trees almost made a tunnel in the dark woods where the road crossed the broad creek. Tom wheeled his horse around, leaned forward and crossed both arms on top of his saddle horn. "This is the place, boys. My idea is to take the outrider first...Should be stickin' pretty close to the stage when it crosses the bayou."

Frank and Jack pulled up beside him.

"Jack's a dead shot with a long gun," commented Pierce.

"That'll do...Hide that paint of yours back in the woods a ways...Sumbitch sticks out like sore thumb."

Jack gave him a look. "He's damn fine in a tight...Got legs and plenty of bottom."

Tom chuckled. "Be that as it may, slick, don't need nobody spottin' us before we start shootin'…Take out the scout soon as the stage gets into the middle of the creek…got it?"

"Like taking candy from a baby."

"Me and Frank will step out and plug the driver and messenger. Team shouldn't try to shy past us if we do it right."

Jack nodded. "What if the passengers start shootin'?"

Tom's tanned face cracked a wry smile. "That'll be their last mistake, I promise you."

Frank looked down at the creek crossing. The water flowed clear over the rocky bottom. It was sixty feet wide and only three deep. "Let's water the horses first…Should help keep 'em quiet when the stage comes."

"Good idea," Tom agreed as he pulled out his gold pocket watch and snapped the cover open. "We got thirty minutes or so to get set up…assumin' the stage is on time." He looked to the west. "Keep a close eye on the road behind us…Last thing we need is some pilgrim ridin' in at the wrong time and throwing a hitch in our little welcome party."

The lone outrider approached the Walnut Bayou ford at a road trot. He bumped his chocolate brown gelding back to a walk—then to a halt at the water's edge and looked around. He was a good hundred yards ahead of the stage.

He waved the driver on and squeezed his knees against the horse's ribs to enter the creek.

His mount stopped and took a long drink as the water swirled past his fetlocks.

"Come on, son...ain't got all day." He slipped his boots out of the oxbow stirrups and held them out front. "Let's go." He clucked.

The gelding pressed forward cautiously, looking down at the rocky bottom as the water came up closer to his belly.

Jack peered from his hiding spot, the '92 Winchester at the ready. *Two gun rig. Boy's loaded for bear.* A smile came to his lips.

The outrider pulled his knees high as he could as the horse sloshed through the deepest part of the creek—water lapped at the bottom of the saddle skirt and soaked the woolen blanket.

Wonder what size them boots are? Long glanced down at his own feet. *Could use a new pair.*

The six horses pulling the stagecoach responded to the tug on the ribbons. They came to a walk a few yards before the crossing and entered the creek exactly as they had dozens of times before.

The road guard waded up the gradual embankment on the far side. He reached the more level section of the road, reached into his saddlebag and withdrew a wax paper pouch of loose-leaf chewing tobacco. He wadded up a bunch of the moist leaves into a ball and pushed it into the side of his mouth.

Tom gauged the stage to be exactly in the middle of the creek. He thumbed the hammer back on his Colt and centered the shotgun messenger above the front sight. Making sure his bullet would clear the double-barreled shotgun cradled in his arms, he squeezed off a round.

His shot echoed up and down the heavily wooded lane, followed almost instantly by Jack and Frank's. The guard rocked back against the top of the coach, and then slumped forward and crumpled down into the boot.

Hit in the chest—only inches from the buttons on his shirt—the driver let the reins fall slack as he clutched at the burning bullet hole. He coughed once, pulled his hand away and saw his gloves covered with foamy red blood. His eyes rolled up and he tumbled off the seat, splashing into the creek below.

The hapless outrider was struck between the shoulder blades—the well-placed shot severing his spine. He rolled out of the saddle. His horse bolted forward. The gelding galloped forty yards down the road and halted when he stepped on one of the split reins.

"Bandits!" A passenger inside drew a .38 caliber pistol from underneath his long morning coat. He stuck it out the window and aimed at the wispy cloud of gunsmoke on the creek bank.

A single .45 caliber shot rang out sharply from forty yards away, striking him dead center in the forehead with a popping sound. The chrome-plated gun dropped from the lifeless fingers straight down into the creek as his body fell back into the coach and disappeared below the side windows. Across the aisle, a young bride to be, screamed at the sight of blood tricking down his nose and onto his starched white shirt.

"You in the coach! Throw out your weapons! You ain't got a chance!"

The reluctant passengers did as they were told. Two sidearms plopped into the crystal clear water. Story moved closer to Pierce and whispered, "Keep 'em covered while I get my horse."

Frank nodded. Jack stepped out of his hiding spot in the brush and joined him.

Tom opened the loading gate and dumped two spent rounds next to his horse. He reloaded and holstered the pistol before leading the mount through the woods onto the road. He swung up into the saddle and reached back to grab a flour sack from his saddlebags.

With the white-cloth sack in one hand, he drew his sixgun again, eased the horse down to the creek and eased up alongside the coach.

"Gimme all your valuables...watches, rings and foldin' money. If'n I suspect for one minute you're holdin' out on me, you'll end up like this hero there." He pointed his muzzle at the deceased salesman on the floorboards, and then tossed the sack inside. "Make it quick, now...ain't got all day." He chuckled.

The five passengers dutifully dropped their belonging in the sack. The woman looked out at his cold blue eyes burning a hole in her over his red bandana mask.

"Mister, I can't get this engagement ring off. I'm too nervous!" her voice cracked.

Tom waved his pistol at the man seated beside her. "Help her…or I can use my knife, if you'd rather."

"No, no! I'll get it for you!" The man took her hand and brought it to his mouth, wetting the ring finger with his saliva. He whispered to her softly as he twisted the ring free and dropped it into the sack. "Sorry, Ma'am."

"Toss it here." Tom caught the bag and slipped a rawhide string around the top, pulled it tight and looped it on his saddle horn. He took one look at the beautiful young blond with tears streaming down both cheeks. "What a shame."

Without warning, he fanned six shots through the window in the door. The six-horse team lunged. He wheeled his roan about and caught the wheel lead by the headstall as they climbed the far side of the creek bank. "Whoa…whoa boys. Easy now."

Jack ran over and grabbed hold of the nigh-side opposite Tom. "What the hell did you go and do that fer? That wadn't part of the deal!"

"You got wanted dodgers out on you?"

He shook his head. "'Course I do…That's the reason I left New Mexico."

"Well, I don't...Wannna know why?...I don't leave witnesses...ever."

Frank stepped up. "What are we gonna do with the bodies?"

"Dump 'em in the creek...Turtles gotta eat, too."

He grinned and pulled down his mask. "We'll clean out the strongbox here and sink it down the creek a ways...Leave the stage a mile or two west of here...Hell, they may never find the bodies the way that bayou's a flowin'...Might float all the way to the Mississippi."

Frank nodded. "Never would thought of that."

"I know." Tom released the reins and reloaded his pistol. He picked up his empties and dropped them in the flour sack. "The fewer things that can tie you to a crime, the better. Best get a move on...we're burnin' daylight."

After dumping the bodies in the middle of the creek, they pulled the heavy strong box out of the boot and blasted the lock open. Tom stepped back.

"Frank, your idea...You get the honors."

"Gladly." He lifted the oaken lid, banded with straps of steel riveted to it. Inside were bundles of newly printed cash and a couple of cloth bags of gold coins. "Jackpot, boys!"

"You said it! We're rich, by the Lord Harry!" Jack grinned from ear to ear.

"Not bad for a couple days work. Don't waste time countin'...Toss some in each of these and let's move out." Tom held out two more tightly-woven cotton flour sacks.

Jack dumped cash in each and handed one to both of his partners. "Got my eyes on them boots the outrider was awearin'."

Tom shook his head. "Hell, you can buy yourself a new custom-made pair over in Nocona, now...Reckon I'd get that horse he was a ridin', though, was me...looked plenty sound and not near as recognizable as your paint."

"Good idea, Mister Story." Jack picked up the empty strong box and waded out in the creek a few yards. He flung it to the center. It floated clear of the crossing before he blew a hole in the lower right corner with his handgun. The box continued to drift away, listing as it took on water.

Tom tied his horse to the back of the coach, and then climbed aboard. Taking the reins in his hands, he snapped them over the team. "Get on up, there...Hyah!"

With a creak of the thick multilayered leather straps suspending the coach from the frame, the rig rolled away from the scene of the heinous crime.

They abandoned the stage off to the west and rode back to the creek.

"We'll ride the bayou in the shallows along the west side for a mile or so…long as the bottom stays rocky, an' then exit one at the time back to the west."

"West? How come?" asked Frank.

"'Cause we're gonna go down to the Red, make camp for the night and ford at the old John Chisum Cattle Trail on the west side of Sivells Bend, of the mornin'."

"Oh, I see you…hidin' our trail, huh?"

"Damn, you don't miss much, do you Frank?"

"Well…" He ducked his head thinking Tom gave him a compliment.

SIVELLS BEND

Tom slung his double-skirted Collins and Morrison saddle on his roan's back, pulled a bubble in the blanket and cinched him up.

The sun was well above the tree line as Frank and Jack were breaking camp and dousing the morning fire.

"You two can head on over to Dexter," Tom said as he let his mount air down, pulled the lattigo one notch tighter and swung up into the saddle.

"Whatcha gonna do?"

"You're right nosey there, ain't you, Jack?…But since you asked, I'm going to make a stop in Gainesville…Need to check out somethin' at the Painted Lady."

124

BASS AND THE LADY

COOKE COUNTY COURTHOUSE
COUNTY CLERK'S OFFICE

Millie Malena had her back to the counter while was replacing an eighteen inch square ledger in its slot against the far wall.

"Need some help with that, little lady?"

The five-two brunette wheeled around at the sound of the familiar voice behind her.

"Bill!...You startled me...You do that all the time, can't you bump into something or scuff your feet when you come in?" She smiled broadly. "I wasn't expecting you."

Deputy US Marshal Brushy Bill Roberts ducked his head. "Sorry darlin', force of habit. Learned some time ago to move quietly...fella tends to live longer that way."

He paused and gave her a big grin. "I wrapped up the case I was working on over in Paris an' caught the train. Thought I'd come over for a little visit...Got a carriage rented outside whenever you can leave."

"I'm just about ready now...that's why I was replacing the ledger...Pick up, cleanup and straighten up at the end of the day, you know?" She looked at the Biedermeier clock on the far wall and smiled. "Almost closing time."

Bill helped Millie up into the Stanhope buggy, untied the bay mare from the iron post ring on the east side of the Court House.

He strode to the other side and stepped up into the seat beside her.

"Well, how about a steak over at the Painted Lady? Bass told me they got the finest Porterhouse north of Fort Worth."

"Love one. I've always wanted to eat there, but it's not a proper place for a lady to go into by herself."

"I think we got that covered." He double clucked at the mare.

PAINTED LADY

Bill and Millie sat at a table near the stage while they waited on their order. They were close enough to hear the entertainer going over her music with the piano player.

"Oh, my, isn't she beautiful? Wonder who she is?" commented Millie, as she appraised the tall dark-haired woman in a red satin dress standing next to the colored piano player.

"The sign in the window said, Starla Marston from New Orleans."

"I wish I could get my hair to do that."

"What?"

"Well, one, it reaches almost to her waist and the ring curls are just perfect. And two, when I try to do that they fall out in about thirty minutes and it's straight as a board."

"I happen to think your hair is absolutely gorgeous…It shines like the morning sun."

Millie blushed. "Oh, you…Thank you, but I know better."

"She must be teaching the player her music."

"How can you tell?"

"I can hear her hum the melody and he's nodding his head. Five'll get you ten he doesn't read music, but can play anything by ear."

"Now that's talent. My son could do that with his mouth harp, he…" She stopped as a cloud seemed to come over her face.

"I would have loved to have known him. Bodie said he was special…was gonna be a good lawman."

The cloud vanished and she smiled at the memory. "Oh, he was…he was indeed."

"I'm…" Bill stopped as the corner of his eye caught a tall man with light hair enter the front door.

The man's blue eyes covered the entire room without moving his head. They came to rest on the shoeshine stand in the corner to his left where a young colored man in a white jacket sat on the edge of the platform. He stepped over, mounted the step, sat in the padded seat and placed his dirty boots on the pedestals.

"…Uh, oh."

"What is it?" Millie looked over in the direction of his gaze.

"Trouble."

"That man in the shoe shine chair? How can you tell?"

She watched as the colored man brushed the dirt off the man's boots with a stiff brush, and then rubbed them down with saddle soap using a smaller round one.

"You been in my line of work for as long as I have…bad actors just have an air about them. Can spot 'em a mile off…The way he wears his gun…and he eyeballed every person in the room in less than five seconds…He's wrathy."

"What's wrathy?"

"On the edge all the time…quick to anger. Got killer's eyes…believe me, I know."

"Oh."

Bill also was aware that the entertainer took notice of the stranger, too, but not from attraction. "There's also more to her than meets the eye."

Millie glanced back at Starla. "How do you do that?"

He grinned and took a sip of his iced tea. "It's a gift."

"Well, see you got yourself a job." Story took a thin cheroot from his vest pocket and stuck it in his mouth.

Bennie grabbed a match from a shot glass under the chair, struck it on the side of the cast iron foot pedestal and lit it when Tom bent over.

"Yassir. Mister Tim, the owner…he has me shinin' boots fer tips an' I cleans up after closin' fer a dollar."

Story had a wry grin. "Whole dollar, huh? Why you'll be openin' your own saloon before you know it."

128

"Sir?"

"Nothin'...You been keepin' your eyes an' ears open like I said?"

"Oh, yassir. Peoples is inclined to talk whilst I shine their shoes 'n boots."

"And?"

Bennie grinned. "Hear tell they's a open horse race comin' up in 'bout ten days...Prize money of a thousand dollars! Kin you 'magine? A thousand dollars...They's a sign over behind the bar an' one on the front winder over yonder." He nodded toward the opposite side of the saloon. "Gonna hold it over to the fairgrounds."

"A thousand dollars? You don't say?"

"Yassir, I do say. Heard a Mister Sullivant...he raises horses...talk about it when he brung the posters in...Say's ain't a horse in Texas kin beat his horse."

"Don't suppose you heard the name of his ranch?"

"Oh, yassir, I did...The Rafter S."

Bennie slathered the black wax polish over Tom's boots with his fingers, and then took a long cotton cloth and started buffing them—popping the rag every three or four times.

Story took a big draw on the stogie and blew a white cloud over his head as he glanced out the large flat sheet glass window on his right.

Farmer & Stienke

NORTH COOKE COUNTY

Bill flicked the ribbons over the mare's rump and bumped her up into a smooth ground-eating extended trot as they headed toward Millie's home from Gainesville. The best road was the old Butterfield Stage road to Callisburg, then north on the Bourland Ranch road to Dexter.

It was nearing sunset as they traveled along the tree-canopied road halfway between Callisburg and Dexter. They paused at Hickory Creek to stretch their legs and allow the mare to drink. They had just crossed through the water when two masked gunmen stepped out of thick copse of persimmon trees on the left side of the road. Both held six shooters in their right hands.

"Halt or suffer yer death!" said the taller one, a step ahead of the other man.

"Whoa up there, girl." Bill pulled the mare to a stop. "What's all this then?"

"Jest git out of the buggy an' don't give us no sass."

Bill laid down the reins and stepped to the ground. "Boys, I do believe you're making a big mistake."

The road agent eyed Roberts' tailored morning coat, gold brocade vest, silk cravat, gray striped trousers and dark bowler. "Naw, it's you that's makin' the mistake, Mister Dandy Pants...I said no sass. Now hand over yer wallet...an' that trollop's purse whilst yer at it."

Bill glanced back at the frightened Millie, shook his head and frowned. "Dadgum, I really wish you hadn't said that."

"An' jest why is that Mister Fancy?" asked the shorter outlaw.

"Because not only have you brigands frightened my lady, but you've also insulted her...Now, I'm going to have to kill you both."

The two highwaymen looked at each other and laughed.

"Haw! Did you hear what he said, Albert? He said..." The taller man never finished.

Almost faster than the eye could follow, Bill drew his Colt Thunderer from the armpit holster under his suit coat and snapped off two shots, striking each man in the center of the chest. They both staggered back and collapsed to the road like wet paper sacks.

Roberts walked the ten paces to where the two men lay, kicked the guns away from their hands and knelt down beside the one called Albert who was still breathing. "Told you."

"Damn you...You've kilt us...kilt us both." He gasped for a breath. "Who are you?"

"Deputy United States Marshal Brushy Bill Roberts." He leaned down close to the man's ear and whispered some more.

Albert stared up at Bill's face and his eyes got big. He shook his head. "No...no." The last word ended in a death rattle.

He picked up the men's pistols, walked back to the buggy and laid them on the floorboard. "I apologize for that, Millie."

She was patting her chest with her hand and trying to catch her breath. "How did you...I mean, how did you do that?...I... never saw you draw."

"They didn't either...It's called distraction."

"What did you say to him?"

"Oh, not really anything..." He looked back at the bodies. "I gotta go move 'em out of the road...Don't guess I can inform the authorities till tomorrow. Who's the county sheriff now?"

"Chief Deputy George Rudabaugh is the acting Sheriff until they can hold an election. "They're trying get Mike Compton to come out of retirement, but I don't think he's having any of it."

Bill nodded. "Big Mike's a good lawman. He's earned his retirement...You know, may have to figure a way for you to live somewhere else besides Delaware Bend. Its reputation is just about as notorious as Tombstone or Leadville."

"I know...but where would I go?"

"Well, I might have an idea." He grinned and stepped toward the bodies.

SUGAR HILL SALOON

Tom tied up his horse at one of the few open spots at the hitching posts directly outside. He loosened the girth a bit and walked into the saloon—a thick cloud of cigarette and cigar smoke had collected up at the fourteen foot embossed tin ceiling. The place was already noisy with the Friday night crowd, and the piano player tried to keep the mood lively.

Story spotted Frank and Jack standing at the far end of the bar. He made eye contact with the leader of the gang, but Pierce nodded toward the far wall, where Stephanie sat at a round table with three locals who were drinking beer and playing poker.

He made his way across the room and stepped up to the table. "Evenin', Ma'am, gents...Anybody join in?"

The oldest of the three, owner of the Foster's Mercantile store looked up at him. "Don't see why not...long as your money's good."

He grinned and winked at the woman as he pulled out a chair. "You're looking quite lovely tonight, Miss Stephanie."

She smiled. "Flattery will get you anywhere, Tom...The usual?"

Story nodded. "And bring us some more glasses if you would, please. My new friends here might like a taste of the good stuff."

The other players, a local blacksmith and a surveyor exchanged glances, and then grinned.

Tom took a ten dollar bill from his wallet and laid in on the table. "What's the game, boys?"

By eleven o'clock, the skinny surveyor had partaken of a bit too much of the free bourbon. He looked down at his cards and then at the four dollars left in front of him. "Tarnation...gonna have to fold. Lady Luck has forsaken me tonight, gentlemen...I best get headed to home 'afor ya'll skin me smooth out...My old lady's gonna raise Billy hell with me as it is."

Tom grinned and glanced down at his hand as the besotted man pushed back and staggered to his feet. "Better luck next time." He tossed five dollars in the pot. "I see your five and call."

"I got two pair...Jacks high," said the oldest man.

"Sumbitch...Think I got yours beat there, Arlen." The blacksmith grinned broadly. "Three of a kind." He spread out the cards showing an Ace, a Queen and the nines."

Tom chuckled. "Three ladies, boys, read 'em an' weep...Wondered which one of you had my other Queen." He poured himself a drink and held out the bottle. "Who's thirsty?"

"Had about all the fun I can handle tonight. Imagine I'm down about fifty." He pushed back from the table.

The sullen-faced blacksmith shook his head. "Sixty-five to me. Talk about a run of bad luck...Huh? Damnation, thought I'd take you on that last pot...Gimme one last taste of that whiskey 'for I head to the house."

Tom obliged the man. He downed it and turned for the door. Story raked the winnings in, separated the bills by denomination, and stuffed them in his wallet.

Stephanie beamed. "Goodness gracious, I love to watch you play."

"Kinda like to have you on my shoulder. Maybe you're my Lady Luck."

She smiled and ran the tip of her tongue over her pearly white teeth. "Maybe so."

He reached into his vest pocket and brought out a carved ivory cameo in an 18 carat gold setting on a matching chain. "You know what, pretty lady? I saw this little bauble and thought it would look just perfect on you."

Her eyes flew open wide. "Tommy! Nobody ever bought me anything like this!"

"Like it?" He opened the tiny clasp and reached around her slender neck.

"Are you serious?...I love it." Her eyes locked on his as he fastened the necklace.

"They asked me if I wanted it boxed up." His perfidy was convincing as he smiled. "Told 'em no thanks...I was gonna give it to you personally."

She lifted the delicate oval keepsake and stared at it for a moment. "I...I don't know what to say..."

He winked. "Oh, I imagine you'll think of somethin'."

She wrapped her arms around his neck and gave him a big kiss.

PAINTED LADY

Across the street in front of Stienke's Gun Shop, an old hunched-over colored man shuffled along the brick sidewalk, pulling a wooden child's wagon filled with junk items, discarded clothing, some tin cans, old shoes and phosphate bottles. He was wearing a dark tattered sack cloth coat and a worn slouch hat pulled down to his ears. The area was lit only by the gas lights inside large round globes set on cast iron posts on both sides of the street every fifty feet.

He stopped, painfully bent over and picked up a lost copper penny, studied it for a moment, and then put it in his pocket. He looked up and saw a young colored man through the window of the Painted Lady Saloon and Steak Emporium shining shoes.

He observed the lad for a long moment until one of the sporting ladies from the Chickasaw Parlor House upstairs shouted at him—thinking he was watching her and several of her friends enjoying the evening air out on the cast iron railing enclosed balcony.

"Don't just watch, honey! If that was a dollar you just found, bring it up here…maybe we can work something out."

She and the other working girls laughed.

He ducked his head and shuffled down Commerce Street in the direction of Broadway. Unseen by the ladies of the evening and under the shadow of his hat, a single tear rolled down his chocolate cheek.

***

CHAPTER SEVEN

SKEANS BOARDING HOUSE

It was a little after midnight when a dark figure entered the carriage house. He reached up to the red painted kerosene globe lantern hanging on a post and turned the wick up. The interior of the barn took on a warm glow, but with multiple dark shadows.

The man straightened up his back and stretched from side to side, removed his dirty, misshapen hat and placed it on top of the items in the little wagon. The disheveled rag picker took the lantern from its hook and, pulling the wagon, opened the door to the tack room at the end of the aisle-way nearest the back of the house and went inside.

A few minutes later, Bass Reeves—now wearing a brown canvas jacket over tan trousers with his twin .38-40 Peacemakers strapped about his hips in cross-draw—opened the door to the kitchen at the back of the boarding house and stepped in. "Got'ny more of that coffee, Fiona?"

She looked up from reading the latest edition of the local newspaper, The Gainesville Daily Register. "On the stove…Where've you been? Almost gave you up for lost."

"Jest been doin' a little nosin' around…How did yer evenin' as the new Painted Lady songbird go?"

"Darn you Bass Reeves. How did I let you talk me into this? I'm going to have to get a new parasol tomorrow before my first show."

"Come again?

"Had to whack a couple of cowboys that tried to get a little handsey…if you know what I mean."

Bass chuckled. "Bet they's some good ol' boys with knots on they heads this mornin'."

Fiona nodded. "Better than a hole in it, though."

"You packin'?"

She looked askance at him from her newspaper. "Now what do you think?…'Course it's only a .41 rimfire, but it does have two rounds."

He smiled. "You kin ask Annabel…"

"Ask Annabel what?" The petite blond said as she walked in the kitchen wearing a forest-green chenille robe above her swollen belly. Her hair was in a long single braid down her back—the way most women with long hair wore it for sleeping. Well?"

"Jest gonna mention the little set-to you had with Bart Shefield over to Kingfisher County."

The young very-pregnant woman turned pale. "Please, Bass...I really don't want to revisit that awful experience. I only did what I had to do...There was no way Theresa and I were going back with those animals."

Bass nodded. "The short version is Ardmore Deputy Sheriff Willie Agee was takin' Annabel and Miss Theresa to safety after we got 'em back from the Griffin gang an' he got hisself bushwhacked by one of the gang members...Well, seems that Miss Annabel here saved him and her friend to boot with her little bitty peashooter."

"Theresa married sweet Willie after he healed up...We had a double weddin'," added Annabel.

"I do feel a little naked without my matched Colts," said Fiona.

Bodie walked down stairs wearing his longjohns and riding pants. One of his gallus straps was hanging off his shoulder. "Heard voices down here...Ya'll know what time it is?"

"Is this here gonna be a quiz?" deadpanned Reeves.

Fiona grinned. "Bass was trying to reassure me about the power of my Remington derringer I keep up inside my parasol."

The sleepy ranger shook his head and yawned. "Yep, my Annabel's a regular heroine with hers."

His wife gave him a look. "Cover your mouth when you yawn, dear. Have you no manners at all?...Bless your heart."

He ducked his head. "Yessum...What are you doing down here? It's past midnight."

"I had this overwhelmin' craving for pickles and sweet-cream." She blushed.

Bodie made a face. "I've heard of strawberries and cream even peaches and cream...but pickles and cream?"

Bass laughed. "Son, oncst you done had as many chilrens as me and my Nellie Jenny, you find they's gonna eat things what ain't fit fer man ner beast when they's pregnant."

"A cravin' is a cravin'." Annabel looked at Fiona. "Do you have any children?"

She pressed her lips together and shook her head. "No...my husband was murdered before we..."

"Oh! I am so sorry...how terribly inconsiderate of me. Please do accept my apology."

"Not necessary. How could you have known?" She looked over at the dark window above the sink, and then turned back to Annabel. "I did so want children, though."

She patted the brunette's hand. "You're still young, there's..."

Fiona shook her head. "I have something I have to do before I can even think about it."

BASS AND THE LADY

Annabel could tell by the look in her steel-gray eyes that this part of the conversation was over.

Fiona turned to Bass. "I think I saw that Tom Story this evening. A man fitting his description came in and got his boots shined by the colored bootblack. They..."

"That was Bennie."

"You saw him?"

He nodded. "I was undercover as a ragpicker. Went by this evenin' on t'other side of the street...Seen 'im in the winder."

"Who's Bennie?" Bodie inquired.

Bass glanced at him. "My son."

He frowned. "And?"

"He's on the run...Got paper on 'im fer killin' his wife."

Annabel brought her hand to her mouth. "Oh, my sweet Lord."

"Why didn't you go in an' arrest him?"

Bass looked at Bodie again. "On account he's travelin' with that gunfighter rustler feller I tol' ya'll 'bout the other night. Figured they might show up 'round here. That's why we set up that race...Reckon we was right, since Fiona thinks that wuz him tonight an' even more so that he wuz talkin to my boy...Got no warrants on 'im, so we gotta let the hand play out.

US MARSHAL'S OFFICE
ARDMORE, IT

The young boy rode to the office and looped his lead rope around the hitching rail. He made his way inside and approached the front desk as Deputy Loss Hart poured his first cup of coffee from a pot on the wood burning stove in the corner.

"Telegram for Marshal Lindsey."

Selden stuck out his hand from the other desk. "That would be me, boy." He was a big broad-shouldered man, standing six four—smelling of stale coffee and tobacco—as he opened the yellow flimsy, slipped on his reading glasses and began to read.

The messenger stood by with notepad in hand in case there was to be a reply.

"Lord have mercy...Listen to this Loss: Thursday Stubblefield stage from Marietta to Fort Sill missing with Army payroll aboard. Stop. Chickasaw farmer Horace Maytubbe found coach bloody and abandoned between Simon and Eastman. Stop." He continued, "Three stage line employees and four passengers unaccounted for. Stop. Foul play suspected. Stop."

Hart stepped over to the desk and looked over Lindsey's shoulder. "Ain't much of nothin' out there...just a few Injun folk trying to scratch out a livin.'"

"'Spect yer right." Selden spat out a stream of brown juice into a nearby spittoon and glanced up at the Regulator wall clock. "Son, see yer ready fer a reply. Send this:…Marietta Stubblefield Stationmaster. Stop. Leaving on morning train. Stop. Will require passenger manifest and witnesses. Stop. Selden Lindsey, Deputy United States Marshal."

The Western Union messenger read the reply back to him.

Selden dug in his vest pocket and tossed him a quarter and a dime.

"Thank you, sir!" He spun around and bolted for the door.

Loss drained his cup, made a face and closed one eye. "Shoulda poured that nasty crap out and started a new pot…Yesterd'ys warmed-over coffee's enough to turn a man's stomach."

"Or use as paint thinner." Lindsey pushed back from the desk and slowly got to his feet. "Well, shake a leg…If we get a move on, meby we can stop by May's General Store for some supplies afore we ride out. Got a feeling this is gonna be a bad one."

Hart pulled out the drawer below the gun rack and grabbed a full box of 12 gauge buckshot and another with fifty rounds of .44 center fire cartridges for himself. He tossed a box of .45-70 to the older marshal. "Anythin' else?"

Selden shook his head, pulled his black coat off the hook and slipped it on. He grabbed a long-barreled lever-action rifle from the rack and stuck the box of ammo in his right front outside pocket.

Loss dragged the double-barreled Greener shotgun from the rack. He followed him out the door and locked it behind them as Selden slid the new '86 Winchester into the well-worn scabbard.

MARIETTA, IT

Deputy Hart led his horse out of the livestock car and down the cleated plank ramp. He joined Selden, who was checking the cinch on his saddle.

"Think we have time to stop and get a bite 'fore we leave town?"

"Dammit, Loss...you ever think 'bout anything but food? Swear to God...act like you never had breakfast...an' I know I watched you down a half dozen fried eggs, half a pound of bacon an' a stack of flapjacks!"

"That was three hours ago...Just a growin' boy." He grinned.

Lindsey patted him on the stomach. "Meby so, but it sure as hell ain't taller...shorty." He smiled. "'Sides, it makes you a bigger target."

The grin disappeared as Loss looked down at his belly.

They led their horses down the boardwalk to the end of the red-brick depot and tied them up outside the office for the Stubblefield Stage line.

The manager got to his feet as the taller marshal opened the door. "So happy you could come so quickly, Marshals. This thing has got us all on edge."

"Quite understandable." Selden introduced himself and Loss.

"Micah Thornberry, Marietta Station manager...I took the liberty to wire the bank and request the serial number ranges on the currency in the payroll...company standard procedure, as you know." He handed him a handwritten copy of the return telegram. "And here is the passenger manifest. Sorry, I can't give you much information on the through passengers from the railroad. They got off the northbound from Dallas and left as soon as the connecting baggage was boarded."

Loss spoke up. "I 'spect we can find out their point of origin from the Gulf, Colorado and Sante Fe if we need them."

Micah nodded. "I'm sure they will have that information...Wait...I can't believe I forgot to mention that we had a local passenger aboard."

Selden's eyebrows lifted. "And what do we know about him?"

The door opened and a blond-haired couple entered the office. They were in their mid-forties and of slim Nordic build. Both had a look of deep concern etched upon their face. The woman wore her hair in a long golden braid under a black handmade lace shawl. She carried a picture frame clutched to her chest.

The manager recognized the pair immediately. He motioned them over to his desk. "Gentlemen, this is Gregory and Olivia Hansen. Their daughter Birgit was on the way to Fort Sill to get married."

Lindsey stuck out his hand. "Sorry to meet under these circumstances."

Gregory shook it firmly.

Selden tipped his hat to his wife. "Ma'am."

Tears had streaked her suntanned face on the way over from their dairy farm on the outskirts of town. She nodded slightly to acknowledge his greeting and then held out the picture. "This was taken a few veeks ago in her vedding dress." Her voice cracked and faded as emotion overcame her.

Hansen wrapped his arm around his wife's shoulder. "She vas to marry a lieutenant in the cavalry." His eyes filled with tears.

Selden studied the picture. The formal portrait was taken seated with the white gown flowing around her feet. The young bride to be had her hands crossed gracefully in her lap, as was the fashion in the Victorian era. He took note of a piece of jewelry hanging down on the lace below the high collar. "Your daughter is quite beautiful. I see she takes after you, Ma'am...By any chance, was she wearing that necklace when she left?"

Both of her parents nodded. "It vas a gift from my mother to me. I gave it to Birgit as a present on her twenty-first birthday...something to remember her grandmother by." Tears began to flow anew. "It vas a cameo carved in ivory, set in a gold locket vith a gold chain...My mother brought it here from Stockholm." She sniffled as her nose began to run.

Selden reached inside his coat and produced a freshly pressed linen handkerchief. "I know this is hard for the both of you. Right now your daughter is only missing...Marshal Hart and I will do our level best to find her...That's my solemn promise."

She dabbed her eyes and nose, but said nothing.

Gregory swallowed hard, trying to make the lump in his throat go away. "She vas vearing an engagement ring as vell and a gray traveling dress."

"Linsey-voolsey skirt with a matching vest over a vhite cotton blouse," Olivia corrected him.

Selden turned to Loss. "Gettin' all these details down?"

"Uh huh." He fumbled in his pocket for a pencil and a small spiral notebook, and then mumbled as he wrote, "White cotton blouse."

The door closed behind the Hansens as they left. Selden looked over at the glum-faced manager. "Know somethin'? The hardest part of this job ain't dealing with the criminals...Got to where I don't hardly give them a second thought...But having to look a mother in the eyes and tell her I'll try to find her daughter, when I know in my gut she's dead or..." He inhaled deeply and let it out. "Think we got about we all we need to get started."

Thornberry stuck out his hand. "Appreciate all that you gentlemen do for us."

The two lawmen turned for the door.

"Say, aren't you the marshals who shot Bill Dalton up at Elk?"

They spun around as one and gave him looks that made him wish he had never opened his mouth. Selden's black mustache curled down in a hair horseshoe, his eyes narrowed into dark slits. "That's what the papers say."

It was a full thirty seconds after they left before Micah dared to breathe. "Lord have mercy on those outlaws...'cause those men won't."

WALNUT BAYOU

It was a quarter past one when the deputy marshals came up to the crossing. The wind had laid and the clear waters had not a ripple as they flowed slowly past the roadway. They spread out and walked their horses slowly, trying not to stir up the silt or sand. It was Loss who first spotted something.

"Hold up there! Is that a pistol on the bottom?"

"Where you talking about?"

Hart held up his gloved hand to block the sun's reflection on the surface, and then he pointed. "Closer to me than you, 'bout twenty feet out. Looks like a nickel-plated shooter to me."

"Believe you're right. I'll let you do the honors since I'm senior."

"Hell, the water's waist deep. It'll take half a day for my boots to dry out."

Lindsey laughed. "See? That's why they teamed you with me...Someone to teach you the thinking part. We ride across and you strip down to your longhandles...I'll hold your horse."

"Don't do me no favors."

Selden scouted around the crossing as Loss removed everything but his union suit. He backtracked a set of hoof prints into the woods. *Uh huh, Here's where he tied up. Hello, what's this?* He reached down into the leaf debris and pulled up a spent pistol cartridge. "A .45...gonna have to do a better job than that if you wanna hide your tracks." He slipped the empty brass into his coat pocket.

Loss broke the surface of the stream with a shiny silver sixgun in one hand and two blued revolvers in the other. "Hey! Found three of 'em! Look brand new to me."

"Good work. I'll keep a sharp eye out for water moccasins." He tried to suppress his grin, but it was hidden anyway, under the thick black pelt on his upper lip.

"Moccasins! You know how I hate snakes!" Loss splashed the final forty yards to the bank as fast as he could. The crotch of his soaked long underwear hung down almost to his knees as he stood with his arms out trying to drip dry.

"Lemme see those." Selden held out his hands.

"Gladly." He used his hands to try to wipe as much water out of his soaked cotton clothing as he could.

Selden flipped the cylinder out on the Smith and Wesson .38 Special, and then closed it. He pulled the hammer to half-cock on the nickel-plated Colt Frontier. Rolling its cylinder around, he counted five loaded rounds and one vacant spot where the hammer normally rested—the Colt Lightning was the same. "Yep, figured…Owners never fired a shot. These have only been in the water for a short while."

"Reckon whoever stopped the stage got the drop on 'em and killed 'em even after they surrendered?"

"Even money on that." Selden spat a stream of tobacco juice into the creek. He watched it disperse and float downstream. "We know the bodies ain't in the coach…May never find 'em if'n they buried 'em."

Loss shook his head slinging the excess water from his hair. "Most criminals are too damned lazy to dig graves…lotta time and effort. 'Spect they might have dumped them in the water and let nature take care of 'em?"

Lindsey looked down at the boot prints leading to and from the water. "Meby our perpetrators ain't smart as they think they is...Cold-blooded bastards." He looked at Loss. "Get dressed, son...Think we'll follow this creek down to the Red...They may have tried to hide their tracks in it."

The sun was hanging low and both men were swatting at mosquitos pestering them as they rode in knee-deep water near both sides of the creek. Selden spotted a difference in the moss growing on the bottom rocks. "Whoa...found the place where the first one cut off west...Two are still working south."

Several hundred yards later, he spotted the second trail cutting through a opening in a clump of willows. "Number two goin' west."

Coming around a bend in the bayou, Loss spotted something light-colored up ahead. As he rode closer, the golden blond hair of the bride who never was became clear. "Oh, sweet Jesus...gonna kill that poor mama back in Marietta."

The bloated body was caught on a pecan deadfall that had succumbed to a flood a year earlier. Loss stepped down from the saddle and water filled his boots. He steeled himself and rolled the body over. Sightless blue eyes stared at him as he fought the urge to throw up. He lifted her left arm and checked the ring finger. There was a mark where an engagement ring had once been, leaving a slight depression fair skin.

Loss looked around. "Selden! Selden!" There was no response. "Dammit." He pulled out his sixgun, held it high overhead and fired three evenly spaced shots.

A second later, he heard three in reply.

"What are we gonna do with her?" Loss looked up as Selden rode up.

"I made that woman a promise...Not that far from the Red. Camp out there and take the body into Gainesville in the morning. They got a medical examiner there...'Member Doc Wellman?"

"Don't take an expert to see the bullet hole."

"I know...Still gotta have a death certificate. I knew when we found that sunk strongbox, those highwaymen decided to use the water to hide their evil doin's."

"More like their undoin's...Bet they left a trail all the way to Texas."

"Uh huh...Told you they weren't so damn smart...We'll need to make a travois to get the body to town...Got a hatchet in my bags." Selden untied the latigo string holding his lariat to the saddle. He pushed the loop through the honda and made it big enough for the girl's body. "Get it under her arms if she ain't too stiff." He tossed the rope and a couple of coils down to Loss.

"Got it. She already passed through the rigor mortis, I reckon." He snaked the loop around her shoulders and then near the waist, before lifting each of the once-delicate beauty's arms and bringing it just under her breasts. Hart moved the honda to the middle of the back. "Take up the slack."

Selden complied, backing Dan up slowly until the rope was taut and the body pulled clear of the tree. "Best we haul her out on the west side…Where the robber's tracks are."

Loss waded back to his horse and mounted up. "No sense in lettin' the bastards backtrack and lose us…I want the scum who did this."

Selden said nothing, but reined the big black around and let him slowly pull the body across the slow moving creek.

A clump of willows on the bank yielded three straight poles they used to create a travois frame. Loss donated his blanket for the bed while Selden sacrificed his rope to lash the rig together. They wrapped the body in Lindsey's tarp he used for a ground cloth and tied it to the Indian-style sled.

Since Dan was the larger and more powerful horse, Selden backed him up to the twelve foot main poles and used the long latigo saddle strings on the skirt to hang the rig on each side.

"Easy there boy. Nothin' to be scared of." He patted his neck before forking the saddle. "Take the lead. Give him somethin' to keep his mind occupied."

"Alright." Loss mounted up and walked his horse around the cadaver.

They followed the trail of four horses. Thirty minutes later the tracks crossed a barren spot where lightning had burned off the grass on a hillside.

"Hold up here," Selden called as he dismounted.

After studying the tracks closely, he swung back into the saddle. "Just as I thought. Only three of 'em had riders. Wadn't fer certain back in the creek, but I damned sure am now." He spat a stream of tobacco juice.

"Don't seem likely that they woulda brung a pack animal with 'em. Foldin' money ain't all that heavy."

"They didn't bring it with 'em. Purty sure they stole the messenger's mount. That Chickasaw farmer didn't say nothing about a seventh horse."

"I see you."

SUGAR HILL SALOON

A dark-skinned man wearing a sackcloth suit and Tom Bull hat pushed past the swinging doors and looked around the barroom. He had a white scar running from his left ear to his chin—the look in his eyes let anyone know in an instant he was not a man to be trifled with.

He bellied up to the bar and addressed the only person he knew. "Tom or Pink Lee, Ed…They here?"

Steine wrinkled up his forehead. "You ain't been around in quite some time, Cal…guess you never heard the news."

He shook his head.

"Pink got hisself killed on a job over in Lindsay along with his brother Jim. Tom's set to hang for a couple dozen counts of murder."

"Huh…been away long. Not hear."

Ed drew a beer from the tap and slid it across the bar. "First one's on me…Looking for work?"

Cal lifted the mug and nodded once before taking a long sip. He used the back of his hand to wipe foam from his upper lip.

Ed tilted his head toward the end of the bar. "See those two? Taller one is Frank Pierce…was the Lee's cousin. He and the other feller are kinda takin' things over…Might could use a man of your talents."

The Cherokee outlaw grinned. "Unnn…Many thanks." He moved down the bar, looking carefully at the other patrons and stepped up to Frank. "Hear about cousins. Sorry not here to help."

Pierce looked him over. "I know you?"

The man shook his head. "Work with Jim Lee in Nations…cattle business…Sometimes me sell whiskey for Ed. Called Cal Mankiller." He looked Frank in the eye. "Cherokee…Full Cherokee."

"Cattle business, huh? Breeder?"

Cal grinned. "No…Collector."

Frank chuckled. "What brings you down to Texas?"

Mankiller looked over his shoulder. "We sit…talk alone?"

"Sure. This is one of my top men, Jack Long. Let's get a table."

"…That when Mankiller decide come Texas for time."

"Till things cool off a mite?"

His nod was almost imperceptible.

Frank glanced over at Jack. "We could use a couple of hard men. If Ed vouches for you, that's good enough for me…Sent a letter up to the Nations over a week ago, trying to get in touch with Doe Lee…Supposed to be gettin' here sometime tonight."

"Mankiller know Doe. We work horses and cattle for Jim last year."

"That's good. Only one you haven't met is Tom Story. He's down to Gainesville checking out what's goin' on in the big city."

"Me hear of Tom Story…Good with gun."

CHICKASAW NATION

Loss pulled up near the banks of the Red River. He glanced over his shoulder at the setting sun. "Looks like they camped here for the night. Gittin' kindly dark to track…What say?"

"Good place to call it a day. Already got a fire pit and plenty of grazin'."

Hart hobbled his horse over on the lush grass, jerked his saddle and carried it over near the pit. He glanced around, saw a partially burned stick and poked around the fire embers—found three charred bits of leather. "Bastards are gettin' mighty sloppy...Bet these are the wallets of their victims."

Selden lowered the travois to the ground, unsaddled Dan and rubbed him down with the top blanket—walked the big black over near Loss' blood bay gelding and hobbled him, too.

He returned to kneel beside Loss. "Yep, they think they're home free...Love to be there when Maledon drops a noose around their necks in Fort Smith."

***

CHAPTER EIGHT

GAINESVILLE, TEXAS
LUCIUS WELLMAN, MD

"Real sorry to have to do this Doc...Know it's not in your County Medical Examiner's jurisdiction, but it's a Federal case an' all.

"It's all right Marshal Lindsey...Such a pity. It is obvious she was lovely." He clinched his jaw for a moment. "What kind of animal would do this?"

"Wadn't no animal, Doc...Don't know of any type of animal would stoop this low...This was some kind of aberrant excuse of pure human excrement that could..." Selden stopped as he began to choke up and just shook his head.

Wellman nodded. "Yeah...I'll have the full autopsy by tomorrow, but I can tell you one thing right now."

"What's that?" asked Loss.

"The shot to her chest would have killed her."

Selden broke his reverie and looked the doctor in the eye. "What do you mean...would have?"

He pulled the white sheet that was covering the body down to her chest and pushed one of her eyelids up. "See that?"

"What?"

"The subconjunctival hemorrhage."

"The what?" asked Loss.

"The visible veins in the white of her eye...You would call it bloodshot."

Selden leaned over for a better look. "Alright...What does that mean?"

Doctor Wellman looked at the two marshals for a long moment. "She was still alive when they threw her in the creek...She drowned."

COOKE COUNTY SHERIFF'S OFFICE

Marshals Lindsey and Hart opened the front door and came face to face with a ruddy complexioned heavyset man.

"Deputy Rudabaugh..."

"Acting Sheriff Rudabaugh, Marshal Lindsey...What can I do for you?"

"Right...Acting Sheriff Rudabaugh...Ranger Hickman in his office?"

"He is, but he's busy right now."

"Oh?"

"He's talking to Marshal Roberts."

"Brushy Bill?" exclaimed Loss.

"I understand that's what he's called."

Bill stuck his head out of a door to an office on the north side of the room. "I heard my name...Well what do you know?...Selden, Loss!" He turned his head back inside. "Hey, Bodie, you won't..."

Hickman appeared beside him. "I heard...Ya'll come on in."

"Looks like you gentlemen have this situation well in hand, I have to go take care of some county business Marshal Roberts dropped on me...Good day." Rudabaugh snugged his bowler down on his head and closed the front door behind him.

"What was that about?" asked Hart as he and Selden stepped inside the Ranger's office.

"Oh, yesterday evening a couple of miscreants had the poor judgment to try to rob my lady and me over in Delaware Bend. Had to terminate their existance...Left 'em beside the road for Rudabaugh."

"You shot 'em?" asked Loss.

Bill just nodded.

"Onlyest guaranteed cure for stupid I know 'bout," said Loss.

"Say, why don't ya'll come with me over to the boardin' house...got somebody want you to meet," mentioned Bodie.

"You reckon Miss Faye's got another couple of places fer supper?...We missed out on lunch."

Hickman shook his head and grinned. "I 'spect so, Loss. She's fixin' early today on account one of the folks I want ya'll to meet has to perform this evenin'."

"Perform?"

SKEANS BOARDING HOUSE

The four law officers stepped up on the wide gray painted verandah, Bodie opened the white gingerbread screen door and stepped into the foyer.

"Don't let that slam. Faye'll peel yer head like a onion. She might have a cake in the oven," he cautioned, Loss Hart.

"I know, my mama was the same way...You say cake?" He eased the coil spring-loaded door closed behind him and followed the others into the parlor.

"I said, might..."

Bass shot to his feet. "Well looky here, looky here what the cat drug in the dog wouldn't have." He turned to Fiona, who was sitting on the love seat with a glass of tea. "This is a hellova hand to draw to. Some of the finest lawmen I know...You've met the young pup already, but that there's Marshals Selden Lindsey and Loss Hart."

The two men whipped off their hats.

Bass continued, "They's the ones that taken out Bill Dalton over to Elk last year an' you've heard me mention Marshal Brushy Bill Roberts before...Fellers, this here is Fiona Miller...Deputy Marshal F.M. Miller."

Bill recognized her from yesterday, raised his eyebrows, and had already doffed his hat too. "You're F.M. Miller? I had no idea you were a..."

"Woman?" Fiona set her tea down on a doily, smiled, got to her feet and held out her hand. "Have been as long as I can remember...It's pleasure, Bill. Heard tell of you...Saw you with your lady yesterday having dinner at the Painted Lady." She shook hands with the three of them. "Good to meet you gentlemen, too."

Bill nodded. "Uh, huh, saw you too. Told Millie there was more to you than met the eye the way you sized up that man getting his boots shined."

"Lord a mercy! Knowed Jack was laid up with that leg, but didn't know that the judge teamed you up with...I mean I thought F.M., uh...didn't know you wuz a wo...uh, lady, I mean..."

Bass roared. "We know what you mean, Loss. Better stop before you dig yerself so deep a brace of mules won't be able to pull you out...Oh, an' just as a word of caution don't call her Ma'am...an' you shore don't want piss her off...I seen her shoot."

Fiona smiled again. "I usually don't dress this way, but both Bass and I are working undercover. I'm doing stage shows at the Painted Lady as Starla Marston from New Orleans...as you already know, Bill...And Bass is working out at the Rafter S."

"Who are ya'll after?" asked Selden.

Bass spoke up, "Tom Story and..."

"Story! I heard tell he's faster than the Sartain brothers," interrupted Loss.

"Yeah, but Bass here is forked lightnin'," added Bodie.

I understand that he and Jack took care of those grandiloquent twins," added Bill. "I believe Tom Story to be of the same cut."

"An' nobody kin git anythin' on him...Slicker'n a greased pig. Seems like there's never anybody to file against him...no witnesses ner nothin' to his rumored nefarious deeds," added Selden.

"Well, we're layin' out a little bait fer 'im..." Bass turned to Selden and Loss. "What're you fellers doin' down thisaway?"

The two lawmen looked at one another.

"Mayhaps we oughta sit down fer this tale...ain't gonna be purty," said Lindsey.

"...So hers was the only body we found." Selden pulled a small piece of paper from his vest pocket. "This here's a sketch of a carved ivory cameo her mama said she was wearin'...it wadn't on the body." He passed it around for every one to have a look.

"It was in a gold settin' an' chain...'Spect they took it along with her diamond engagement ring.

"Figure the other bodies 're somwhere 'twix here and Shreveport...One of the most callus and heinous crimes we've ever investigated. None of 'em had a chance...I just dread telling that little lady's momma and daddy." His face darkened as he finished filling everyone in.

Bass had pulled out his well-worn rosewood pipe, filled it from a doeskin pouch, lit it and took a long slow draw. It was his way of thinking. "Sel, you say ya'll tracked the three perpetrators across the Red into Cooke County?"

"That's right, lost their tracks when they joined the main road to the Red River ferry north of Gainesville."

Reeves turned to Bill and Fiona. "An' ya'll think that feller gittin' his boots shined was Story?"

They looked at each other and nodded.

"You don't think..."

Bass interrupted Bill. "Well, now, studyin' on it a right smart, I jest don't hardly believe in coincidences...Where there's a stink...best start lookin' fer somethin' or somebody rotten...The other two coulda been headed over to Dexter."

"Supper's on," said Faye as she entered the parlor from the dining room. "Oh, goodness more company." She smiled big. "Well, it's a blessing I fixed a big pot roast...Bill, Selden and Loss, ya'll are always welcome...'Course I'm not sure I have enough for Mister Hart, though."

"Aw, Miz Faye."

"Is supper ready?" asked Tom Sullivant from the foyer.

"Well, yes, I was beginning to think ya'll weren't going to show," responded Faye as he, Walt and Francis Ann entered.

"Is that peach cobbler I smell?" commented Loss pointing to the wicker basket in Durbin's hand.

"We couldn't come empty handed, so I brought Bodie's favorite desert...The freestones were ripe," said Fran.

"Oh, yum." The Ranger jumped to his feet. "I can't wa..."

"Only one serving this time mister...I'm not letting your pants out again."

Bodie looked at Annabel. "Yessum...Maybe someday they'll figure out how to put that stretchy stuff in my suspenders in pants."

"I wouldn't count on it," replied his wife.

"Does just havin' one servin' of that there cobbler apply to me too, Miss Annabel?"

She laughed. "No, Loss. I swear to goodness, I do believe you could eat ten servin's and you wouldn't gain a pound...Are you sure you don't have a hollow leg...bless your heart."

"No Ma'am, don't think so. Been thisaway long as I kin 'member. Don't seem to matter how much or what I eat...everthang just seems to stay the same."

"Oh, how wonderful that would be," commented Faye.

"Say, Bass, how's Flash comin' along? He gonna be ready for the big race?" asked Bodie.

"Looks like it, Fran is leggin' him out twice a day."

"You're not going to ride him in the race, are you?" asked Faye.

"She is not. That's n-o-t, not...If I have to hog tie her," stated Walt emphatically.

"I agree. Leggin' up is one thang, but a hell-bent-fer-leather all out race fer a mile...not good. You're three months along, Miss Fran...Ain't like him, but what if he stumbled er pulled a stifle?" added Bass. "I kin ride 'im."

"Aren't you over two hundred pounds?"

"Not sure, but I 'spect so, Fiona. Why?"

"Well, for one, there's a chance of you being recognized and two, the less weight Flash has to carry, the better...How about I ride him? I only weigh around one hundred thirty or so."

"Race open to anybody?"

"Of course, Selden, why do you ask?" answered Sullivant.

He looked at Bass and grinned. "Well, thought it might be interestin' to see who's the fastest...Flash er Dan."

"Who's gonna ride him, Sel, you weigh as much, if'n not more'n me?" said Bass.

"Well, reckon Loss kin ride 'im...he don't weigh a hundred fifty soakin' wet."

BASS AND THE LADY

"Huh?" Loss looked up from his second bowl of cobbler—some of the fresh cream Faye had poured on top had coated the bottom of his mustache.

NORTH COOKE COUNTY

Bennie Reeves stepped down from his bay gelding at the bank of Hickory Creek and loosened the girth. He wanted to allow the horse to drink its fill before heading on in to the Painted Lady for his job. He had to be there at 5pm for the evening crowd.

He glanced at his horse sucking up the cool water with a slurping sound. "Yer lookin' a some better, Ted…Reckon that bait'a grain you been gittin' twict a day I been able to buy with my shine money's startin' to fill you out a tad…Ain't near as gainty as last week…Well, ain't you got nothin' to say, like thank you or 'preciate it?"

The horse raised his head, water running from his mouth, looked at his master, and then put his muzzle back in the creek and drank some more. Bennie squatted down beside him, picked up a number of flat stream-washed pebbles and skipped one across the surface—it hit the top of the water three times before sinking.

"Damn, used to do better'n that when I was a kid."

He skipped another—it only ricocheted twice. Bennie had a look of deep concentration on his face as he watched the rock sink and the ripples disappear in the slow moving creek. His jaw muscles worked, rippling the short nappy beard like grain in the wind.

He glanced at Ted again as the horse had turned away from the water and was cropping the bluestem grass growing just above the latest waterline. "Ol' son, what am I gonna do? Cain't go to jail…just cain't. Pray to God they don't send poppa after me."

He looked briefly at the late afternoon sky, paused as a tear rolled down his cheek, and then skipped another rock…it glanced once from the surface and sank. "Not gonna let 'em take me, jest ain't…not alive anyways."

He threw the entire handful into the water, making Ted jump. "Gotta git away from Story somehow, someway…man has no heart…Aw hell, what am I sayin'? I done kilt my own wife. What does that say about me?"

He cinched up his horse, mounted and clucked him up into a trot toward Gainesville.

PAINTED LADY

It was just after sundown as Tom Story studied the sign in the window:

OPEN HORSE RACE

ONE THOUSAND DOLLAR PURSE

Cooke County Fairground

Distance - Two Miles - Steeplechase

BASS AND THE LADY

September 14
$50 Entry fee
See Rube Jolley at the PAINTED LADY
To sign up.

He stepped over to the front door and went inside. Bennie jumped up from the shine platform, at the end of the thirty-five foot bar, where he was sitting. "Shine mister?"

Story walked over to him. "Later, boy...Gotta see the bartender first." He propped his foot on the brass railing six inches off the floor and leaned over the dark green polished marble bar top.

A portly man with mutton-chop whiskers—hair parted in the center and slicked down with pomade—walked from serving a couple of cowboys a few feet away. He wore dark trousers, a white shirt with a red bow tie and matching arm garters—there was a white apron tied around his waist. "What'll it be, mister?"

"You Jolley?"

"'Bout what?"

"No, I mean is that yer name?"

Rube chuckled. "Yeah, I couldn't resist...It was when the day started...won't guarantee nothin' come closin' time."

"Yeah, heard that one before...Want to enter the horse race."

"You or your horse?"

Story finally cracked a smile. "Reckon I'll enter my horse...this time."

169

Rube smiled back, turned around and got a printed form from the back bar, next to the large ornate brass cash register.

"Fill this out and bring it back with fifty dollars and you'll be all set to go."

Tom took the form and looked it over. "Got a pencil?"

"Got that too." He took a stub of a yellow number two out of a pocket in the front of his apron. "'Preciate that back."

Story nodded. "Pour me a shot of your best sour mash and I'll fill it out over…" He turned and saw the entertainer next to the stage talking to the piano player. "Is she about to do her show?"

"Yes, sir, Miss Marston is due to go on in ten minutes," he said as he filled a shot glass with Old Taylor.

"Just give me the bottle and another glass. I'll fill out this form over by the stage."

"Very good, sir…Don't blame you. She's something, all right." He screwed the cap back on the bottle and pushed it and the glass toward Tom.

He couldn't take his eyes off the dark-haired beauty as he walked to a vacant table near the front of the stage. She was dressed in a red satin low-cut gown trimmed with black Chantilly lace around the bodice, the three-quarter sleeves and bottom of the skirt. There was a matching parasol protruding from the pocket sewn to the side of the gown near her knees.

Her hair was down in long flowing waves. She glanced up from her conversation and smiled as he took a seat. He smiled back, nodded, removed his flat-brimmed hat and ran his fingers through his sandy hair.

He looked directly at her eyes again, held up the empty glass, tilted his head and raised one eyebrow. The subtlety was not lost on her as she leaned over, whispered something to Jake, her player, and walked the five feet over to his table.

"If that's for me, I'll take it," she purred as she sat down.

"Anyway you want it." He didn't wait for an answer, but started to pour the amber liquid into the glass.

She held up her hand. "Easy now…Just a splash. I do have to perform, you know."

"As you wish."

Fiona picked it up and looked at the half-inch of bourbon in the bottom. "I do love a good sour mash…Here's to women and horses…and the men who ride them."

She took a small sip. "Mmm, that's nice…It's very good for the throat, you know…in moderation." She winked. "Relaxes the vocal cords." She sat the glass back on the table, settled back into the chair and ran the tip of her tongue over her upper lip, savoring the last drop of the Old Tayor. "I'm Starla."

The *goddess effect* on Tom was electric. He found himself momentarily short of breath—as if he had somehow forgotten to breathe. He coughed once into the back of his hand. "Excuse, me, Starla. The name's Thomas…Tom Story…Interesting toast."

"Pleased to meet you Thomas…Tom Story. New in town?"

He chuckled. "You're quick...real quick. I like that in a lady." He downed a shot of bourbon and poured himself another. "To answer your question...yes, just got here a few days ago."

"Something we have in common...Been here less than a week myself...You like music?"

He nodded. "Depends. If it's good...I like it."

Fiona smiled broadly, her white teeth glistened in the light of the overhead crystal gas chandelier. "Hope you like my singing."

Tom sat back and smiled at her. "If it's anything like the rest of you, I expect I'm gonna love the show." He had regained his composure slightly and was beginning to get back into his cocksure self-confident manner.

Across the street in the alley between Stienke's Gun Shop and Street's Pharmacy, an old colored ragpicker watched through the windows of the Painted Lady from the shadows. He paid particular attention to the young man at the shoeshine stand.

After a while, he changed his focus to the raven-haired beauty strolling across the stage in front of an enthusiastic packed house, twirling a red with black trim parasol on her shoulder as she sang a popular tune of the day. He couldn't quite hear the music, but was betting it was *Daisy Bell*.

He noticed the man he believed to be Tom Story sitting at a table near the front of the stage between the piano player and the three short steps that led up from the floor to the raised platform. His back was to the north brick wall of the saloon so he could not only see the performance, but also most of the balance of the room. *Smart...er paranoid...er both.*

Fiona, aka Starla, curtsied to the thunderous applause of the audience, closed her parasol and slipped it into a ready-made pouch on the side and moved—no, glided down the steps and over to Story's table. He pulled a chair out for her on the opposite side of the table.

"Thank you, kind sir." She sat and dabbed the moisture on her upper lip away with a soft white linen handkerchief she kept in one of the slash pockets of her gown.

The evening breeze kept the room relatively cool and free of smoke as the fourteen foot ceilings and the three foot tilt-in transoms created a natural wind tunnel for ventilation.

He reached for the bottle of bourbon.

She shook her head. "No, thanks, I still have two sets...I would take a glass of water, though."

He waved down a waitress. "Miss? Can we get a glass of water for Miss Marston?"

The buxom girl nodded and headed for the bar, passing an inebriated cowboy who was headed to Starla and Tom's table.

He stepped up, leaned over and exhaled his liquor breath in Fiona's face. "Dang, you shore are purty. Purty as a flax-maned pony. How's about you comin' upstairs with me? Ol' Arlie kin show you a real good time."

"The lady is with me, cowboy. I suggest you head back over to the bar," Tom said quietly.

"Naw she ain't." Arlie grabbed Starla's arm and started to pull her up from the chair when he caught the barrel of Story's Colt across his forehead, sending his hat flying and him to the floor like a pile of dirty laundry.

Rube stepped up with a baseball bat in his hand and looked down at the out-cold cowboy. There was blood starting to ooze from the burst skin above his eyes.

"Looks like you beat me to it, Tom. I was fixin' to knock him into next week with Betsy." He slapped the fat part of the bat in the palm of his hand. "Told him not to come over here."

"Time and effort will take care of ignorance...but stupid is apparently forever," commented Tom.

She smiled. "That's something my father used to say."

"Well, since you're here, Rube, you can drag him out back until he wakes up...He's a bit odoriferous."

"I can do that." He motioned for Bennie to come over to help.

They each grabbed a boot and dragged him across the floor toward the back door.

Starla turned back to Tom. "Thank you. That's one of the disadvantages of entertaining in a saloon." She glanced at the form on the table. "I see you're entering the big race Saturday. You must be pretty confident about your horse."

Tom looked her in the eye. "You could say that. Never been beat before...Like greased lightnin' in the stretch."

"Is that a fact?"

"Come to think of it, I would really enjoy you watchin' me win that purse. What would you say about accompanying me to the soiree?"

Fiona batted her eyes. "Why, I declare...that is so very sweet of you to ask...I'm sorry, but I already have a previous engagement for Saturday."

The look on his face telegraphed his disappointment. "Maybe next time."

The waitress returned with a tumbler of cool water and set it down in front of her.

"Thank you so much, Betty Lou...Singing song after song takes it out of you." She took a sip.

Story grinned. "But you are so very good at it...Surprised I've never heard of you before."

"I suppose I'm still waiting for my big break."

SKEANS BOARDING HOUSE

Fiona and Tom climbed the steps to the verandah and stopped in front of the door.

She turned to face him. "Thank you for escorting me home."

175

"It was an honor and a pleasure, my sweet lady. Might have been another amorous cowboy hanging about."

She nodded. "Will I see you tomorrow?"

"Wild horses couldn't keep me away from your show."

He leaned forward to kiss her, but she turned and offered him her cheek a split second before his lips could touch hers. A fleeting frown passed over his face. She reached for the brass handle to the screen door, but he was quicker. He opened it and stepped back.

"Until it be morrow." He doffed his hat and bowed theatrically.

She curtseyed slightly. "I do believe that's Juliet's line: 'Yet I should kill thee with much cherishing. Good night, good night! Parting is such sweet sorrow, that I shall say good night till it be morrow.'...End of Act Two, Scene Two, Romeo and Juliet...William Shakespeare." She smiled.

His face flushed slightly, his mouth twitched, but he recovered quickly. "Ah, caught red-handed."

"One must be careful when purloining things...Don't you agree?"

He flushed again and clenched his jaw. "I suppose you're correct...Good night then." Tom turned on his heel and strode down the steps and out the brick sidewalk into the darkness.

She watched him disappear into the night, grinned, entered the foyer, hung her dark-red woolen shawl on the oak halltree just inside the door and walked to the kitchen.

BASS AND THE LADY

Bass stood at the stove, pouring a cup of coffee as she came through the swinging door from the dinning room.

"Well, pour me one too while you're at it...You'll never guess who walked me home."

Bass didn't look around as he grabbed another white porcelain mug from the cabinet and filled it. "Tom Story."

"How did...?"

"Watched most of yer show from across the street an' follered ya'll here...I'm kindly hard to see in the dark." He grinned. "Slipped around to the back when he wuz atryin' to make advances on the porch." He handed her the cup.

She raised her eyebrows. "Well, what if he had tried to attack me?" She sat down at the table in the center of the kitchen.

Bass laughed. "Mighta had to rescue *him*...Naw, looked to me like you had him wrapped around yer little fanger an' wuz aturnin' him ever whichaway but aloose...Don't think he knew if'n you was atellin' 'im to sic 'um er come 'ere."

He also sat down and began thumbing through a copy of the latest Sears and Roebuck catalogue lying on the table Faye had received in the mail that day.

"Thought you couldn't read?"

"Cain't...Like to look at the pictures, though." He leaned over closer to the book and pointed. "Would you looky there! A feller kin order a whole house, ready-made. They ship the entire kit and caboodle in boxes on a train. You jest slap it together when you git it...Haw! Ain't that passin' strange?"

Fiona took a sip of her coffee. "I'm sure that's nice if you want a cracker-box house."

"Naw. Look at this'un...A two story with all sorts of gingerbread...Does that say nine hundered and fifty dollars?" He touched a figure on the page.

"Uh, huh...Don't you want to hear what went on this evening?"

He leaned back in his chair and cradled his cup in both of his huge hands. "Figured you'd git 'round to tellin' me when you wuz ready."

Fiona closed her eyes and shook her head. "Wonder what the penalty is for killing a Deputy US Marshal?"

Bass grinned. "'Spect it's 'bout the same as killin' 'nybody else."

She looked back at him over the rim of her cup. "Unless it's justifiable homicide."

"Ya'll make enough racket to raise the dead."

They both looked up to see Bill coming in, pulling his suspenders over his shoulders. He was only wearing pants, his union suit and was barefoot.

"Any coffee left?" He rubbed his face with both hands.

"They is, but I ain't waitin' on you."

Roberts stepped over to the stove, grabbed a cup from the cupboard on the right and filled it half-full.

"You kin fill it up. We've had ours," said Bass.

"Uh uh, won't be able to get back to sleep."

"Is that what you've been doing while Bass and I were working?"

He blew across the surface of the coffee, took a sip and sat down at the table. "I'll have you know Marshal Miller, that Selden, Loss and I had dinner at over at the Fried Pie and divided up what we needed to be doing...thank you very much." He took another sip.

"And that would be?" asked Bass.

"There's one thing I've learned in my years bein' around outlaws...on both sides of the fence...and that's if they come into a right smart of money...they will spend it."

"Now that is a truism," said Fiona.

"We decided it was time to do some good old lawman work and wear out some boot leather. We're gonna start canvasin' stores tomorrow...Loss took Dan out to the ranch to get him ready for the race."

"Where's Selden?"

"Upstairs. Swear to God, you could set a bomb off under the bed and wouldn't wake him up, plus he snores like a freight train...That's why I heard ya'll."

"You kin share my room if'n you like," Bass said.

"You snore?"

"Don't rightly know...Never sat up to listen."

Bill furrowed his brow and then looked at Fiona.

"Don't look at me, I have no idea."

He looked back at Bass. "Might as well." He looked at the brunette again. "You know Shakespeare, huh?"

"Were you spying on me, too?"

"Nope. Our room is right over the front porch. Had the window open."

"Well, since you asked, yes I do, Keats, Browning and Hawthorne as well."

"I almost busted out laughin' when you caught that mountebank trying to take credit for that line. I could hear the embarrassment in his flannel-mouth voice...That was classic and you being so insouciant."

"What er ya'll talkin' 'bout? Wish you'd speak American."

Fiona grinned. "Some men are like a rooster, Bass...They think the sun comes up just to hear them crow."

"Now that I understood."

***

CHAPTER NINE

SUGAR HILL SALOON

The mid-afternoon crowd was a tad thin as Bennie Reeves stepped inside the door and waited for a second for his eyes to adjust to the darker conditions. He spied Tom, Frank and Jack seated at a table near the back of the bar and walked quickly to join them.

"Well, what did you find out, boy?"

If Bennie took offense at Tom's question, his face didn't reflect it. "They's eight horses in the race besides yor'n, Mister Story...so far. All tol', folks be gettin' mighty worked up about it."

"That's what I wanted to hear." Tom took a deep draw on his cigarillo and let out a huge cloud of blue smoke. "Get yourself back to work and keep your ears open. I need to know who the favorite is and what breed they're ridin'. Be in a little later for the show."

"Yassir." Bennie spun around and made for the front door.

Frank took a sip of his bourbon. "You know, I think that idea 'bout robbin' the race receipts is a damn good one."

A smirk came to Tom's lips. "Hell, yes, it is. Figure close to ten thousand people payin' a buck apiece to get in, plus the pot on the race wagers...we're lookin' at ten to fifteen thousand...maybe more."

Jack grinned. "That's more than a lot of banks keep on hand."

Tom laughed. "I knew you boys would see the brilliance in my plan." He slammed down a shot of whisky and poured himself another. "Got me the perfect alibi...Thousands of folks are gonna see me ridin' for that purse...You'll be knockin' off the main gate and the bettin' money while everybody's watching the race. Besides, it will give us some well-used currency in small bills to play with until the heat is off the stage job."

"We got us a couple new hands..."

Story interrupted Frank. "Couple of new hands? That's something you failed to discuss with me." His pale blue eyes seemed to turn to ice.

"Well now, don't git yer dander up, it jest kinda happened. One of my cousins, Doe Lee, is a good hand with horses, come in last night from the Nations. And 'nother feller, a full-blood Cherokee on the run, Cal Mankiller, come by yesterdy...he's worked with Doe. Easy to recognize...got a big-assed scar on the left side of his face...Ugly as a burnt boot."

"Uh, huh...heard of him. Can tolerate other Indians and whites...but hates half-breeds. A cold-blooded killer...from the front or the back." Story nodded. "We might can use him at that."

CALIFORNIA STREET
GAINESVILLE, TX

Brushy Bill stepped out of Pulte's Hardware store and looked across the street. Selden was walking out of the bank and waved over at him. Bill waited for the trolley to pass and crossed over to the far side of the aptly named thoroughfare. "Anything?"

Selden shook his head. "No dice...Don't look like anybody's been passing the new notes yet."

"Same over in the stores. It's easy to pick out new crisp currency...What's next?"

"Think I'll drop by the Painted Lady and register old Dan for the race, since we got Loss out to the Rafter S helpin' Little John exercise him along with Flash." He lifted his US Marshal's badge off his vest and slipped it in his pocket.

"Don't want to spook Bass' boy off, I see."

"Nope...Kid don't know me from Adam's ox. Just as soon keep it thataway...till Bass decides to make his move. Learnt long ago to trust his instincts. That man's got the patience of Job...Anyways, I'll register usin' my first and middle names only." He chuckled. "Selden Trullery oughta throw 'em fer a loop."

Bill grinned. "Got everything wrapped up over in Paris for the time bein'...I'll finish the other side of the street and check with 'em at the depot. Somethin's bound to break loose on this case...Got a feelin' 'bout it."

Selden nodded and turned north toward the Painted Lady.

PAINTED LADY

Bennie strolled out of the linen closet with his clean, starched, white jacket—his employee uniform—and headed to the shine stand at the front of the room, near the front door. He checked his supplies and brushes as a broad-shouldered man in a big black hat was at the end of the bar with Rube filling out a form.

The stranger finished, pushed it over to the bartender, dug in his vest pocket for two double eagles and a liberty, and then stacked the gold coins on top of the form.

"How's that?"

Rube looked at the form and scraped the fifty dollars off into his palm. "Looks just fine, Mister Trullery...just fine. Good luck, Saturday."

184

"Has more to do with the steed than luck, my friend." He nodded, touched the brim of his hat, turned around and stepped to the door.

"Shine mister?"

"Maybe next…" He looked down at his scuffed and dirty mid-calf stovetop boots. "Think you can do anythin' with these?"

"Yasser, make 'em shine like a new dollar."

"You do that an' I'll give you a dollar. How's that?"

"Golly! Fer a dollar, I'll make 'em where you kin shave in 'em, sir."

Selden climbed up into the big chair and put his feet on the stands. "What's yer name, boy?"

"Willie, sir…Uh, Willie Spencer."

"Well, git it done, Willie."

Ten minutes later, he popped the long cotton shinecloth one last time and tapped the bottom of Selden's foot to let him know he was finished. "There you are, sir."

Lindsey looked down at the black boots. "Sonofagun, do believe a feller could shave in those, Willie…Good job." He fished a silver dollar out and flipped it to him.

"Thank you, Mister Trullery." He looked down at the new Morgan in his hand. "My poppa's partial to these, too."

Selden looked at him hard. "That a fact?" *They happen to be Bass Reeves' callin' card.* He had the hint of a wry smile.

185

Embarrassed, Willie looked away and stepped back so the man could step down. "Thank you, again, sir."

Lindsey nodded, glanced over at the bartender, touched his hat again and strolled out the front door.

Bennie stuffed the dollar in his pants pocket, turned around and walked over to the bar. "Afternoon, Rube, how's it agoin' today?"

"Fine, Willie, fine as frog hair...so far. Don't want to git cocky though." He wiped over the already cleaned bar top out of habit with a small white towel.

"How's come?"

He chuckled. "Ain't over."

"Hey, that's a good one...Ain't over. Gotta 'member that...How's that there race thang acomin'?"

"Real good...Got ten now, countin' the Rafter S's own entry."

"Uh, what all's kinda horses air they?"

Rube picked up the stack of filled-out forms from under the bar and shuffled through them. "Well, let's see here...There's one...no, two Saddlebreds...Your customer that just left signed up a second. Now, here's a Morgan, a Mustang, an Appaloosa..." He laid part of the stack down. "...a Thoroughbred, a Missouri Fox Trotter? Huh? Oh, well...A Walker...and two Standardbreds."

"Who be gittin' the smart money?"

BASS AND THE LADY

Rube checked his tally book. "That would be the Rafter S Saddlebred...so far. Gonna have to get the honorable Judge Leander Algernon Miles, III to hold the stakes...Gettin' to be quite a pile." He shook his head and grinned.

COOKE COUNTY COURTHOUSE

Millie glanced up at the Biedermeier wall clock. The polished brass pendulum swung back and forth as the precision German-made instrument clicked the seconds away like a mechanical heartbeat. *Ten minutes till closing time...Better get started with the pick up, clean up and straighten up.*

She moved to the stacks of heavy ledgers scattered around on the tables in the county clerk's office and closed the first one. It was three foot by two feet and almost six inches thick.

"Hello, pretty lady. Need a hand?"

She spun around at the sound of a familiar voice. "Bill Roberts! You nearly scared the life out of me, again! How do you get in here without a sound?"

He chuckled. "Practice...Comes in mighty handy in my line of work." He lifted the hinged section of the counter and stepped inside. "What kind of man would let such a beautiful creature as yourself tote all those heavy books?"

"My boss doesn't seem to have a problem in that department."

"Where is the old goat? Perhaps I need to have a discussion with him."

"No you don't…Besides, he took off early…as usual."

"Just like an elected official. Never around when you need 'em." He stuck out his hands. "Load me up. Just tell me where you want 'em."

Millie smiled. "You're spoiling me, you know that?"

"A gentleman's prerogative. Chivalry is alive and well…regardless of what the newspapers say."

The attractive dark-haired widow shook her head and placed three of the heavy record books in his arms. "By all means, please your sense of chivalry." She spun around. "Follow me, kind sir."

"I shall follow you to hell and back, should the need arise, my dear." Leading Bill to the heavy oaken shelves where the county's records were stored, she pointed to the bottom one. "The one on the top goes down there in the U through Z section."

He knelt down and slid it off, placing the ledger where the spine was visible.

"Have you ever heard such a commotion about anything like this horse race on Saturday? A person would think that we never have a single social event around here…ever."

Bill got to his feet. "I know I'm looking forward to it. Got friends entered in the deal."

She pointed to the middle shelf. "L through M. I'll swan...I don't have a single thing to wear."

Bill chuckled. "Every woman in the whole world says the same thing. It's amazing we don't see more females walking around buck nekkid."

Millie swatted him on the shoulder. "Keep your mind out of the gutter, mister!...What I mean is that all my clothes are staid...out of fashion...frumpy, dowdy things a person wears to work."

He smiled. "You look beautiful to me...Got an idea. There are plenty of ladies shops here in town. What is the chance you take off a little early tomorrow?...It so happens I picked up a little reward money this month. Love to buy you a new outfit for this shindig."

"You would?"

"My word is my bond...maybe some of those fancy Saint Louis shoes to go with it."

Millie's eyes flew open wide. She wrapped her hands around his head and pulled him close for a passionate kiss.

PAINTED LADY

Tom Story settled into the chair in a table in the second row. He glared at the four men seated between him and the stage. *Dammit. Knew I shoulda got here a little earlier.*

189

Betty Lou spotted the new arrival and walked quickly to the table. "The usual, Mister Story?"

He nodded. "With two glasses." As she walked away, he glanced back over to the shoeshine booth. Bennie had one customer in the chair and another waiting nearby. Tom checked his watch and looked up to see the piano player check his list of songs for the evening. *She's running late tonight...Usually here by now.* He found himself getting uncharacteristically nervous as he looked to the front door again and frowned.

The waitress returned with a cork-lined tray, a bottle of Old Taylor Bourbon and two clean glasses. "Here you are, sir. Would you like to see a menu?"

"Nope, ate earlier. Miss Marston here yet?"

"I believe so...She's probably in the dressing room touching up for the performance."

"Would you let her know I'm here?"

"Certainly, sir." Betty Lou smiled and walked down the hallway behind the stage. She knocked twice on the door.

Fiona was reviewing the lyrics to the songs she planned to perform that night. She set the music down and spun around on the swivel stool in front of the makeup mirror. "Come in."

Betty Lou stuck her head in. "Your number one admirer wants you to know he's here again."

"Tell him I'll be out shortly...I'm powdering my nose."

"You got it, sister."

BASS AND THE LADY

After she closed the door, Fiona chuckled. *Always keep 'em waiting. Drives men crazy.* She looked at the clock on the wall. *Another five minutes won't kill him.*

OUTSKIRTS OF GAINESVILLE

The lone rider wearing a black Tom Bull hat with a red-tail hawk feather in the beaded band, watched the sun set as he passed the first few houses on the edge of town. He maintained a road trot on his horse and kept a sharp lookout for holes and deep ruts in the dirt street. Dusk was settling in as he approached the Smith Brothers wagon yard and corral.

A young man lit a lantern and hung it on a hook outside the office door. He spotted the dark-skinned rider as he pulled rein. "Overnightin' your pony?"

"No. Only half hour or so. How far Painted Lady Saloon?"

He pointed west. "Three blocks thataway and turn right on Commerce Street. Jest listen for the music…Cain't miss it."

"How much for horse?"

"A quarter'll do."

Cal Mankiller dug in his vest, pulled out a silver coin and handed it the teenager. "You water horse, give hay?"

"You betcha." As he watched the stranger with the obsidian eyes walk away, a cold chill rattled his spine.

PAINTED LADY

Cal Mankiller entered the front door and looked around the crowded room. He glanced at the brunette entertainer on stage singing a popular ballad of the day that he was totally unfamiliar with. Listening to white man's music was definitely not a pastime for the renegade. He sauntered over to the young colored man at the shoeshine stand. "Where Tom Story?"

Bennie's eyes got big as saucers as he looked up at the dark-visaged Indian. "Uh…That's him over to the stage…uh, light-haired feller sittin' by hisself." He pointed. "But I don't know if'n…"

Mankiller ignored the rest of his answer and started making his way through the tables toward the stage.

"'Take me back to London, as quickly as you can, Oh! Mister Porter, what a silly girl I am'," Starla Marston sang the last lines of the chorus of *Oh, Mister Porter,* and then curtseyed to the audience to thunderous applause.

She looked up and saw Cal Mankiller heading in her direction. For the first time since becoming a marshal, she froze for a split second. *Oh God, why now?* Her heart started pounding like a trip hammer. She eased her hand down into the top of her parasol in the gown's side pocket.

Two days earlier, she had decided keeping her derringer under her garter around her thigh wasn't very functional. She

192

had twisted another elastic garter around the shaft at the center of the parasol and attached the small, but deadly, pistol there.

"If you will excuse me, I'll take a short break. The next show will begin in fifteen minutes…Thank you."

Mankiller's eyes met hers momentarily. Was there a flicker of recognition? She palmed the tiny two-shot gun, curtseyed again and exited stage left. Fiona realized she had been holding her breath after she was offstage—she exhaled. *Not the time or place.*

The Indian stopped at the table. "You Story?"

Tom looked up at the big Cherokee, his eyes went instantly from the black eyes to the large white scar that ran from his left ear to the point of his chin. *Damn, looks like it was made by a cavalry saber.*

"Mankiller, I take it."

"You take good." He pulled out a chair and sat down.

"Don't remember asking you to have a seat," Tom said sharply.

Cal ignored the statement. "Mankiller need money."

Story glanced around. He couldn't see Fiona watching from the shadows between the purple velvet curtains and the side of the stage. "Why the hell couldn't you wait until I got back to Dexter or get it from Frank?" he said sotto.

"Hungry…no eat since yesterday. Frank and Jack say you take all money in poker game…Mankiller no wait."

"Well, that's true." Tom tried to smile, but his face wouldn't let him as he looked at the dark soulless eyes of the rabid killer. He involuntarily shivered and slipped his hand past the handle of his Colt under his frock coat. *May have made a mistake adding this psycho.*

"Where hand go?"

He pulled a couple of double eagles from the side pocket of his vest and laid them on the table. He tilted his head slightly. "Just getting some money."

Cal scraped the gold coins into the palm of his hand and slipped them into the side pocket of his black sackcloth jacket.

"Don't ever come in here again," Story hissed.

The Indian got to his feet. "Mankiller go where Mankiller want." He turned and meandered toward the front door.

Tom watched him all the way out and suddenly realized he was sweating. He pulled a white kerchief from his pocket and dabbed his forehead.

"Who was that?"

He jerked the cloth down and looked up as Fiona pulled out a chair.

"Oh...just an Indian I hired to...uh...help me with my horse for the race."

"I don't like him...Keep him away from me...You known him long?"

He shook his head. "Actually, just met him."

"There's something evil in his eyes."

He glanced at the door, and then back. "Yeah, I noticed...You look as if you could use a drink."

Fiona forced a smile. "I know it's against my rules, but...maybe a little one."

Tom poured each of them a fresh shot.

COOKE COUNTY COURTHOUSE

Brushy Bill escorted Millie back from their abbreviated luncheon date. He glanced up at the clock on the wall. "I'll be back at two o'clock sharp for our little shopping extravaganza."

She shook her head and laughed. "Don't really think a dress and a pair of shoes would fall into the category of an extravaganza...do you?"

He grinned. "Depends...Some lady folk make a mountain out of a molehill when it comes to buyin' clothes." He winked. "Present company excepted."

She pointed at the door. "Go on, you. Permit me to get back to work or I will not be ready to leave here early."

Bill doffed his hat in a chivalrous manner and bowed at the waist. "Yes, m'lady. Parting is such sweet sorrow." He grinned and tugged his hat back in place.

Bill left the courthouse on the north side and turned right on the California Street brick sidewalk. He stopped just over a block east, outside Kinne's Jewelry Store and looked both ways before entering. The fourteen foot high interior walls were stacked with glass shelves filled with sterling-silver coffee sets and serving pieces.

Inside, a pretty dark-haired young woman addressed him from behind the U shaped counter, "Welcome to Kinnes...May I help you?"

Bill walked around the glass display cases. "Maybe so...I want to buy an engagement ring...Ya'll got anything like that?"

Gina Wiese smiled back. "Of course...My father is a master jeweler and if you don't see anything that suits your fancy, I would imagine he could make one that does."

Forty minutes later, Bill decided on an engraved gold band with a small diamond set in white gold.

"Do you have an idea about what ring size she wears?"

Roberts shook his head. "Not really...her hands are pretty dainty. Perhaps you know her...She works over in the county clerk's office..."

Gina gasped and her eyes flew open wide. "Millie Malena? I haven't heard the news!"

"I haven't asked her yet...It's kind of a surprise."

The saleswoman leaned closer. "My lips are sealed. But I do know her and she wears a size 5 on that finger."

Bill slipped the velvet-covered ring box in his outer coat pocket and stepped out into the mid-afternoon sun. *Just enough time for a shoeshine and a cool beer.* He crossed California on Red River street after the trolley went by heading west to the train depot. He had a spring in his step and whistled a tune all the way to the Painted Lady Saloon.

CHAPMAN'S LADIES READY TO WEAR

Millie looked at herself in the mirror. The tight-fitting bodice accentuated her hourglass figure and yet was classic in design. It went to her ankles and required three crinoline petty coats to keep the skirt portion flared out. She smiled and spun around. "This one fits like a glove...I don't think we'll have to do anything to it...What do you think?"

Brushy Bill was seated in a leather arm chair and nodded as a huge grin came to his face. "I say you will be the most beautiful woman at the fairgrounds...Wrap it up."

She rushed over to him and gave him a kiss full on the lips. "William Roberts, you are the most generous and wonderful man I know. Thank you, thank you, thank you."

"It gives me great joy to make you happy. Now all we have to find are some shoes...I saw a fancy pair in the window at Norton's."

Millie squealed with delight. "Give me a minute to change."

STIENKE'S GUN SHOP

Jack Long looked around at the new guns beneath the six foot long counters. Colts, Smith and Wesson and Iver Johnson revolvers dominated the offering in handguns, but behind the counter were racks of new and used lever guns, single shots as well as pump and break-action shotguns.

The tall man behind the counter walked down to the end and spoke up, "Show you anything, Mister? Might be somethin' you cain't live without."

"Meby later. Right now, need to stock up on some pistol ammo."

"Got that too." He pointed to the shelves in the center of the store. "Over in the middle row, on this side we have Stevens, Remington and Winchester Western. What caliber you lookin' for?"

"Need two boxes of .45 Colt and one .44 Winchester."

"Got plenty of both...Lead-tipped, self lubricatin'...good stuff."

Long stepped over to the eight foot tall shelving and picked up a three boxes. "This oughta do." He walked back to the counter and set them down next the brass cash register.

"Need any buckshot or birdshot?"

"This 'bout covers it."

Stienke quickly totaled the purchase in his head. "Three at six and a half is nineteen-fifty." He stacked the heavy rounds neatly inside a heavily-made brown paper sack.

Jack pulled his wallet from the back pocket of his tan canvas pants. He slipped out a crisp new twenty dollar bill and handed it over to the proprietor who rang up the sale and gave him two quarters in return.

"Pleasure doin' business with you. Come back and see us, sir."

Long grinned. "See you down the road." He turned and walked out into the bright afternoon sun on Commerce Street.

Bill backed out of Norton's with an armload of boxes and held the door open for his sweetheart with his foot. "You getting hungry yet?...It's almost five."

She grinned. "Thought you'd never ask...Wherever you want to go."

"Let's try somewhere different. There's a steak place over on Main."

Jack rounded the corner onto the Broadway sidewalk and headed east for the wagon yard and corral near Pecan Creek. He met a couple walking his way and his eyes were immediately drawn to the attractive female.

The two were talking excitedly as they approached the corner. She had her left arm draped through his right—his hands were full of boxes with colorful ribbons tied around them.

Mere steps before they passed, Jack allowed his gaze to drift to the man. Something about the way he wore his hat looked familiar. The slightly built man also had rather distinctive, protruding ears. He focused on the stranger's eyes, which were obviously looking at his lady as they passed by.

It took a full second for Jack's memory to kick in. After all, it had been fifteen years since the stranger had ended up on the opposite side of a range war in New Mexico. At one time, they had been friends, and then became mortal enemies.

Billy the Kid! Son of a bitch...Figured Pat Garrett was lying when he said he kilt you! He spun around as his hand went for his sixgun. "Bonney!"

Brushy Bill dropped the packages as he untangled Millie's arm from his own. He went for his gun as he wheeled to his right to face the shouted challenge.

Millie saw the murderous look in the cowboy's eyes as he aimed at Bill. She lunged instinctively between the two—her hands out in front of her.

Bill tried to push her away as he snatched the Colt from his shoulder holster. "No!"

The sounds of two shots rang out almost simultaneously and echoed up and down the city street.

Millie rocked back, her eyes wide with surprise. She grabbed for Bill's outstretched hand and slumped to the pavement at his feet. Her white bodice was stained with crimson spreading from a dime-sized hole between her breasts.

Jack fell back hard to the sidewalk, as bright red blood spurted from his carotid artery. His hat was knocked off and lay two feet away as he tried to move, but only the heel of his left foot drummed against the brick.

Bill held Millie's hand as he knelt beside her and laid his pistol on the sidewalk. Tears filled his eyes as he looked at her wound—knowing it was mortal. "Why...Why'd you do it?...That bullet was meant for me."

She gasped twice. "Why did he call you Bonney?"

"I was gonna tell you...just never was the right time."

"I...love you, Bill."

His breath was a ragged sob as he took the small box from his pocket and opened it. "Millie Malena. I love you with all my heart and I want you to..."

Her face lost all expression as the spark of life faded from her beautiful dark brown eyes—her head rolled to the side.

"No...not now. Oh, God...no." His shaking hands slipped the ring on her finger. His body trembled with emotion as he lovingly kissed her one last time—using the tips of his fingers, he softly closed her eyes for all eternity.

Bill's chin rested on his chest for a moment—he picked up his Colt and pushed himself to his feet. He turned and faced the man who had killed the love of his life. Cocking the hammer back, he stepped closer to him. "Who the hell are you?"

Roberts tried to blink away the tears, but had to resort to using the back of his left hand. He looked down at the cowboy lying motionless in a growing pool of blood. "Jack? Jack Long...You worthless bastard."

Bill kicked the pistol away from the man's outstretched hand. It didn't really matter. Long was paralyzed and bleeding out anyway. He knelt down beside him and whispered in his ear, "Told you I'd kill you if I ever laid eyes on you for bushwacking John Tunstel and now you've killed my bride to be." He got to his feet and aimed at Jack's forehead.

The fear in Long's eyes was apparent, but Brushy Bill lowered the hammer. "You ain't worth the bullet. Go ahead and bleed to death, you back-shootin' scum...Take your time."

A passerby came up. "What happened?"

Bill just shook his head. "Man murdered my fiancée and I killed him. Could you go get the town marshal?"

He took one look at the Deputy US Marshal's badge on Robert's vest. "You bet...Be right back."

In less than ten minutes, the man came back with a stocky, chiseled-faced mustachioed town marshal in tow.

"Harvey, go get Doc Wellman...tell him to bring his wagon."

"Yessir, I'll go git my horse." He strode off toward the wagon yard.

He stuck out his hand. "Kenneth Farmer, Town Marshal."

"Bill Roberts...Out of the Paris office."

Farmer nodded, glanced at Millie. "Harvey said this man shot your fiancée trying to kill you, that right, Marshal?"

"That's correct."

He looked over at the other body, lying in a large pool of his own blood. "Who is…uh, was he?"

"Jack Long…Outlaw from New Mexico…killer, rustler."

"You from there, too?

Bill nodded. "Some fifteen years ago. 'Spect if you contact the Lincoln County sheriff, you'll find there's papers on him… Arizona Rangers probably have some dodgers too…No federal warrants on him that I know of."

"Who's sheriff there now?"

"No idea, since Garrett retired."

"What the hell was this riffraff doin' in my town?" He knelt down by the body, rolled it over and removed a long wallet from his back pocket.

"I'd like an answer to that question myself, Marshal." He looked down at the crumpled body of his love and his eyes began to fill with tears.

Marshal Farmer pulled out a number of twenty dollar bills. "Huh…well looky here, looky here, brand new paper money. Now where do you suppose…"

***

CHAPTER TEN

BROADWAY STREET

Selden walked up as Doctor Wellman drew rein in a buckboard being pulled by a single roan gelding. He waded into the crowd that had gathered. "Make way folks, make way...lawman comin' through."

Bill had taken his jacket off and laid it over Millie's body. Her legs stuck out from beneath the long dark coat.

"Heard the shooting. Loss and I were halfway across town, canvassin' stores." The look on Brushy Bill's face told him most of the story. "Damnation, son...Cain't tell you how sorry I am...That the bastard what shot her?"

Bill was still in a state of shock. He nodded, and then took a deep breath.

Town Marshal Farmer moved closer and handed Selden a pair of crisp new twenty dollar bills. "Found these on the deceased." He pointed to Jack. "Marshall Roberts says he was wanted in New Mexico and that the serial numbers match those taken in the Stubblefield stage holdup and murders up in the Nations."

Selden frowned, his dark mustache took the shape of an inverted U. "Well, I'll be a suckegg mule...Why'd he take an' shoot Millie?"

"He recognized me from New Mexico...Millie and I were talking and I...I guess I let my guard down." He sighed and shook his head. "He called me out after we passed by...Millie took the bullet...meant for me." Bill's lower lip began to tremble.

Lindsey put his hand on his fellow lawman's shoulder. "God rest her soul, Bill...She was a brave woman."

Doc Wellman stepped down from the wagon and stode over to Bill. "My deepest condolences, Marshal. I really liked her."

"Thanks Doc. Everybody did."

"Can you men give me a hand? I'll get them loaded up and do what has to be done."

Bill raised his hand. "Hold on, Doc. If you don't mind, I'd rather not see Millie ride in the same wagon with the man that killed her."

Wellman nodded. "See your point. Two trips won't be a huge imposition...considering the circumstances."

"Appreciate your kindness." Roberts walked over to Millie's body and removed his coat.

A murmur erupted from the assembled gawkers.

Selden stepped in between the body and the crowd. "Ya'll move along now. Show some respect."

The look on his face and tone of his voice gave the impression that it was more than a suggestion and they began to disperse.

Loss Hart joined them as Doc, Bill, Selden and Farmer got on each side and lifted Millie from the sidewalk. They carried her to the back of the wagon. Loss stepped up into the bed and supported her head and shoulders as they slid the body in on a blanket the doc had spread out.

Bill turned around and stared at the boxes lying beside the pool of blood for a moment. "Doc...Hold on." He stepped over to the packages and picked them up. "She looked beautiful in her new shoes and dress. It would be fitting if she was buried in them. Would you see that the funeral home gets them." His voice cracked a bit and trailed off.

Wellman became misty-eyed as Bill laid them in the bed beside her. "I would be proud to take care of that for you, Marshal Roberts."

BASS AND THE LADY

SKEANS BOARDING HOUSE

Faye embraced him, stepped back and held both his hands in hers. "I am so, so sorry, Bill. We loved her too. I know there is absolutely nothing anyone can say or do to ease your pain at this time. But, we are all here for you...I think we've all been there at one time or another...Has the funeral been scheduled?"

He shook his head and whispered, his voice barely audible, "Thank you, Faye...I've sent word to Father Miller. I suspect it will be next week sometime. I know she would have wanted the last rites..."

"God's merciful love is greater than our hearts and isn't bound by the sacraments of the church...I think you can feel confident that she's with her son now in Heaven." She hugged him again.

He nodded his thanks. Bill's face seemed to be made of granite as his gaze appeared to be a thousand yards away.

"I'll go get you some tea." Faye gave his hands a final squeeze, turned and walked through the two-way swinging door into the kitchen.

Bass, Bodie and Selden shook his hand and patted his shoulder in turn. Annabel and Fiona each hugged him. No one said a word—they all felt Faye said everything that was needed.

Bill took a deep breath, exhaled and sat on the dark green Chesterfield sofa next to Fiona. She patted his thigh.

"Well, we know one thing...Long was one of the coach murderers. Now, just gotta find the other two. You still think Story was the leader, Bass?"

The big man leaned against the mantle with a Mason jar of iced tea in his hand. "I do Sel...I do indeed. Like I said, jest don't believe in coincidences."

"And now that miscreant, Cal Mankiller, is in the mix. I really don't think he was part of that holdup."

"How so, Fiona?" asked Bodie.

"Story didn't seem to know him...I mean, he knew who he was, but I don't think they had ever met. Plus I saw him slip him some money...gold coins. He told me...for what it's worth...he had just hired him to help with his horse."

"Right...and soon as they drain the Palo Duro, it'll be perfect for farmin'." Bodie chuckled at his own joke.

"Once I found the new cartridge boxes in that sack the late Mister Long was totin', I stopped by the closest gun shop and asked a few questions." He grinned. "Buck Stienke couldn't have been nicer...Knowed him from when he was up in Ardmore. But he didn't have nothin' else that would help us...Anybody got any ideas who the third man might be?" Selden looked at the others.

Bass' face clouded over. "Jest pray to God it wadn't Bennie."

"What time should we all get out to the fair grounds tomorrow?" asked Bodie.

BASS AND THE LADY

Bass shook his head to dispel the thoughts of his son being involved in that heinous crime. "I'm gonna tell Tom to have Little John and Fats take the horses out there about ten of a mornin'...Race ain't till two. Give 'em time to settle in with the crowd an' all...I'll still be undercover so's my boy don't recognize me...'case he's there. Seems like where Story is...Bennie's there too...not a good sign."

"Who er what you gonna be, Bass?" asked Selden.

"Gonna wear some extry paddin' an' be a grounds keeper. Folks generally don't pay no mind to either coloreds er trash collectors."

"Well, I'd say you had both avenues covered then."

Bass looked at Fiona for a long beat, and then grinned. "Yes, Ma'am."

She threw one of the small green velvet throw pillows from the couch at his head. He snatched it from the air with his massive hand and flipped his wrist, sending it back at her like a ball bouncing from a wall—she wasn't ready. It hit her full in the face with a soft whap and fell to her lap.

"Better be glad I'm not heeled, you big galoot."

PAINTED LADY SALOON

Fiona finished her first set and took a seat across the table from Tom Story. He had arranged to have a glass of tea waiting for her.

209

She lifted it up and toasted him. "Thank you, kind sir. Very chivalrous."

"My pleasure. You look absolutely ravishing tonight."

She took a sip and set the glass down before carefully blotting her lips with her white linen sleeve hanky. "You know, I never got around to ask you about which hotel you're staying in…Is it the Turner down by the depot?"

He grinned and shook his head. "Sometimes I wish that were the case. Actually, I took a room in the first town I came to after I crossed the Red River at Preston's Ferry…the Dexter Hotel."

She smiled. "I've never been that far north…Once the train from New Orleans pulled in here, I got a room with Faye Skeans and have been working ever since…Is Dexter a big town?"

Tom shook his head. "Used to be, they tell me." He downed a shot of bourbon. "They say it was a lot bigger than Gainesville at one time…but kind of died on the vine when the railroad went south through Woodbine and passed it by…Funny how that works. Seen it happen more than once."

"You must have a lot of interesting stories with all your travels…I'd like to hear about them sometime."

He chuckled. "Well, don't mean to brag, but I have covered me some country. But saddle sores are not much to be proud of…if you know what I mean."

"I suppose. Perhaps, it's only a case of the grass is always greener." She glanced at his handsome profile as she took another sip of tea.

"I do know I like to listen to you sing." He winked. "Kinda fond of watching you, as well…God, you are one beautiful woman." He leaned forward on his elbows and stared at Fiona.

Her gray eyes locked with his pale blues. "And you are quite the lady's man with a velvet tongue." She sighed, shook head and smiled. "I appreciate your compliment…Women like to hear nice things said about them."

Fiona glanced over her shoulder at Jake sitting back down on his swivel stool at the piano and flexing his long fingers. "Guess it's time to get on with the next set. The natives will be getting restless."

Tom slid his chair back, got up and pulled hers out as she stood. "Go, my little nightingale…Show everybody what a real singer sounds like."

COOKE COUNTY FAIR GROUNDS

Luckily, Saturday morning dawned clear and bright. The ticket takers at the gate opened promptly at ten. The town mayor, Jarrod Hatcher—a trim man in his fifties with mutton chop whiskers—had decided to turn the race into a full-blown county fair type event. The crowd, he surmised, should exceed ten thousand souls and with the admission fee for adults set—by him—at one dollar, the city coffers would get a needed infusion. Immediately just inside the gate, Hatcher had erected a tan twenty-by-twenty army surplus tent as his executive office. Inside, were two tables, one for the gate receipts—to be added to the vendor fees. His personal secretary would be manning one while the other was for the honorable Judge Leander Algernon Miles, III and his court assistant.

The venerable judge had been chosen to set the odds and hold the bets with his court assistant keeping the tally book. There was already a line forming outside ready to make their wagers. It was only a little smaller than the line of folks who failed to get tickets from a local merchant and were waiting to buy theirs at the gate.

The vendors, in a one hundred yard long stretch near the start and finish line, were getting their wares set up. The kettle popcorn booth had its fire at the proper level for the coals.

The meat sandwich stand—next to the fried catfish tent—opened up, manned by Fletcher Davis up from Athens, Texas. He created what he called a hamburger steak on a yeast bun with mustard, a Bermuda onion and a slice of Brick cheese. The sandwich was served with Irish and sweet potato wedges fried together in a big cast iron wash pot of boiling lard, salted and covered with a thick sweetened tomato sauce.

The word *hamburger,* Davis said he got from some German immigrants from Hamburg a few years back for a fried or grilled ground meat cake patty or steak that was a favorite back in the old country. Old Dave, as Fletcher was called, would take his dish to the St. Louis World's Fair in 1904. The *hamburger* would become a national icon in a very short time.

Next to Fletcher's was the very popular ice cream stand. There were ten wooden ice cream freezers already being cranked by local teenagers. The proprietors, two middle-aged ladies from the small town of Muenster—only five miles to the west—were writing the flavors on a three-by-four foot slate blackboard. Listed were: Vanilla, Dutch Chocolate, Strawberry, Peach, Buttered Pecan and a local favorite—Watermelon Rind Preserve, made from the very sweet local Black Diamond watermelon.

The other booths included vendors selling, lemonade, hand pulled taffy, buffalo jerky, several pie stands—located conveniently close the ice cream tent,and homemade chocolate. Handmade goods such as quilts, pottery and wooden toys.

The Gainesville Tuba band with their red, trimmed in gold parade uniforms—were drifting in with their instruments and some were beginning to tune up. The drummer unloaded his big bass drum from a wagon.

SKEANS BOARDING HOUSE

Fiona finished lunch and tied her hair back in a low pony tail. She was wearing black canvas riding pants with a one piece leather insert on the inner thigh and seat, and a light blue chambray button-up shirt. She dabbed a bit of rouge on her upper lip, pressed them together and smoothed up with her little finger. *That's all I'm doing today...It's a horse race, not a beauty pageant.*

She glanced down at the tiny Remington derringer on the sideboard and stuck it in her pants pocket. Fiona opened the bottom dresser drawer and removed her matched nickel-plated Colts.

She opened the loading gates on each, pulled the hammer back to half-cock and slowly rolled the cylinders a full turn to confirm they were properly loaded. She eased the hammers down on the single empty chamber and slipped both back into the cross-draw rig before stowing them snugly inside a carpet bag. She left it in her room for Faye to bring in the wagon.

Fiona tapped on the door to the room down the hall.

Brushy Bill stepped out a few seconds later, his saddle bags slung over his shoulder. His eyes were sad, bloodshot and still a bit puffy from recurring crying jags that seemed to come upon him in waves.

"I Appreciate you riding out with me, my friend."

"Got to do something…Can't stop thinking about her."

She placed her hand on his shoulder. "I know what it's like to lose the love of your life. Believe me…I know."

"I'll be all right in a day or two…Once the funeral is past."

214

BASS AND THE LADY

Fiona tried to force a smile, but it didn't feel right. "Let's get going. The fresh air will do us both some good."

COOKE COUNTY FAIR GROUNDS

Contestants for the big race were almost all checked in as the Rafter S wagon pulled through the gate with two magnificent American Saddlebreds tied to the back of the buckboard. One was coal black and the other an almost white dapple gray.

Little John Boutté, a short stub of a man, handled the reins, with his coworker, Fats Ward, an extraordinarily skinny colored man, beside him on the wagon seat.

"Wooboy, Fats, smell that?" Little John sniffed the air as they passed the booths.

"Lawdy, lawdy, I does, I does...Mayhaps need to take a stroll down by the food vendors after we git the horses settled in...Gots me some of last months pay that's 'bout to burn a hole clean through my pocket...'Sides, believe I could eat the ass-end out of a leather duck."

Little John guffawed. "When cain't you?...We kin take turns. Bass said we wasn't to leave the horses alone, no...That's why they's two of us."

"Ain't nobody gwanna touch my babies...I'll see to that." Fats patted the old Navy Colt revolver high up on his hip.

"Kin you hit an'thin' with that, my fran?"

"Don't rightly know...But 'ny nabob wantin to cause some mischief ain't gonna know if'n I can er cain't when I'm a pointin' it in his direction an' ear the hammer back."

Little John nodded and pointed at a cut-down Greener by his left leg. "My twice barreled ten gauge shootgun will make they eyes bug out to double they size...I gaurontee," said the short Louisiana native.

Fats chuckled. "Yeah, son...be like lookin' down into the gates of hell they own selves."

The two men failed to notice the shabbily-dressed, portly gray-haired old colored man with a large burlap sack hung over his left shoulder by a short piece of rope, shuffling along the vendor row. He carried a four foot length of broom handle with a headless nail driven in one end and sharpened to a point for stabbing loose paper. But, they did notice a big, scar-faced Indian leaning against a tree, smoking a roll-your-own.

"Damnation, Fats, that Injun over yonder looks like he jest plumb hates the world, don't he?"

"Meby he jest needs a good dose of Yagoda's Bitters...Hear tell it kin take care of thangs when you cain't do yer mornin' business."

Little John nodded. "I'm here to tell you. *Laissez les bon temps roulez.*"

"What in hell does that mean? That some of that coonass talk?"

216

"Let the good times roll, my ver good fran…let the good times roll."

"Ain't it the truth."

Little John flicked the reins over the big sorrel mare's rump, clucked at her and headed toward the corrals set up for the contestants.

Fiona and Bill rode up to the corral together. He swung down and opened the gate and let her inside, quickly following behind. He loosened the cinch on his horse, Tippy, and tied it to the railing.

"There's Flash…They're gettin' that little bitty saddle strapped to him…Looks like Dan already has his on."

"Never rode an English saddle before. Looks lightweight enough."

Bill chuckled. "Oh, yes, Ma…Fiona. Don't hardly weigh anything. Easy on the animals…mighty slippery though for the rider. You might want to get a little practice in before the race. The little scudders don't have a horn to hang on to in a tight."

She raised her eyebrows. "I see that. It'll be like trying to ride on a postage stamp…And look at those metal stirrups. There's nothing to them."

"Those Englishmen think they're the biggest bloody toad in the puddle for ridin' to the hounds and such nonsense. They even jump with 'em."

She nodded. "We might have occasion to do that on the course. I'm sure there is at least one creek to cross."

Thirty minutes later, Selden and Loss trotted their horses through the gate, flashing their badges at the attendants. Lindsey had borrowed a handsome sorrel gelding Saddlebred from Tom Sullivant since his Dan was entered in the race.

They nodded at Marshal Farmer and Acting Sheriff Rudabaugh and stopped.

"How's it goin' Marshal...Acting Sheriff?"

"Fine as chicken teeth, Selden...fine as chicken teeth. We're just makin' the rounds discouragin' any grifters what mighta drifted this way lookin' for some easy pickins."

"We're also on the lookout for confidence men..."

"Means the same thing, George."

Rudabaugh glanced at the town marshal. "Uh, huh, well, the fair grounds is under the jurisdiction of the County Sheriff's office."

"Uh...not exactly...Town Council voted just last Monday to incorporate this area into the city...for tax purposes, you understand?"

Rudabaugh slammed his bowler to the ground. "How's come nobody ever tells me. I'm always the last to know anything."

BASS AND THE LADY

A gust of wind picked up his dark green bowler and sent it bouncing across the bare ground toward a juggler on stilts practicing with three Bowie knives.

"Oh, damn!" The corpulent law officer waddled after his hat. "Hey, you, grab my hat," he yelled at the juggler.

The performer glanced down at the round-topped bowler as it tumbled and rolled near his position. He stopped spinning the knives, catching two in his left and the third in his right hand. In one smooth move, he flipped the single twelve inch blade knife, spearing the hat through the crown and pinning it to the ground beside his foot.

"Got it, Sheriff."

Rudabaugh stumbled to a stop, glanced at his new hat with the Bowie knife handle sticking out of the top, and then up at the juggler with a look that would melt steel.

"Want to hand me my knife back, Sheriff?...Cain't get down that low."

George bent over, grabbed the handle, pulled it out of the ground and slid his hat from the blade. He stuck two fingers through the wide gash in the top as he handed the knife back to the juggler. "It's *Acting* Sheriff," he said as he jammed the bowler back on his head and stalked away toward the fortune teller's table.

Loss and Selden grinned, shook their heads and directed their mounts to the contestant's corral over near the oval track and pulled rein beside the Rafter S wagon, Bill and Fiona.

219

Big Dan and Flash were each in a twelve by twelve stall. They had already been given a half bucket of water apiece—all they would get until after the race.

"What's that on Dan and Flash's back?" asked Loss.

Fats chuckled. "That's called an English saddle, Marshal Hart...Missy Fran loves to ride 'em."

"Don't look much bigger'n a wash rag."

"Think about the horse, Loss, not yerself," commented Selden. "I'm gonna walk back over to the main tent and check on the bettin' odds. Wanna come along, Bill?"

"Might as well, can't do anything here. We need to scope out the folks comin' through the gate anyway."

"Let's mount up, Loss and take them into the warm-up arena with some of the other riders and get the kinks out."

"Of them er us?"

"Your choice," replied Fiona with a smile.

The two undercover marshals had mounted up and were loping their steeds in large circles in the practice or warm-up arena.

"Ding, dang, feller really has to concentrate on stayin' in the center of this tiny slick-assed saddle...pardon the expression."

Fiona grinned. "Heard worse...You forget I've been wearing a deputy marshal's badge for several years now...Just keep your eyes between his ears and you won't have any trouble. Remember to press your knees in and raise up just a bit when you go over a jump."

220

"Jump? What do you mean, 'jump'?"

"Didn't you read the race rules?"

"Naw. Figured we just ride hell-bent-for-leather out to the turn-pole an' then back."

She chuckled. "Well, not exactly."

"What does that mean?"

They rounded the far end of the arena and loped back toward the center, still side-by-side.

"It means this is a cross-country race. Across creeks, jumping dead falls, ditches and split-rail fences, over hills and through the dale...In Ireland, it's called a steeplechase."

"What's a 'dale'."

"The low ground between hills...You know, a swag or coolee?"

"Why didn't you just say so?...A dale...huh." Loss grunted.

Fiona looked over as a buckboard with three people inside and two horses tied behind pulled up to the arena—Tom Story was driving. She nudged Flash over to the fence and reined up. "Good morning, Tom...Willie."

"Miss Starla! Didn't hardly recognize you," the young colored man exclaimed from the bed of the wagon as his eyes quickly focused on the big gray stallion.

ADMINISTRATION TENT

Selden and Bill strode toward the big tent passing a cart vendor just outside.

"Git yer dogs on a roll! Red hot! Right here!" the vendor hawked.

"Hey, Bill, want one of those dachshund sausage's on a bun? Folks say they're really good."

"You buying?"

"Reckon so, since I brought it up." He raised his hand. "Here you go, son."

The young man pushed his cart over to them. "Yessir, how many?"

"We'll take two…got 'ny chow-chow?"

"Yessir! Mustard too."

Selden looked at Bill.

"Sounds good. What are these things called?"

"They been sellin' 'em at baseball games up north fer a couple years now…callin' 'em hot dogs on account of…"

Roberts nodded. "Yeah, I get it…Some of that mustard and chow-chow on mine too…you don't mind."

"How much?" asked Selden.

"Ten cents each, sir…Go good with beer they say…Booth right over yonder." He pointed down the vendor isle.

Selden gave him a quarter when he handed them the two butcher paper wrapped hot dogs. "Keep the change, boy."

"Wow! Thank you sir." He turned and continued through the increasing crowd. "Hot dawgs! Right here!"

The two marshals unwrapped their confections and each took big bites off the end.

"Wonder how these'd taste with chili on 'em," mused Selden.

"Be a little messy, I imagine. Kinda like trying to eat a soup sandwich...Doubt it would ever catch on." Bill took another bite. "Besides, why ruin a good thing?"

"Uh, huh."

They walked between the two lines at the entry into the spacious tent and moved over to the big blackboard set up at the betting table. Marshal Farmer had a short piece of chalk and was filling in the odds on entry number nine—there were a total of eleven.

"How's it comin' Marshal?"

The stocky lawman turned around. "Oh, mornin' again, Selden...Bill. Just updatin' the odds board...Gotta do it 'bout ever fifteen minutes."

"How do you figure 'em?" asked Bill.

Farmer glanced around, and then leaned over closer to the two men. "By gosh an' by golly mostly...but if'n anybody asks...very scientific with that abacus thing layin' on the table there. Borrowed it from the high school math teacher, Mister Griffin. He says it come from China...Problem is, I ain't got a dang clue how to work it, so I just get the total amount on each horse from Mervin there…" He tilted his head in the direction of the judges twenty-something assistant. "…an' see who's gittin' the most bets." He glanced around again to see if anyone else was close enough to hear. "Then I jest make a wild-ass stab at what looks right."

Selden grinned and shook his head. "Sounds good to me."

"Who's getting the most bets?" asked Bill.

"Well, it's a tossup 'tween yer horse, Dan and that Rafter S grey…Howsomever, did git a sizable bet jest a little bit ago on a red roan Standardbred geldin' named Red Dawn, at six to one…He's a total unknown."

"How much?"

Farmer glanced over at the tally book, and then back at Selden. "Five hunderd dollars."

"Woowee, sounds like somebody knows somethin', don't it."

"I'd say so, Selden, I'd say so…Who made the bet?" asked Bill.

The marshal glanced at the tally book again. "A Tom Story."

"Uh, huh…and whose horse is it?"

Farmer turned around and picked up the contestant list and ran his finger down it. "Well, well…" He looked up at the two marshals. "…Tom Story."

Roberts grinned and nodded. "Well, well, indeed."

Selden scratched the side of his nose. "Sounds to me like Mister Story has somethin' planned…"

"Or else he's trying to stir up the betting," interrupted Bill as he and the other two marshals exchanged glances.

"Could be...Here's a double eagle on Dan." Selden laid the gold twenty dollar coin in front of Mervin, the judge's assistant.

"Yessir." The bespeckled slight young man put the money in a small steel box and wrote the bet down in the tally book. "All done, Marshal."

"Obliged...When's the judge comin' in?"

Mervin pulled out a stainless steel inexpensive Waterbury pocket watch and popped the cover. "In about an hour, sir."

***

CHAPTER ELEVEN

COOKE COUNTY FAIR GROUNDS

Tom and Francis Ann Sullivant drove through the gate in their black Stanhope buggy, with the top down.

"Come up, Rosie." He clucked and popped the snappers above the rump of the four-stocking sorrel Standardbred mare as they pulled away from the attendants.

Fran's husband, inactive Texas Ranger Walt Durbin and four of the Rafter S wranglers riding behind nodded and touched the brim of their hats as they also passed through. Following them were Bodie, Annabel and Faye Skeans in a two-seated Spring wagon. The Ranger's line-back dun, Lakota Moon, was tethered to the rear beside Fiona's black and white Appaloosa, Diablo.

BASS AND THE LADY

The convoy of Rafter S employees and supporters unloaded and tied up in a grove of scattered white oak, cottonwood and pecan trees near the administration tent. They watered the horses with buckets they had brought along, loosened their tack, and then strode in the direction of the tent to place their bets.

The telegraph agent from the Santa Fe Depot, Percy Gilhooley, was directing the connection of a telegraph station between the announcer's platform and the main tent. He had set up a small table just outside with his Morse key on top with the end of the copper wire connected to it.

"Well, looky here. It's First Assistant Texas Ranger Gilhooley," said a voice softly behind him.

He turned to see Bodie, followed by the others, walking up.

"Ranger Hickman! Gollygee." He glanced around, leaned toward him and whispered, "I'm still keepin' my eyes and ears open...sir."

"That's good, uh, Percy. You keep up the good work, hear?" He glanced down at the key on the table and his eye followed the wire up into a red oak next to the tent, and then north in the direction of the creek, draped through the trees. "Well, that's interestin'."

"What's that, sir?"

"Yer wire...strung all through the trees like a grapevine."

Walt, Annabel and the rest all looked up at the wire and back to the young man in the green eyeshade with puzzled expressions.

"Oh, yessir!" Gilhooley beamed. "That's the way they first strung wire durin' the War of Northern Aggression. It was easier if there was a lot of trees and such to hang the wire on the branches instead of plantin' poles...That's where the expression, 'Heard it through the grapevine' come from, on account of the sending and receiving wire looking like muscadine vines."

"You don't say?" commented Walt.

"Oh, I seen lots of it durin' the war," said Tom Sullivant. "Worked fine...Where's this goin'?"

"Goin' out to the turnaround point. There's an agent from Western Union set up out there. When the horses get to the pylon and make the big turn back to the fair grounds...Well, he sends it to me an' I relay it to Marshal Farmer...He'll be standin' on that tall platform next to me...He's got this megaphone and he lets everbody back here know who's ahead and who's dropped out and such. Don't you see?...Just like one of them regular race track announcers."

"Well, I do declare," said Annabel.

Bodie glanced over his shoulder. "Me an Walt are fixin' go inside the main tent and place our bets...Sweetie, why don't you and Francis Ann go over and check out the quiltin' booth? Might find something nice for the baby boy."

"What if Faye's wrong? What if I buy a blue one and the baby is a girl?" Annabel grinned and looked at their landlord.

"Not a snowball's chance, young lady...Haven't been wrong yet."

Walt laughed out loud. "Wouldn't it be somethin' if you have twins...one of each."

Annabel shook her finger at him. "Bite your tongue, Walter Durbin." She looked down at her stomach and patted both sides. "Bodie's been telling everyone that I'm as big as a house."

"Uh, oh, that reminds me, darlin'. My mama and her sister were twins...You never got to meet my Aunt Fannie yet."

"Now you tell me...We only have one name picked out."

Faye glanced down at Annabel's protruding belly. "Just to be on the safe side, you better buy two."

"Yes, Ma'am." She grabbed Francis Ann by the hand. "We best get going before they decide I'm having triplets."

"Perish the thought."

Tom climbed back into the buckboard and clucked the gelding into motion. "Stephanie, my dear, once we get Red Dawn all settled down in the pen area, you'll need to get yourself a seat in the stands. Bennie and I'll be tied up getting ready for the race."

"I can take care of myself, thank you very much...Besides, there are plenty of things to see and do here."

Bennie looked around the fairgrounds that were rapidly filling with people. "All them little cook tents smell purty good. I'ma gonna get me somethin' 'fore the race starts, fer shore."

"After we get Dawn brushed and ready to go...Got a lot of money ridin' on him."

They pulled up to the fence surrounding the corral and pen area. Bennie hopped down and opened the wooden gate. Once the wagon and horses were through, he swung back onto the rear of the wagon. A few of the other contestants were already mounted and limbering up their horses.

PRACTICE ARENA

Fiona wheeled her mount and spotted the newest arrivals. She trotted up to the arena fence as the buckboard rolled to stop. Smiling broadly, she addressed the somewhat astonished gambler and outlaw, "Hello, Tom...Aren't you going to introduce your friend?"

She looked nothing like the elegantly dressed and well-coiffed entertainer. Although her riding clothes were more appropriate for a man in the Victorian age, they left no doubt as to the lady's gender.

"Oh, excuse my manners. This is Stephanie...uh, Ladd, from over at Dexter...Stephanie, this is Miss Starla Marston, the singer from New Orleans."

230

The blonde nodded. "Pleased, I'm sure." She cut her eyes at Tom. "I see where you've been spending your evenings," she said with ice dripping off each word.

Loss trotted up beside Fiona. "Friends of your'n?"

"Oh, yes. This is Mister Tom Story and his, ah, lady friend...Stephanie Ladd...Is that right?" She looked back over at her. "And that's Willie Spencer from the Painted Lady." She tilted her head toward Loss. "This is Loss Hart...he's riding Dan here in the race...Mister Story will be riding that strawberry roan behind his wagon there," she said to Loss.

Hart doffed his hat at Stephanie and his eyes fell upon the cameo broach nestled between her ample breasts for a brief moment. "How do. Pleased to meet ya'll...Nice lookin' horse. He a Standardbred?"

Tom nodded. "That's correct. His name's Red Dawn...the color of the sky at daybreak...Well, nice to meet you, too. Guess we'd better go saddle up, stretch him out a bit and warm him up before the race...Good luck to ya'll."

He turned the bay gelding pulling the wagon to the left and headed down to some trees close to the south end of the arena.

When they were out of earshot, Loss turned to Fiona. "You see what I saw?"

"I did...I did indeed."

"Reckon I better go find Selden."

"I'm sure Bass is somewhere around too...probably being unobtrusive."

"Unobwhat?"

"Hard to see."

Loss turned Dan to trot over to the gate mumbling to himself, "I jest don't understand how's come folks cain't say what they mean the first time."

After Tom parked the wagon and started saddling Dawn, Bennie stepped over to him, making sure that Stephanie was still sitting on the seat, checking her hair and makeup in a small compact mirror.

"Mister Tom," he whispered.

"What?" Story bent over, reached under the stallion and grabbed the long latigo hanging from the offside, brought it over and threaded it through the O ring on the left side of the saddle.

"Uh...you know that gray horse that Miss Starla was a sittin' on?"

"Yeah, what about it?" He made two more wraps through the ring with the cinch strap, looped it around, slipped the end through and pulled it tight, taking the slack out. "Hand me his bridle," he said as he checked the tie-downs on his saddlebags.

Bennie grabbed the D-ring snaffle bit with the copper-coated mouthpiece, bridle and split reins and handed it to Tom.

"Well, that horse..."

"You said that. Nice looking animal."

"Yessir...but, uh, that's...that's my daddy's horse."

"Oh? An' just who's your daddy?"

Bennie hesitated.

"Who's your daddy?" Tom asked again. This time he looked over his shoulder directly at the nervous colored boy.

"Bass Reeves...My daddy's Bass Reeves."

Story spun around and grabbed him by both arms. "What?" he hissed. "Marshal Bass Reeves?"

Bennie nodded.

"God dammit to hell!" He stomped around in a tight circle stirring up little clouds of dust. "You sure that's his horse?"

"Yessir...Knows him anywhere."

Tom looked around. "Maybe he sold him."

"Uh, uh...No way, no day. Daddy would never sell that horse."

"I don't suppose you've seen him anywhere around here?"

"No, sir. That's why I was so shook up...Seein' his horse."

He looked around again. "He's gotta be around somewhere...Must be after you."

Bennie shook his head. "If'n daddy don't want to be seen...ain't nobody gonna see 'im. He's like a ghost...Lived with Injuns fer over two years."

"Why the hell didn't you tell me Bass Reeves was your father?" He grabbed his arms again and shook him. "Huh?"

"Well, didn't think 'bout it, jest wanted to git far away as I could...But if'n my daddy's after me, there ain't no gittin' away. If'n he's got papers on me…he won't never quit…Not never."

Story looked off and thought a minute. "Could be it ain't you he's after. Could be he's after somebody else…Could be he's got papers on that Cherokee, Mankiller…Yeah, bet that's it."

"That Injun what come in the saloon the other night?"

Tom nodded.

"He's scary lookin'."

"Yeah…But you'd better light a shuck anyway. No need in drawing anymore attention to us than necessary. Get on that nag of yours and head out. Meet you back in Dexter…or better yet, Dripping Spring. Pack up my stuff at the hotel…all of it, especially my saddle bags under the bed. I expect we'll be making tracks…Now scat."

After putting Dan back in his pen, Loss headed out toward the main tent and vendor area next to the track. His nose went up into the air as he neared Fletcher's Hamburger stand—he stopped. "Say, Ma'am, how's about one of them meat sandwiches there. Shore smell tasty."

"With all the fixin's?" asked a happy-faced woman behind the counter.

"I 'magine…What all comes on it?"

"A grilled ground beef patty, brick cheese, onion and mustard between two halves of a yeast roll."

234

"Kin you double up on the beef an' cheese?"

"Two beef patties with two cheese slices?...My you're a hungry fellow, aren't you?"

"Yessum...You don't mind...could you add a couple dill stacker pickles on it?"

"Be extra."

Loss pulled a fifty cent piece from his vest pocket and placed it on the counter. "That cover it?"

She grinned a big toothy smile, winked at him and turned back to the expanded metal grill lying over a cast iron wash pot with a bed of hot hickory coals in the bottom. "I 'spect."

"What's yer name, Ma'am?"

"Penny...Penny Whisman...Miss Penny Whisman," she replied over her shoulder as she shaped out two thick patties of fresh ground beef and laid them above the coals.

After a few minutes, she removed them to a table where she sprinkled a couple pinches of ground salt from a small bowl over the still sizzling surface. Penny then placed them and the slices of cheese, mustard, a thick slab of red onion in the middle of the big round bun along with three stacker pickles, wrapped it in a piece of white butcher paper. She handed it to Loss with a paper napkin and a grin.

"Umm, umm, umm, that shore smells wonderful. I reckon nothin' smells better'n grilled meat...less'n it's a apple pie." He took a big bite and with his mouth still full said, "...An' tastes even better. Makes you want to go home and slap yer grandma, it's so good."

Penny grinned a very infectious smile. "I'm glad you like it Mister…"

"Loss Hart. I'm from up in the Nations…You should go into business," he said between bites.

Penny looked around the booth. "Uh, I think Mister Fletcher Davis already has." She giggled.

"Well, ah, meby you could open up a small specialty restaurant up in Ardmore…Just sell these, what do you call em…hamburgers? Along with some of those fried tater slices…What do you think?"

"I'll ask Old Dave…uh, Mister Davis. She smiled again at Loss and shyly ducked her head. "I wouldn't mind."

"I'd probably be yer best customer, Miss Penny. This'd go great with a beer…er one of them phosphates."

She pointed across the venue at another booth. "They say that new drink, Dr Pepper, from down to Waco is awfully good…It's got twenty-three flavors…and is supposed to be a brain tonic."

Loss rotated the burger, dropping the napkin near his foot. "How's come so many? Meby they oughta stick to just one."

"No, they combined twenty-three different flavors to create a new taste."

"Oh, why didn't you just say so."

"I think I just did," she replied and turned to wait on another customer at the other end of the plank counter.

Hart bent his head over to take another big bite just in time to see a broomstick with a nail in the end stab the napkin right beside his foot. He jumped. "Great sufferin' horny toads! Watch out with that thang, feller...Almost made me drop my sandwich."

"Just be glad that paper wadn't on top of yer boot, Loss," the stooped-over, paunchy old colored man said softly.

"How do you know my..." He bent over and looked under the floppy battered fedora. "Bass?..."

"Shhhh." He put a finger to his lips while he pulled the napkin off the nail and handed it back to him. "Meet me over to that clump of cedars near the entrance...Gonna meander over thataway."

"Got somethin' to tell..."

"I know...Over there." Bass started shuffling off in that direction, stabbing trash as he went.

Loss shook his head and grinned. "That man never ceases to amaze me."

In ten minutes, Loss had drifted his way over to the copse of cedars and surreptitiously eased his way inside. There was a small open space near the center where he found Bodie, Selden, Bill and Walt already there.

"See he found you, too," commented Bodie.

"Now all we need is him," said Selden.

"Been waitin' on ya'll." Bass stepped out from behind one of the large cedars toward the back side.

"Dang, Bass, if'n you ain't jest like a Comanch, er a spook," Walt said as he spun around.

"Or Apache," added Bill.

"If I'da been a Injun an' this was twenty years ago…you'd a been already dead." Bass grinned.

"That's the damn truth…You spent some time with the Cherokee, didn'tcha?

"Plus Seminole and Creek, Selden. The Seminole was the best at slippin' around without nobody seein'…Good people. Gov'ment never could get 'em all out of Florida."

"Seen yer boy, Bass," said Loss.

He nodded. "Seen 'im too…with Story when they come in. Bennie rode out a few minutes ago, headed northeast…Seen that big ugly Cherokee, Mankiller, too."

"Well, guess what that saloon gal with Story had 'round her neck?"

Reeves looked at Loss. "That stole cameo, I'd wager."

Hart nodded. "Damnere close as yer gonna git."

"You wanta make yer move?" asked Bill.

Bass shook his head. "Uh, uh…Not now. Gut tells me Story's up to somethin', an' they's at least one, meby more with him 'sides Mankiller…Kin git my boy anytime."

"Think they might be after the gate?" postured Bodie.

"Good as any. No way they's here just to win the race," said Bass.

"Got your Colts?" asked Bodie.

He grinned. "What do you think all this here paddin' is hidin'?" Bass looked around at the small, but deadly, group of lawmen. "'Spect everbody, but Loss here, needs to stay close to the main tent."

"Should we say anything to Farmer?" asked Bodie.

He shook his head. "He's gonna be up on that platform, announcin' the race anyways."

"What about that acting sheriff, Rudabaugh?"

Bass had a wry grin on his face and cocked one eyebrow at Marshal Roberts.

"Didn't think so." The slight built marshal nodded.

Frank Pierce and Doe Lee tied their horses to some young persimmon trees just outside the gate.

"Reckon we oughta not loosen their cinches, Frank?" asked Doe.

"Wouldn't think so...We might be in a bit of a hurry to leave...You git my meanin'."

"Wonder what come of Jack?"

"No tellin'. Last I knew, he was goin' in to Gainesville fer ammo an' such. Meby he run afoul of the local law or meby he just lit out...Feller been on the run long as he has tends to be a mite flighty...Not really somebody I want watchin' by backside anyhoo."

Lee nodded. "Could be...Where we 'sposed to meet that big butt-ugly Injun?"

"Story said we was to meet-up in the general vicinity of the gate...'Spect he won't be too hard to find."

"I'd say."

"How's 'bout we grab somethin' to eat...might not have time later," Pierce suggested.

"Whatcha gonna git?"

"One of them meat sandwiches over yonder...You?"

"Gonna try one of them fried catfishes with a stick stuck in it." Lee pointed at a booth down the way a bit from Fletcher's.

After Penny had made a hamburger for Frank, he met Doe back near the entrance.

"How's yer fish?"

"Damn good...They even slathered some of that mustard on it."

"Feller could git addicted to these hamburger things," Pierce said as he and Lee both pitched their napkins to the ground. "Let's go find that damn redhide."

They had failed to notice an old colored man approaching from the opposite direction until he stopped right in front of them, blocking their way and stabbed the litter with his stick.

"Hey, git outta the way nigger…whatin hell you doin'?" Frank blurted.

"Yassir, beggin' yer pardon, sirs…Beggin' yer pardon. Jest collectin' trash, ah is."

"Well, hurry it up."

"I's a hurrin' massa, I's a hurrin'," he mumbled as he pulled the paper from the sharpened nail, shoved it in his gunny sack and shuffled off.

Doe watched the old man move away. "Was that smoke bastard bein' uppity?"

"What do you mean?"

"With that 'massa' stuff." He took a waxed pouch of Horse Head Tobacco from his vest pocket and stuffed a moist wad into his cheek.

Frank shook his head. "Naw, some dumb niggers jest cain't seem to break the habit…an' that suits me fine."

Doe wallowed the loose leaf tobacco around in his mouth until the wad compacted into a masticated ball he allowed to settle on the left side between his cheek and gum.

He felt a surge of the nicotine as his mouth filled with saliva. Taking one last look at the shuffling old man, he let fly the first stream of sticky brown juice. He wiped the dribble from his bottom lip on the back of his hand. "Let's git over to the main tent and check out the lay of the land. Don't want us no surprises when it comes time to make our move."

241

Loss made his way though the milling crowd and opened the gate to the pens. He stepped inside and approached Fiona standing beside her mount. She was stroking Blaze's neck and talking to him in a low voice, trying her best to keep him calm as the noise of the throng of onlookers and the band tuning up got louder by the minute.

"Ain't seen the like of all these folks gathered in a bunch…'cepting meby a big hanging in Fort Smith." He grabbed the lead rope from the top fence rail and snapped it to Dan's headstall.

"I try to avoid those morbid affairs," she replied. "I know it's part of law enforcement…but not quite my cup of tea."

"Know what you mean. Don't like to watch them kicking as they dangle from the noose, myself…Gives me the willies." Loss took out his silver pocket watch and rechecked the time. "Reckon we best git saddled up. Only fifteen minutes till the race is set to go."

"We should warm them up again. Don't want to start 'em off cold."

Bass worked over to Selden, Bodie and Walt standing near the barrier that separated the track from the vendor area. Keeping his head down, he stabbed a few pieces of paper on the ground near them and softly spoke sotto voce, "Heered two fellers say they needed to find Mankiller…'Pears to me to be at least three of 'em now."

Selden, keeping his gaze on Dan over in the practice arena, asked, "What do they look like?"

Bass bent over and picked up a nickel in the dust, studied it and slipped it into his pants. "One is couple inches shy of six feet, 'bout one-sixty, I make it...With a Buffalo Bill mustache an' chin whiskers, wearin' a dark brown sackcloth suit an' the other is barrel chested, in a tan canvas coat an' old black fedora...no mustache, ner nothin'. Ya'll seen drawin's of Mankiller on the dodgers?"

"Have, yessir, I have...one ugly son of a bitch. Hear tell it don't bother him killin' women er children."

***

CHAPTER TWELVE

COOKE COUNTY FAIR GROUNDS

"Attention, all race contestants! May I have your attention?" Marshal Farmer shouted through a large green megaphone he had borrowed from the local high school. "All contestants please bring your horses to the starting line in the track... You have ten minutes."

The riders began to adjust their tack, mount and trot into the track at the south end. Of the eleven entrants, four were with English saddles, six McClellans and the cowboy on the Mustang was riding his square-skirted working saddle.

Fiona leaned over toward Loss as they trotted into the track. "Looks like some of these folks have done this before."

He nodded. "I do believe you're right."

"Well, you folks ready?"

They turned as Story sidled up beside them and slowed Dawn to a walk while they moved toward the starting line, halfway down the track.

"I think so," replied Fiona. "The question is...are you?" She smiled.

"I guess we'll see...and just so you know...I ride to win."

"That's going to make it interesting...so do I," she countered.

"That's why I'm here, too," added Loss.

They all looked up at Marshal Farmer on top of the ten foot high platform on the east side of the track, behind the bleachers. He started the announcement through the megaphone, "Riders, do not cross the line in front of you until I fire my pistol for the start. Any violators will be disqualified."

All the contestants stayed well back of the white line that had been drawn across the track with flour. The horses, sensing the start, began to snort and dance in place. Several reared and others were spun in a circle by their owners to maintain control—the tension was palpable. Everyone was holding a tight rein on their antsy mounts, even Fiona as she patted Blaze on the neck and whispered softly to him.

The Gainesville Tuba Band in the large gazebo nearby, struck up a lively rendition of John Philip Sousa's brand new tune, *Stars and Stripes Forever*, which further stimulated the horses.

"Knock it off, Burton!" Farmer fairly screamed through the megaphone at the band conductor.

Burton McFarland meekly waved his players to stop. "Sorry Marshal," he yelled up at the platform.

"After I start the race!...After!" Farmer yelled back down. "Damn guy's dumb as a box of rocks," he mumbled,

The marshal turned back to the track. "Riders, the course is one mile out to the marker. You will circle the pylon and come back the same way making the race a grand total of two miles. You must stay on the course and in the saddle. Riderless horses crossing the finish line will be disqualified...Riders ready!"

He slowly raised his Colt in the air, held it there for a few seconds, and then squeezed the trigger.

The horses needed no further encouragement. They dug in at the thunderous clap of the marshal's .45 and as a solid group, sprinted toward the north end of the track—loose dirt flying from their back hooves. The opening at the north end had a pole across it at two feet above the ground—the first obstacle in the steeple chase.

The band immediately struck up the rousing march again as the animals were covering the one hundred and fifty yards toward the opening. They had strung out enough and jockeyed for position to go through the sixteen foot gate two and three at a time. They all cleared the first jump with ease—there would be harder ones later.

Loss slid almost out of the tiny English saddle as Dan easily lunged over the low barrier. "Goshdangamighty!" he yelled as he grabbed some of the long black mane and pulled himself back to the center.

"Told you, Loss," shouted Fiona over her shoulder. "Keep your eyes between his ears…especially when he jumps."

"What if he jumps sidewise?"

"Then you're both in trouble."

"Thanks," he grumbled as he leaned forward over the big black's neck.

Story glanced over from the other side at Loss while he was regaining his seat and grinned.

The group of eleven riders spaced themselves out after exiting the track—to give each other running room—as they thundered across the bucolic countryside toward wooded Elm creek, halfway to the turn pylon. The serpentine course was marked with yellow ribbon hanging from either trees or tall stakes planted in the ground along both sides. The marked route was some one hundred feet wide. A rider going outside the ribbons or around a barrier was subject to disqualification.

The next obstacle was a pile of leafy branches stacked three feet in height with a water-filled trench on the far side. Fiona, with her long raven pony tail flying in the wind as Story and

Loss's mounts each cleared the hedge behind her, landing in the water, and then scrambling out of the wide ditch back onto firm ground. Loss had both arms wrapped around Dan's neck.

Two of the pack stumbled and both riders were thrown into the water. The other six made it out of the pool. The hard part would be the return leg when they would have to jump from the water over the makeshift hedge.

The route curved around a cluster of cedar trees only to immediately have a four foot high split-rail fence as the next challenge. The riders only had ten yards after rounding the trees to gather their mounts to make the jump.

Blaze and Red Dawn easily cleared the obstacle while Dan's trailing back hoof clipped the top rail and knocked it down on one section. Track stewards—stationed at each jump—quickly replaced it for the rest of the contestants.

The cowboy's Mustang unexpectedly squatted down on his haunches at a full gallop. His sliding stop, with his nose touching the top rail, threw his rider head-over-heels ten feet on the other side, where he landed with a thud.

The young man blinked, sat up, shook his head, glanced around for his hat, grabbed it and jammed it back in place. He looked at his horse standing patiently on the other side of the fence. "Dadgummit, horse! Had no idee you could stop that quick." He grinned meekly at the judges as he slowly got to his feet.

BASS AND THE LADY

The eight remaining participants pounded down the slope of the swale with Elm Creek meandering through the middle. The limestone-bottomed waterway ran only three feet deep during the summer, but could get to flood stage of thirty feet or more, within hours after a heavy rain. Luckily, there hadn't been much rain in the previous week.

COOKE COUNTY FAIRGROUNDS

The crowd was at a maximum for the facility, a little over ten thousand souls. The stands erected at the track were full of rabid race fans. The vendor area was likewise packed—children of all ages ran amuck.

Frank and Doe shouldered their way through the crowd as they tried to spot Mankiller.

"By the Lord Harry, with all these here folks an' they kids a runnin' 'round, they'll never know we was even here," said Doe.

"Got a point there, cousin…Hey, there that Injun is, over yonder under that red oak, rollin' a smoke." He pointed with his chin.

Easing their way through the throng they obliquely headed in his direction.

"Looks like he swallered a porcupine…He all'ays like that?" asked Frank.

"Long as I knowed 'im."

Frank chuckled and said under his breath, "With that expression an' that there scar, he makes a burnt boot look good."

"But, you know what? He likes it…Thinks it makes folks scared of 'im."

"I kin believe that," Frank whispered as they stepped up to the Cherokee.

"How's it goin', Cal?" asked Lee.

Mankiller took a long drag, threw the rest of the quirly on the ground and exhaled a blue cloud of smoke right in Lee's face. "How what goin'?" His black soulless eyes seemed to look through the man.

"You ready?"

"Mankiller always ready."

"We're gonna slip around and cut our way into the back of the tent, you watch out here in case anybody tries to come in while we're…uh, takin' care of bidness…Count to twenty an' meet us outside the gate."

"No can count."

"Shit…knew that…Uh, one of us will wave from the front openin' when we're done."

RACE COURSE

The eight contestants thundered their way into the creek and splashed through the clear three foot deep water, sending up huge white sheets of spray. Bream, bass and catfish scattered before the pounding hooves. The white limestone bottom and clear water allowed the riders to avoid any large loose rocks and holes as their horses lunged across the sixty foot wide waterway.

They scrambled up the north bank and headed along the markers toward the next obstacle. Each of the riders, as well as their mounts, were completely soaked. Fiona's raven hair and light blue chambray shirt were plastered down and her white bustier was clearly outlined underneath.

"Dang, Fiona, I liked to have drown back there," Loss shouted over at her as he wiped the water from his eyes.

She grinned. "At least you won't have to take a bath now."

Story overheard the exchange. *Fiona? What's he talking about?* He mused.

The next challenge was a series of ten cane poles set in a line—the poles were placed at five yard intervals. The horse and rider must zigzag the line, alternating sides of the poles. Knocking a pole over was a disqualification. The first horse there would naturally lead through.

Blaze just nosed out Red Dawn to the first pole and entered the slalom—Dan was hot on the roan's tail. The next horse, one of the Missouri Fox Trotters, knocked the third pole over at an angle. The obstacle judge waved his red flag, disqualifying the team and he reset the pole—seven horses remained in the race.

The last obstacle before the pylon was a series of ten three foot high jumps set at ten yards apart.

COOKE COUNTY FAIR GROUNDS

Frank and Doe slipped around to the side of the tent nearest the outside fence that encircled the grounds. Lee pulled out his two-bladed Camillus folding knife, opened the long razor sharp spey blade, knelt down on the ground and cut a small slit a little over two feet above the ground.

He spread the opening enough to peek in. There were only two people inside that he could see—a man and a woman—both gathered close to the open front entry, listening for the marshal to announce who was in the lead. The band outside just started up another of Sousa's marches, *The Liberty Bell.*

Frank turned back to Doe, nodded and held up two fingers. He then quickly sliced a man-size opening in the canvas. The two men pulled their bandanas up over the lower half of their faces, drew their six guns and stepped in.

"What's all this?"

Frank spun to his right to see the Judge Leander Algernon Miles, III getting up from his chair behind the betting table and jerking his Pince nez eyeglasses from his nose.

"This is a holdup, old man," said Frank.

Miles blustered. "Preposterous...It most certainly is not. You pestiferous riffraff get out of here...Right now." He pointed to the slit behind them.

"I suggest you sit down, grampa."

"Now see here I'm Judge..."

That was as far as he got as Pierce backhanded him against the side of his head with the barrel of his Remington. He collapsed like a newspaper in a fire.

"Looky there, Frank." Doe pointed to the metal box on the table in front of where the judge had been sitting.

The box was open and large stacks of folding money and several of double eagles were orderly arranged in front of it.

"He musta been countin' the bet money...Kindly convenient for us, ain't it?" said Pierce.

Mervin, the judge's assistant, turned away from the door and back inside. "Hey..."

RACE COURSE

Two more riders were thrown when their mounts stumbled in the sequenced jumps—five left. They charged around the pylon, Dan and Blaze were close as two sides of a silver dollar with Red Dawn just a half-length behind because he had to make a wider turn. The remaining two, the Thoroughbred and the Morgan were seven and eight lengths back, both showing signs of flagging.

The agent from Western Union furiously hammered his key, sending the information back to Percy Gilhooley at the Fair Grounds.

Story swatted the roan across the croup with his two foot long braided-rawhide quirt. The animal surged forward and pulled even with Loss on the opposite side from Fiona just as they approached the sequenced jumps again.

Blaze took the jumps first, followed by Loss and Story running side-by-side. The Thoroughbred made the first five jumps and stumbled on the sixth before finishing the grueling obstacle at a fatigued lope. The Morgan refused to jump and wheeled to one side, dumping the rider and getting the red flag.

Blaze was at a ground-eating rhythmic stride as they rounded the curve just before entering the slalom—Dan was one pole behind her with Story's Red Dawn one behind him.

Fiona bumped the big gray stallion back as they approached the edge of the swag leading down to Elm Creek again. Tom saw his opportunity and pushed his roan up alongside Loss's right just as Dan splashed into the water.

He switched the quirt from his right to his left and backhanded Loss across the base of the throat, knocking him completely out of the saddle and tumbling into the water with a mighty splash. His head was under the water momentarily before he found his footing in and got to his feet, wiping water from his eyes. He saw Fiona's mount splashing to the bank.

"I'm down, Marshal Miller!" he yelled to her. "I'm alright."

Story, just behind, her also heard the shout. She glanced over her shoulder, nodded at Loss and saw a puzzled expression come over Tom's face. *Oh, damn, cat's out of the bag.*

COOKE COUNTY FAIR GROUNDS

Frank eared the hammer back on his pistol. "Hands up...now."

The slightly-built young lawyer's hands shot into the air, high over his head. The middle-aged woman who had been tallying the admission fees for the mayor, started screaming like all the banshees from hell...

Doe reacted by snapping a shot at her from his Colt—the screaming abruptly stopped as she was dead before she hit the ground.

"Damn you! Why'd did you do that?" Frank demanded.

"What do you mean? That caterwauling would have brought half the crowd in here."

"Fool! And that shot won't?...Crap." He pitched him a small flour sack. "Put what you can of the money on that table over there...I'll git the bettin' money."

Outside at the telegraph table, Percy was writing like a man on a mission as he listened to the rapid clacking of his key.

He shouted up at Farmer on the platform, "Flash and Dan even, Red Dawn half-length behind followed by Bob's Folly and then Big Boy...rest are out."

The marshal brought the megaphone to his mouth. "Burton!" he yelled at the band leader and drew his finger across his throat.

McFarland waved at his musicians and they stopped playing the rousing tune so Farmer could announce the standings at the halfway mark.

Bass stood in front of the vendors aisle, between the announcer's tower and the administration tent, peering off to the north trying to see when the horses would come into view for the stretch.

Selden, Walt and Bodie, getting caught up in the excitement of the race, had slowly come together near the base of the platform to get the latest information.

As Marshal Farmer finished announcing the status at the pylon, acting Sheriff Rudabaugh strode quickly over to the tent to inform the judge while the band started back up. Confused that there was no one standing at the door, he went inside the semi-dark tent and stumbled over the body of the woman, barely keeping his balance.

Again, Doe Lee reacted and shot the rotund man in the chest as he was reaching for his gun. The sheriff staggered back out of the tent, turned and fell face first to the ground.

Doe glanced over at Pierce. "Couldn't be helped, that was the Sheriff."

"Well, the milk's curdled now. We got all the money sacked up anyway…Wave at the Injun and let's get the hell outta here."

"Won't need to…that jug-butted sheriff fell back out of the tent…He'll know," said Lee.

Frank nodded and ducked out the slit in the back, followed immediately by Doe.

Simultaneously, Bass and the other lawmen sprang into action, followed immediately by Cal Mankiller.

"It's a robbery!" yelled Percy Gilhooley as he saw Rudabaugh get blasted out of the tent and go to the ground. He pulled a small five-shot .22 caliber pistol from his pocket and ran toward the body.

Mankiller grabbed a high school girl around the waist, picked her up and, using her as a shield, fired twice at the telegraph agent in stride. Gilhooley dropped his gun and tumbled to the ground, his momentum causing his body to flip and end up on his back.

Pandemonium ensued as the crowd responded to the gunfire. Women and children screamed as most of the attendees surged toward the gate in panic.

The lawmen were hamstrung by the number of citizens in a frenzied state—no one could get a clear shot at Mankiller through the crowd as he dragged the girl along with him toward the entrance.

Marshal Farmer saw the other law officer's predicament, but he had no such problem. His vantage from up on the tower allowed him a shot at the outlaw's back.

Mankiller sensed the danger, twisted the girl around and immediately saw the marshal up on the platform fifty feet away drawing a bead on him. Farmer hesitated when the high school girl blocked his shot.

The Cherokee fired three quick rounds—one splintered the railing, one missed and the last struck Farmer in the side. He fell against the two-by-four railing, grabbed at it as it broke away and fell heavily to the ground ten feet below...

RACE COURSE

Story quirted Red Dawn in a desperate attempt to catch Fiona, but she had already rounded the trees, cleared the four foot jump and was headed to the water hazard. He mercilessly spurred his mount around the split rail fence and caught her, bumping into Flash's rump and throwing him off-stride.

Tom eased up beside her and tried to quirt her like he did Loss—she ducked his swing.

"A marshal, huh?...Well, here, take this."

He swung again, but this time, Fiona grabbed the quirt with her right hand and reined Flash to the left with her knees, almost jerking Story out of the saddle. He released his grip, slipped his hand out of the leather loop on the quirt and glanced forward.

Both Fiona and Tom were able to see the chaos at the fair grounds, and then they heard the three quick shots that felled Marshal Farmer.

Story, realizing that either the robbery was underway or had come apart at the seams, made a decision. He wheeled the roan to the right and galloped back in the direction of the creek. *Time to get out of here*, he thought.

Seeing the confusion at the grounds, Fiona decided her duty was there. There would be another time for Mister Story. Off-stride and out of rhythm to make the water jump, she elected to go around, receiving the red flag.

She urged Flash at top speed toward the gate at the end of the track—riderless Dan, wanting to stay close to gray stallion, ran alongside keeping pace. They jumped the final barrier and crossed the finish line simultaneously.

The young man on the only horse left in the grueling race—the Thoroughbred, Bob's Folly. He managed to get over the hedge with his exhausted mount. They trotted to the track, jumped the bar, and then crossed the finish at a walk.

Fiona had already dismounted and given the reins to Francis Ann, Fats grabbed what was left of Dan's leathers after he had snapped them off stepping on them.

"What happened?" she asked Francis.

"Some men robbed the administration tent...Got the bet money, the admission money and shot at least four people."

"Who?"

"Marshal Farmer, the telegraph agent, the acting sheriff and a woman keeping records in the tent."

"All dead?"

Francis shook her head. "The sheriff and the woman...don't know about the other two. Bass and them are over there trying to figure everything out...Go ahead, Little John, Fats and I'll cool out the horses and take care of them...Where's Loss?"

Fiona pointed back down the course. "He's coming...on foot. Story knocked him out of the saddle."

"What?"

"Later." She headed toward the other side of the stands where the law officers were.

As she walked around the bleachers to the crowd of people milling near the tower, she had to push her way through. The strong smell of gunsmoke still lingered in the still air. "Make way, make way, Deputy US Marshal." She pulled her badge from her pants pocket, flashed it, and then pinned it to her shirt.

Bodie was kneeling down cradling the telegraph agent in his arms. He looked over at Doc Wellman, who shook his head.

There were tears in Gilhooley's eyes. "It hurts, Ranger Hickman...hurts real bad." He looked down at the dark, almost black blood—indicating a liver shot—oozing between his fingers from just below and to the right of his sternum. "I...tried to stop 'um. Didn't see the Injun till...till he...he shot me...I'm sorry, Ranger...I let you down."

"No you didn't Percy...No you didn't...You kept him from shootin' other folks." Bodie tried to swallow the lump growing in his throat, but couldn't. "You are a hero, First Assistant Ranger Gilhooley...a real hero."

The young man nodded and tried to smile. "I..."

He didn't say anything else as the light faded and went out in his eyes—he softly sighed his last breath. The tears began to flow unabashed from Bodie's eyes as he gently laid Percy on the ground and softly passed his hand over his face, closing his eye lids. His shoulders shook with repressed sobs. Annabel helped him to his feet and held him in her arms as he cried.

"It's my fault...All my fault he's dead."

She hugged him tighter. "No, it wasn't. He was thrilled that he was helping."

Doc Wellman stood up after examining Marshal Farmer's wound and nodded to Selden to help the man to his feet. "Let's get him in the tent so I can stop that bleeding in his side."

Fiona picked up the marshal's gun he had dropped when he fell from the tower.

Farmer grunted. "Feels like I been kicked in the ribs by a mule, Doc...but it don't hurt near a much as my leg."

"Your leg? You get shot there too? I don't see any bleeding." He looked down.

"Nope...not shot. Think I busted it in the fall."

"Fallin' broke your leg?" asked Selden.

He shook his head. "Uh uh, that sudden stop when I got to that hard ground done the deed."

The two men got under each arm and helped him hop toward the administration tent.

Doctor Wellman addressed a local business man standing nearby. "James, go fetch Barnaby."

Selden glanced over at him. "Barnaby?"

The undertaker."

"I ain't a gonna die, am I, Doc?" asked Farmer through gritted teeth.

"Well, actually, yes...Yes you are Marshal...just not anytime soon."

"Whew, fer a minute there I thought I was in trouble."

"I believe the bullet bounced off your ribs and lacerated the skin and soft tissue on top to a fair-thee-well. Gotta stitch you up and put some turpentine and tallow on it."

"You know about that?" asked Selden.

"Oh, yeah. Got some from Doc Ashalatubbi up at Ardmore...but I guess you know him, don't you?"

"Damn sure do...Patched me up mor'n once. He got it from Angie, Jack McGann's wife, after she doctored his bullet wounds…Durn stuff'll heal up an' hair over a cat's rear in three days…or so I'm told."

"Well, I ain't no cat's ass, I'll have you to know," Farmer snapped. "Now, ya'll quit jawin' like I wadn't even here an' git me fixed up…Got work to do."

"You're not going to be doing anything for a while, Marshal…Trust me on that," said Wellman.

They helped him up onto one of the tables, assisted by Bass and Bill who were already in the tent checking on the two bodies and the theft.

"Doc, need to see to the Judge sittin' over yonder." Bass pointed to the elderly man with a cloth held to the side of his head by Walt. "They pistol whipped 'im…Got a purty good gash that's bleedin' like a stuck hog…His eyes kindly look funny."

Wellman nodded. "Probably has a concussion. Don't let him lie down and keep pressure on that cloth…Head wounds bleed worst than almost any other place. I'll get to him soon as I tend to Farmer…"

"I'll help," came a soft voice from the flap entrance.

They all looked up to see Annabel enter along with Bodie. "You'll recall, Doctor, I assisted you after the bank robbery in Lindsay."

"I do indeed, Annabel and thank you. You'll find compresses, sutures and whatever else you need in my bag...Just keep him awake. The spirits of ammonia are in the small green bottle."

"I know." She smiled that dazzling smile of hers and opened the doctor's black valise.

"Oh, and hand me the laudanum...Farmer's going to need a goodly dose."

"Yes, sir," Annabel said as she opened the case.

"I hate that stuff."

"You'll hate the other worse, Marshal," said Wellman.

"I'll help too, Annabel...Just tell me what you want me to do," said Fiona.

"Bass, if ya'll would remove the deceased outside, the undertaker went to get his wagon." He handed the green bottle containing the brownish liquid to Farmer. "Two swallows."

"Wonderful," he said as he turned the small bottle up to his lips, took the first draught and almost gagged.

"We kin handle that, Doc...Bodie, you, Walt and Bill give me a hand with the bodies...by the by, where be Loss?"

"Right here," the little man said in a raspy voice as he entered. His clothing still had not dried from his drenching in the creek.

"What's wrong with yer voice...an' where yer hat?" asked Selden.

Loss pointed at a large red welt across the base of his throat. "Story whacked me with his quirt," he wheezed. "Hat's probably down to the Trinity River by now, I 'spect…What happened?"

"Bass was right," said Selden. "They robbed it…Judge said they was two come in the back side over there." He pointed to the long cut in the tent wall and we know Mankiller was outside."

"Git any of 'em?" Loss asked.

Selden just shook his head. "Too many innocent folk around."

"Well, reckon I better go see Mister Sullivant and git Ol' Slewfoot."

"Slewfoot?" asked Walt.

"My horse…that's his name."

"Alrighty then…"

Walt was interrupted by a short high-pitched exclamation from Annabel as she grabbed her abdomen. "Oh!…My goodness, I think my water just broke." She looked down at the growing puddle of clear pinkish liquid running down her leg as she stepped back away from her ministrations to Judge Miles.

"Uh, oh…doubt there's time to get you to town," said Wellman, looking up from stitching Marshal Farmer's wound. "Somebody get Faye. I'm going to need towels, blankets and plenty of hot water. Get her up on that other table and remove any undergarments…Now! Do it now," he barked.

"What do I do? What do I do?" Bodie kept repeating, his voice becoming more agitated and higher each time.

"One...my sweet husband, you can get out of here and make yourself...Oooooh." Annabel grimaced in pain as the first contraction hit. "...Useful."

"Come on, Bodie, we'll go down to that quilting booth. Bet those ladies will have plenty of clean quilts and cloth the Doc can use...I'm sure they'll help." Bill grabbed him by the arm and hustled him out of the tent.

"I know where I kin git some hot water," Loss rasped, turned and scurried out too.

"Doc, I done delivered six of my own...an' make that seven, what with Baby Sarah last year. If it ain't back'ards I 'spect I kin help."

Wellman grinned. "I expect you can too, Bass...You and Fiona make Annabel as comfortable as you can and count the time between contractions. I have to set the marshal's leg before it swells too much."

Faye burst through the opening. "I was afraid of this." She headed straight over to Annabel. "How are you feeling, Honey?"

"Bless your heart, Faye, I'm fine...at least so far." She forced a small grin.

"When did you have your first contraction?"

"A little over a minute ago."

"Hard or easy?"

"Hard."

"Oh, my."

"I don't think this is going to take too awfully long," commented Faye.

The doctor handed Farmer his white handkerchief folded over eight times. "Bite down on this, that laudanum will only do so much...Selden, grab hold under the marshal's arms and lean back when I say *now*."

The marshal put the thick wad between his teeth and nodded his head. Wellman grabbed the heel and the top of Farmer's right foot and counted, "One...two...Now!"

The marshal and Annabel screamed simultaneously...

***

267

CHAPTER THIRTEEN

NORTH COOKE COUNTY

Story splashed down the center of the rock-bottomed Elm Fork of the Trinity River headed south. "Sorry to put you through this, old son," he said to Red Dawn. "But, doesn't look like we got a choice. That gal sure put one over on me…I'll let that be a lesson." He looked back over his shoulder for the umpteenth time.

"We'll keep at a walk as long as we're not being chased, cut out of the creek south of Gainesville, circle back around to the north and head toward Dripping Spring. They won't know if we headed west or south in this creek. Glad I told the boys we'd meet up there, since I told whatever her name is I was stayin' in

Dexter." He bumped him to a halt and allowed the grateful horse to suck up a couple of gallons of water.

He lifted up slightly on the reins, the red roan reluctantly lifted his muzzle with water dripping from his muzzle. "That's enough for now. You've cooled off a bunch, but still don't want you drinking your fill…You can have some more in a bit."

He patted him on the neck and nudged him forward once again.

Almost due north of Story's position, Frank Pierce, Doe Lee and Cal Mankiller trotted along both sides of the track in the crushed rock right of way of the Gulf & Colorado Railroad.

"Tom said to foller the railroad to the Red…'Nybody tryin' to track us will play hob doin' it in crushed rock. We'll ford the river, cut over south of Thackerville, head up to Horseshoe Bend and re-cross back into Texas."

""Then what?" asked Doe.

"Said we'd rendezvous at Drippin Spring, divi up an' scatter," said Frank.

"How's he a comin'?" asked Doe.

"Didn't say."

"Mankiller track in broken rock."

Frank glanced over at the Cherokee. "Meby so…but they ain't got no Injuns with 'em…Ain't that what you'd say Doe?"

"I'd say."

COOKE COUNTY FAIR GROUNDS

Loss strode up to Fletcher's Hamburger stand where Miss Whisman had her back to the venue aisle and was packing her supplies.

"Miss Penny?"

She turned around in surprise. "Oh, Mister Hart...you startled me...I didn't recognize your voice."

"Sorry, Ma'am, er Miss, got hit in the throat durin' the ride." He pointed at it.

"I'm so sorry...What with all that shootin' and people gettin' killed...why it's enough to give a body the vapors."

"Yessum, uh...I need a big favor."

"Certainly."

"I didn't tell you the whole truth earlier."

"Oh?...About what?"

"Who I am...Now, Loss Hart is my real name, but, I'm also a Deputy US Marshal assigned to the Indian Territory."

"Oh, my." She put her hand to her mouth and got a puzzled expression on her face.

"See, uh...we got a lady over in the tent what's havin' a baby an' Doc Wellman needs a bunch of hot water..."

She interrupted him. "Silly man, why didn't you just say so? I could have already had it on since I still have plenty of good coals left...Blathering on about who you were...I swan."

Penny grabbed a galvanized bucket half-full of water from under the table and set it on the grill. She picked up an empty one and handed it to Loss. "Now you go down the way...." She pointed. "...to the fair grounds pitcher pump there at the trough and fill this one half full. This first one should be hot enough by the time you get back...Now scat." She shook her head and grinned as she watched him hurry away.

Two ladies—one older and full-figured and the other, middle-aged, skinny as a rail—from the quilting booth followed Bill and Bodie into the tent. Each carried a large soft wicker basket filled with quilts and blankets. The older woman, Sue Land, turned to the two men, and then looked directly at Bodie.

"You're the husband, right?"

"Yessum." He jerked his hat off.

"You don't have any business in here then, so you just skedaddle." She shooed him away with her hand and looked at Bill. "You can go too."

"I'll join you," said Selden. "If'n the doc's through with me."

"I am...Go see what's keeping Loss with that water."

"Here it is," said Hart as he carried the bucket through the opening. "Got another one on the way."

Selden addressed Bill and Bodie, "Fellers, I reckon we need to go out and find that saloon gal with the broach. Don't think she was part of it, but she's at least a material witness and recipient of stolen goods."

"I better go too, Selden, since I know what she looks like." Fiona opened the carpet bag Faye had brought in, took out her twin cross-draw Colts and strapped them around her shapely hips. She took each weapon out, checked the loads, centered the empty chamber under the hammer. She then smoothly flipped them back in their holsters.

"Good idea, Fiona," Selden commented.

The ladies from the quilting booth looked at Fiona, her ivory-handled Colts, and then at the crescent and star Deputy US Marshal's badge on her blue denim shirt.

"You're a Federal Marshal?" asked Sue in wonder.

"So they tell me…Ya'll ready?" She slipped a beaded leather band around her head to keep her hair in place. "This'll have to do since I don't have my hat."

Selden and the others nodded and they all filed out of the tent.

"I swear, never heard of such a thing…a lady marshal," said the skinny woman.

"Nor me," Miz Land concurred.

"Well, I'll tell ya'll one thang fer sure and by golly…That lady will do to ride the river with," commented Bass with a grin as he poured some of Loss' hot water in a basin and scrubbed his hands and forearms with some of the doctor's lye soap.

Annabel groaned with another contraction.

"Bass, check her dilation," said Wellman as he put another layer of wrapping around Farmer's splints.

BASS AND THE LADY

The big marshal dried his hands on a clean cloth handed to him by one of the ladies and reached up under Annabel's skirt as Faye blotted her sweating forehead. "'Bout halfway there, I'd say, Doc."

"Check every contraction...I'm getting close to being done with Marshal Farmer until I can get him to town and put a proper cast on."

"Yessir."

"Was it necessary you had to cut my pant leg off, Doc?"

"Either that or you sit here naked."

"Better'n havin' to buy a whole new suit jest fer the pants...Don't cha know?"

"Gets to where these days folks jest want to complain about 'bout purtnear everthang...'stead of countin' their blessins'," commented Bass. "That bullet been just a hair to the left an' you wouldn't a been buyin' nothin'."

Faye wiped Annabel's forehead and face again. "Are you all right, dear? You're starting to sweat quite a bit."

She managed a smile, despite the pain and discomfort. "Bless your heart, Faye...Southern girls don't sweat...we glisten."

DEXTER HOTEL

Bennie tied his bay gelding in the woods behind the hotel and slipped up the back outside stairs. He pulled the key from his

273

pocket and opened the door to his and Tom's room. After looking around, he determined no one had been in since they left that morning.

He grabbed his gunny sack and put the single change of clothing he had in it, and then got Story's carpet bag. He took it to the chifferobe, opened the side door and started putting his extra shirts and trousers in the bottom. After he placed Tom's toiletries along the sides, he closed it and buckled the latch.

Glancing around the room again to make sure he wasn't leaving anything he headed toward the exit, and then abruptly stopped with his hand on the outside door knob. *Damn.*

He spun around, went back into the room, got down on his knees, reached under the bed and dragged out Story's saddlebags. He laid them on top of the white chenille spread. *That was close. Dang near fergot 'em…He'd a kilt me shore.*

He glanced at the door, slowly unbuckled the straps on one side, lifted it up and peeked inside. He gasped at the sight and smell of stacks and stacks of crisp newly-minted money. "Oh, lawdy, lawdy." He quickly closed it and buckled it back, making sure the tang was in the same hole as before.

COOKE COUNTY FAIR GROUNDS

Annabel screamed, sat partially up for a couple of beats, and then fell heavily back to the table and the rolled-up quilt that was her pillow—she panted heavily.

"Breathe deep, youngun," Bass said. "Breathe deep and blow it out...That's good...Now try to relax."

He reached up under her dress again. "'Bout there, Doc. I kin just feel the...Oh, Lord!"

"What is it?" asked Wellman as he finished up Farmer's temporary cast.

"I thought it was the crown, but it ain't...It's a...heel!"

"I'll be right there."

Annabel raised up. "What is it?"

"It's all right, honey, the baby may be backwards, just lay back down," comforted Faye.

"Backwards?" asked Annabel.

Wellman washed and dried his hands, bent over and felt in the birth canal. "No question, that's a heel...That means not only is the baby coming backwards, but has one leg up and one leg down." He stood back up, shook his head and dried his hand again. "I'm not equipped to do a cesarean here."

He paused. "There's two options...one, try to deliver the baby...and I have to tell you, there may be two of them...And I don't know that her pelvis can separate far enough for a breech birth...Or two, get the baby turned around."

"How do you do that?" asked Faye.

"Sometimes by a procedure called an external cephalic version where I massage the baby around, but the problem here is there's already a leg in the birth canal...so it has to be done from inside."

Bass shook his head. "My hands is way too big for her, Doc."

Wellman nodded. "As are mine, Bass…She's very tiny and it's complicated by the fact the baby is about a week early so she hasn't fully separated yet."

"It must have been the excitement of the robbery."

The doctor looked at Faye and nodded.

"I think I can help."

They all turned to see Francis Ann standing in the opening with her father—she strode on inside.

"I think my hands are small enough, plus I've gone up inside more mares than I can count to turn a foal around…How much different can it be, Doc?"

"None, except for room."

Annabel screamed again, even louder this time.

"I don't see we have any choice. Wash up, Fran," said Wellman. "I'll help with external massage…I need some oil, lard, anything."

"I have several gallon tins of peanut oil down at my booth," said Penny who had just brought in another pail of hot water.

"Perfect," said the doctor.

"Be right back."

"Better put on some more water, too," Wellman added.

She nodded. "Come on Loss, you can go fetch the water and put it on while I bring the oil back." They left the tent together.

BASS AND THE LADY

Francis finished drying her hands and nodded to the doctor. He had Penny pour a little of the clear light-yellow oil in his palm and he rubbed his hands together.

All the women in the tent circled the table to give Annabel a degree of modesty as Francis and Wellman went to work after pushing her skirt up to her waist.

"We have to do this quickly between contractions," he said.

Fran nodded and with her tiny hands, she was able to get one completely in the birth canal and push the leg back into the womb.

The doctor started massaging in a circular motion with the fingertips of both hands. Slowly he worked the baby's rump around to the top until he could feel the firmness of the head moving to its more proper down position.

"I can feel the crown!" Francis reported.

"Now, push, Annabel, push!" the doctor directed.

NORTH COOKE COUNTY

The three outlaws moved over the tracks as they neared the river in order to ford at Brown's Crossing—about a quarter of a mile east from the railroad bridge. They worked their way down the incline to the bank and waded their mounts out into the slowly moving muddy waters of the Red.

"'Spect it'll take us till nightfall to git up to Horseshoe Bend...don't you, Doe?"

"'Magine so."

"We'll stop at Brown Springs, water the horses and give 'em a blow."

"Mankiller no need stop."

"We might be needin' these horses, we git into a chase...We'll rest 'um."

"Do like Apache brothers...Ride horse till die, eat horse, then go on foot. *Torwv hvtke* no catch."

"What's *torwv hvtke?*" asked Frank.

"Cherokee for white eyes."

"I knew that," lied Doe.

SOUTH COOKE COUNTY

Story halted Red Dawn again and allowed him to drink once more, and then exited the creek on the east side immediately south of Gainesville and just after the confluence of Pecan Creek with Elm. Shortly, he crossed the same Gulf and Colorado Railroad tracks that his cohorts had before they got to the Red.

He spotted an area thick with young western red cedars. "Well, boy, looks like a good place to take a blow. We'll rest there for about an hour, and then head north...It'll be after dark before we can get to Dripping Spring anyway."

BASS AND THE LADY

Tom guided Red Dawn through the copse until he found an open area that also included some blue stem and gramma grass, dismounted and stripped the tack from the horse.

"You know son, these cedars wouldn't be here if it weren't for the white man. He drove the Indians out who used to burn the land off to create better grass for the buffalo...Now these cedars cover nearly half the grasslands. Times they are a changin'...You not goin' to comment?"

Dawn was too busy grazing to bother.

Tom hobbled him, and then built a hat-sized smokeless fire with dead, bone-dry wood and boiled some Arbuckle.

COOKE COUNTY FAIR GROUNDS

Annabel screamed again and rose back up into a curl. Faye on one side and Penny on the other assisted her in staying in that position.

"Push, Annabel!" Wellman encouraged. "Breathe and blow...now push again."

She grunted and pushed harder.

"I can feel the shoulders...Just a little more," prompted Francis Ann.

"Ahhhhhmmmm." Annabel pushed with the next contraction.

"I got my fingers under the armpits. Just once more," urged Fran.

279

With the next contraction, the baby emerged from the birth canal.

"It's a boy!" She eased the bloody, mucus-covered child out and held it while Doctor Wellman quickly cut the cord with his surgical scissors, tied a knot in it and washed it with a dilute solution of carbolic acid.

"See, Aunt Faye told you."

He took the baby boy by the heels and held him upside down to allow any fluids to drain from his lungs, made sure his mouth was clear with his finger, and then pulled back his hand to slap the little behind, when he started to scream bloody murder.

"Well, no need for the swat, it's quite obvious he's breathing on his own…One of you ladies take him, clean him up and oil him down with a light coating of that peanut oil."

Sue took the child from his hands. "We have some white flannel for a navel band, do you want us…"

"Of course. You ladies know what to…"

"There's another one!" shouted Francis.

Wellman spun back around. "Coming all right?"

RACE TRACK

Fiona, Selden, Bodie and Bill approached an apparently confused Stephanie Ladd as she scanned from the north entry of the track to the myriad people still milling about.

"Stephanie?"

The blonde turned. "Oh, Miss Marston, have you seen Tom?"

"That's what we're here to talk with you about. My name is not Marston, it's Fiona Miller."

"I...I don't understand." She appeared to become more confused when she looked at the badge on her shirt and the badges worn by Selden, Bodie and Bill.

"Perhaps we should step over to the stands and we'll try our best to explain," said Marshal Lindsey.

A few minutes later, with tears running down her cheeks, Stephanie reached behind her neck and unclasped the gold chain holding the cameo. "This was the nicest gift I...I ever got...Should have known it was too good to be true...I knew Tom didn't always ride on the right side of the law, but he said he bought it special just for me...Oh, that poor, poor girl." She handed the broach to Selden, and then buried her face in her hands and wept.

Fiona put an arm around her and hugged. "There was no way you could have known."

She nodded. "I feel so bad for that girl's mother and father."

"You will have to stand as a material witness, Miss Ladd," said Selden. "We would appreciate it if you wouldn't leave the area."

"Of course…I don't have any place to go anyway." She looked up at the big marshal with her tearstained face.

"Yessum. It's just somethin' I have to say…We'll be in touch with you in a few days…soon as we catch Story and the others. By the way do you know who he was associatin' with?"

She blotted her eyes with her hanky. "Yes, Frank Pierce…He was cousin to Tom, Pink and Jim Lee and another was their brother, Doe…Just a couple of days ago, this big ugly Indian, Cal somethin', joined up…There was one more, a Jack Long from New Mexico…But he disappeared. They figured he didn't want no part of the deal."

Bill shook his head. "Well not exactly…Long shot my fiancée." Roberts took a deep breath and tried to swallow the lump that formed instantly in his throat. "I killed him."

Stephanie put her hand to her mouth, and then said, "Oh, I'm so sorry for your loss." Her tears began to flow again.

"Did you hear any of their plans?" asked Fiona.

She shook her head. "No, they would quit talkin' business when I came up."

ADMINISTRATION TENT

Annabel pushed and moaned again.

"I've got a head," said Fran. "This one's coming easier…Got the shoulders."

"Once more, Annabel…Almost there," entreated Wellman.

After the shoulders, the baby abruptly squirted out into Francis' waiting hands.

"A girl! It's a baby girl," she squealed.

Wellman repeated the same procedure with the baby girl that he did with her brother and handed the crying infant to Sue and the ladies. "Francis can you take care of the afterbirth?"

"No problem, Doc. Too bad we're not like horses…they eat it."

"Oooh, yuck," chimed in every other woman in the room including Annabel.

"Just sayin', is all. It does stimulate their milk."

Annabel looked at her swollen bosom. "I don't think I'm going to need any help."

Selden, Bodie, Bill and Fiona stepped back into the tent. Bass looked around first.

"Well, hello, daddy," he addressed Bodie.

The young ranger stepped over to his wife who already had the baby boy on her chest nursing him.

"Is it…?"

Annabel smiled and nodded. "It's a boy."

"Hot dangomighty!"

Just then, Faye brought another bundle over and laid it on the other side of Annabel's chest. "And here's his baby sister."

Bodie's knees buckled slightly before Bass grabbed his arm to steady him.

"Holy cow," he said as he bent over trying see the little tike's tiny faces. He leaned a little further and gave Annabel a kiss. "You done good girl...twins. Wow!"

She smiled. "Well, I think you had a little something to do with it, too."

"Yeah, but you did all the hard work." He grinned like the proverbial Cheshire cat. "I'm a daddy! What do you know about that? Wait'll I tell mama."

"Do you have names?" asked the doctor.

Bodie and Annabel looked at each other and simultaneously said, "Bass."

"I wouldn't be here at all if it weren't for Bass rescuing my friend Theresa and me from the Griffin gang a couple of years ago," related Annabel.

"Aw, jest doin' my job, Ma'am." He ducked his head. If his skin could have shown it—it would have been obvious he was blushing.

"All right, then what about the girl," asked Faye.

"What rhymes with Bass?" asked Annabel.

"Cass," offered Fiona.

"How about Cassie Ann." The new mother looked at Francis. "In honor of Francis Ann making their births possible."

The beautiful redhead also blushed. "Oh, I did no such thing...I just did what had to be done."

BASS AND THE LADY

"It's not open for discussion, girl...Cassie Ann it is...and how about Edward for Bass' middle name after my great uncle Robert Edward Lee?" said Annabel.

Bodie nodded.

"Good choices...I'll make notes of that for the birth certificates," said Doctor Wellman. "They'll be ready sometime tomorrow...I'd suggest you ladies remove Annabel's wet petty coats and fix something for an under garment, she's going to be draining for a day or so."

"We know, Doctor Wellman, we know. We'll take care of it," said Faye. "Come ladies."

"Well, reckon that handles that," said Bass, and then he looked at Selden. "Did ya'll take care of that other matter?

Lindsey nodded, reached in his pocket, pulled out the cameo broach and held it up. "Yep, Miss Ladd is more than happy to stand as a material witness against Tom Story...She also gave us the names of his cronies, but didn't know of their plans."

"Let's saddle up gents, we got us some trackin' to do, 'fore they scatter like a covey of quail," said Bass. "N'body see what kinda horses them three nabobs what done the robbin' an' killin' wuz ridin'?"

"Mankiller rides a claybank dun...I'd know him anywhere," commented Fiona.

"Shod?" asked Bass.

She nodded. "Much as he hates the white man and half-breeds, he does adapt some of our practices."

"Good, shod horses er a bunch easier to track than barefoot."

"How so, Bass?" queried Bill.

"When outlaws is on the scout er the run, they's al'ays think they kin ride over rock an' hide their trail. The head of the nails holdin' them steel shoes on their feet stick out just a mite on the bottom. Count on 'em scratchin' the rock some...even when walkin'."

"What about if they put sacks over their hooves?" asked Bodie.

Bass chuckled. "Works great fer 'bout a hunderd yards. You know how much a horse weighs?"

"Dependin' on the breed, nine hundred to twelve hundred pounds, I reckon," answered Bodie.

"Uh huh. Let's say a thousand pounds average...That makes purtnear two hunderd an' fifty pound per foot...don't take long 'fore them nails wear through the cloth, er hell...beg pardon ladies...even leather...Most trackers give up when they lose the trail on account of it, don't you see...but they's jest a mite early on the quit."

"Glad you're doin' the trackin' Bass...I thought I knew something about it, but I see I'm just a newborn babe...to coin a phrase." Bill grinned and looked over at Annabel nursing both her babies.

"We need to gather up some wagons. I need to get Marshal Farmer to my clinic so I can put a proper cast on...the judge, I need to put to bed a while so I can watch him…plus need an easy rider for the mother and babies," said Wellman.

"I can take care of that," said Tom Sullivant. "Be right back…Oh, I'll have Fats and Little John bring ya'll's horses up. They've been rested, grained, watered and groomed."

" Much 'bliged, Tom," said Bass.

***

CHAPTER FOURTEEN

COOKE COUNTY FAIRGROUNDS

The law officers stood around Bass, kneeling on the ground studying the tracks where Frank and Doe had tied their horses outside the fence.

"Anything unique, Bass?"

He got to his feet and brushed the dirt off his knee. "They's all unique, Bill...Hoss and folk tracks is jest like lookin' at a pitchur, fer me...each one's different." He glanced at the others. "You kin tell the difference 'tween a pitchur of yer momma an' yer' daddy, cain'tcha?"

"Well, sure," commented Bodie.

"Tracks is the same fer me...Ya'll know how each of us tend to wear out boot leather in different ways?"

"How do you mean?" asked Loss.

"Wellsir, some wears out the ball of they foot first an' some the heel…An' they's different patterns on each one…some to the inside, some to the outside. One foot one way, the other…somethin' else…All in all, tracks jest tell me a story…Where they been, where they goin'…even to what mood they in."

"What mood?" asked a bewildered Walt Durbin.

"Shore. These fellers here was a mite agitated…shufflin' around, jerkin' on they horses…Musta been everthang didn't go quite like they planned."

"Probably didn't figure on Rudabaugh pokin' his head in the tent," said Bodie.

Bass nodded. "That would be part of it, I 'spect." He pointed to a third set of tracks. "Now, these here belong to the Injun."

"How so?" asked Fiona.

"Cherokee like to roll the toe on a shoe…curl it up jest a bit. It's like the natural wear pattern on a wild horse…all'ays wear the toe off first since they do a sight more runnin' than kept horses…Injuns try to duplicate the way a horse is in the wild…thinks it makes 'em faster. Plus…" He picked up a half-smoked handmade cigarette. "Mankiller wadn't happy either…He only smoked half of his quirly an' throwed it down when he rode up."

"What's the brand?" asked Selden.

Bass smelled of the butt, but Fiona beat him to the reply.

"Bull Durham…He always smokes Bull Durham. Been trailing him for two years."

Bass nodded and mounted a rested Blaze.

"What about Story?" asked Loss.

"'Spect we foller these miscreants, we'll find him too…They got the money."

"Which way did they go?" inquired Bodie.

"Northeast," was all Bass said as he squeezed Blaze up into a collected trot.

The others glanced around and followed.

BROWN SPRINGS
CHICKASAW NATION

The three outlaws pulled rein at the spring just a couple hundred yards on the other side of the Red River. The clear, fresh spring water flowed out of the ground above a limestone outcropping and formed a pool over twelve feet in diameter—partially covered with water plants. The overflow ran off and formed a lagoon almost an acre in size, and then off to join the Red.

They stripped the gear from the horses and let them drink from the pool. Doe got his canteen from his saddle, knelt down at the edge of the water and began filling it. He jumped up and fell backward with a shout.

"Damn!"

Frank and Mankiller both drew their weapons.

"What is it?"

Doe pointed at the water where the huge head of an alligator snapping turtle that was almost the size of a wash tub, was sticking above the surface, it's mouth wide open and making a hissing noise.

Frank cocked his Remington and aimed at the prehistoric reptile.

The Cherokee laid his hand on Pierce's arm. "No! Bad luck kill water beast." He looked around the vicinity and noticed an area on the north side of the pool that had been an ancient Indian burial ground.

He literally began to shake and even for an Indian, turned pale. "Mankiller no like here. No stay." He grabbed his saddle, threw it back on his horse and cinched up. "Mankiller go."

"Wait a minute, Injun, what the hell are you talkin' about..."

Frank was interrupted by the sound of loud knocks from the thick woods, as if someone or something was banging on a hollow log with a large limb. They both froze.

"*Uktena*," the Cherokee whispered, looking around.

"What's *Uktena*?" asked a nervous Doe.

Mankiller stabbed his foot in the stirrup. "Man beast. Evil spirit. Kill many." He wheeled his mount and spurred him to a gallop, giving the old burial grounds a wide berth.

Frank and Doe looked at each other just as a large rock arced from the thick brush on the opposite side of the pool and splashed into the water. The rock was followed by a loud roar like all the banshees from hell were loosened.

"Hey, wait up, Injun!" yelled Doe.

The two men saddled and mounted in record time, and then followed after Mankiller, whipping and spurring their horses to top speed.

NORTH COOKE COUNTY

The posse stopped at the railroad right of way just north of Gainesville after following the outlaw's tracks from the fairgrounds. Bass leaned over and studied the loose fill rock.

"Which way did they go, Bass?" asked Walt.

"North." He pointed at the right of way. "See…some of them rocks be a tad darker…That was on the bottom side that horse's hooves turned over."

"I'll be danged…I see that now," said Bodie. "How do you do that?"

Bass grinned. "Just look for somethin' that shouldn't be there…Like the tracks of Story's horse we crossed back about a mile that went south."

"Why didn't you say nothin'?" asked Loss.

"Wadn't no need…We follow the money."

"Why did Story go south?" inquired Fiona.

"I mind to throw us off the trail…They'll come back together, by an' by." He nudged Blaze to the north, alongside

292

the rock bed and occasionally glanced down at the tracks in the gravel. It was only seven miles to the Red.

"Crossed over to the east side here." Bass pointed.

The others were learning what to look for. Fiona moved Diablo to the other side of the railroad tracks. "One was already on this side…Mankiller. I can see the rolled toes where his horse stepped out of the road bed and onto the adjacent soil." She trotted on toward the east, following the sign.

Bass looked at the lengthening shadows being cast across the ground by the mixed hardwoods that grew in the Cross Timbers area.

EAST COOKE COUNTY

Story pulled rein at the edge of an east-west running railroad track. He looked off to the west and saw plumes of smoke drifting up into the air from numerous homes scattered throughout the woods—increasing as they got closer to town. "Must be the KATY coming from Denison…I'm makin' good time."

He looked back west again at the sun barely touching the far horizon. "Well, ol' son, just as well find a place to stop again and fix something to eat. I imagine you could use some more rest…I know I could."

He found a secluded place along the banks of a small creek almost due east of Gainesville and setup camp. After Story put the coffee on, he dug a bottle of Dr. Tobias Venetian Horse Liniment from his saddle bags and gave each of Red Dawn's legs and back a good bracing. "Well, that ought to feel some better."

He hobbled the roan on some good prairie grass. "Couple hours and we'll move on north...Should get there 'bout daylight." He looked over at the eastern horizon. "Moon should be comin' up by then."

DRIPPING SPRING

Bennie had covered the seven miles from Dexter to the spring in three hours on his exhausted gelding. The sun was setting on the western horizon with a reddish-gold glow and the moonless night would provide little comfort. After watering and picketing his horse on some luscious grass near the water, he set about building a small fire beside an embankment.

He fetched a gunny sack from his saddle, pulled out the battered old coffee pot and set it close to the fire after filling it with water and throwing a handful of ground coffee inside.

Bennie dug out his small six inch tin frying pan, sliced some of the salt pork he had left and set the skillet on a flat rock at the edge of the fire.

Coffee and fried salt pork would be all he would have to eat as he had neglected to get supplies. In fact, it never dawned on him that his father would be in Gainesville—regardless of the reason—and he was unaware that Story and his henchmen had robbed the race.

Bennie chewed the crisp fried salt pork slowly, and then took a sip of the stout trail brew. He stared at the small pool of water formed by the spring and watched a large bullfrog snatch a dragonfly in the air with his long tongue.

He set his tin cup down, stepped over to Story's saddle bags and opened them again. He took out one of the thick bundles of twenty dollar bills, studied it for a moment, and then turned it over. The other side of the thick paper band wrapped around the stack read: *United States Army*.

"Oh, my sweet Jesus." He dropped the money back in the pouch as if it had burned his hand and looked up at the myriad stars twinkling overhead like thousands upon thousands of campfires. "I's didn't mean to kill her...you knows that, Lord, and I's so sorry I done it...Jest come in there an' found her betrayin' me an' I guess...I got all nettled...But that money's somethin' else...They's somethin' evil 'bout it. I kin feel it...I doesn't know what to do...Like bein' deep down in a well an' cain't see no way out."

He sat down next to the fire for a long while, and then pulled the .38 Smith and Wesson from his pocket and studied the weapon for a moment. Then, with tears rolling down both cheeks, he slowly cocked the hammer back and brought the barrel up under his chin…

NORTH COOKE COUNTY

"I know of a spot 'tween here an' Brown's Crossin', Bass. It's an old home place…house burnt down five or ten years ago, but there's a dug well that I checked a while back…got good water in it."

"Sounds good, Bodie, lead out."

They stopped on a grass-covered knoll some forty feet above and overlooking the river as she curved back to the north. There was a native rock-cased well with boards laid over the top near one side of the clearing.

"I'll set up a picket line over yonder next to the trees," said Walt.

"Keep a good eye out for copperheads…Last time I came by here when I was trackin' those rustlers, found three big'uns by the well," cautioned Bodie.

Walt glanced back over his shoulder. "I'll do that…Hate snakes, 'specially copperheads and cottonmouths…At least rattlers you can hear when you're close to 'em."

"Make ya'll a deal, I'll do the cooking, ya'll do the fire building and clean up…I know how Bass cooks and if the rest of you are of the same ilk...Well, enough said," commented Fiona as she stripped the gear from Diablo.

"Hey, looky here. A summer pear tree...an' they're gittin' most ripe," exclaimed Loss as he was scouring about for firewood at the edge of the tree line.

"Pick some...they'll make a nice desert. I think I have enough fixings to make a cobbler," directed Fiona.

"Hotdiggitydog, yum-yum." Loss took off his hat and started filling it with some of the large sweet roundish pears—Bodie came over to help since he was at least six inches taller than Hart.

Bass set about building a fire for Fiona to cook on while Selden gathered rocks to form the pit and keep the flames from the grass.

"Son-of-a..." Walt yelled, jumped back and drew his Colt and aimed at a three foot long orange and black copperhead coiled up by some deadwood.

"Hold it, Walt," admonished Bass, walking over. "No shootin'. Don't know how close those montebanks are." He drew his eight inch Bowie and flipped it end over end, pinning the deadly viper's head to the ground.

"If you'll skin it, I'll add it to the stew," said Fiona.

Walt grinned. "Say, that'll work...We cook up rattlers all the time down in south Texas...Tastes kinda like chicken."

After everyone had finished their supper and trail cobbler, Bass grabbed the coffee pot and made the rounds filling cups.

"That was mighty fine fixins', Miss Fiona, mighty fine…'Specially that cobbler, uh huh."

"Thank you, Loss, glad you enjoyed it."

Selded chuckled. "Never seen a meal yet that Loss didn't enjoy. I swear he could make dinner out of chewin' on a ten year old piece of rawhide."

"Aw, that ain't so. Meby five year old…but not ten."

The rest joined in with Selden's hearty laugh.

"Not sure what that has to say about my cooking," stated Fiona.

"Oh, don't git me wrong, Fiona, that was an outstandin' meal…We jest fun Loss 'bout his eatin' habits ever chanct we git," said Selden. "On account of it plays hob with his attitude if he misses one."

"How come we didn't keep on their trail? We might coulda caught 'em."

Bass took a long pull on his old rosewood pipe and blew a cloud of blue aromatic smoke over his head before he answered, "Been cogitatin' on that, Bodie…not much sense in it. One, gits purty hard to track in the dark and two…got me a good idee where they be headin'."

"You gonna tell us er just keep us in the dark?" asked Loss from the shadows on the other side of the fire.

"You tryin' to be funny, Loss?" countered Selden.

"What do you mean? I wuz just wantin' to...Oh, that's good...it is kinda funny, ain't it?" he said as he looked around at the darkness surrounding the campsite.

"What I wuz gonna say is we crossed my boy Bennie's tracks back when we left the fair grounds, headin' due northeast."

"What's up northeast?" asked Fiona.

Bass looked at her and smiled. "Delaware Bend...an' Dexter."

"That's where Story was staying, at the Dexter Hotel," blurted Fiona.

Bass grinned. "I know."

DRIPPING SPRING

"Hello, the camp!"

Bennie quickly dropped the pistol down by his side and scooted back away from the fire. "Come ahead."

Frank, Doe and Mankiller entered the campsite from out of the darkness leading their lathered-up horses.

"Got'ny grub?" asked Frank.

"Little...got coffee on."

"Brush down and water our horses, nigger...while we fix ourselves somethin'."

"Yasser." Benny got to his feet, surreptitiously uncocking and slipping his gun back in his pocket. He led their horses over

299

toward the grassy area where his was. He glanced back over toward the fire as the three men helped themselves to the coffee.

When he had finished with the horses—leaving them hobbled to graze—Bennie walked back into the firelight.

"This sowbelly all you got?" demanded Frank.

"That's it...Mister Story didn't say nothin' 'bout us leavin'. Jest told me before the race to light a shuck, git his stuff an' meet here...An' that's what I done."

"Where's he now?" asked Doe.

Bennie shrugged and shook his head. "Jest said to meet him here."

Frank glanced over at the tack and carpet bag lying under a tree just at the line of the firelight. "That his gear yonder?"

The young Reeves nodded.

Frank pitched the remains of his coffee in the fire where it hissed, strode over, squatted down and opened the bag.

Bennie shot to his feet. "I mind Mister Tom wouldn't like you diggin' through his thangs."

Pierce shot him a mean look. "I don't give a rat's ass what you mind, nigger...Now sit yer black ass down."

Bennie slowly squatted back down with a look of consternation on his face. He glanced at Doe, and then at the Cherokee whose scowl never seemed to change.

"Does African get part of loot?" Mankiller asked.

"What loot?" Bennie looked at Frank.

Doe Lee held up two flour sacks. "We knocked off the race…the admissions money and the bettin' money…Must be ten er fifteen thousand dollars here."

He turned to Cal. "And nope, the nigger don't git none of it…Aw, hell." He reached inside one of the bags and pulled out a twenty dollar gold piece and flipped it to Bennie. "Here, don't say we never give you nothin'." He laughed loudly. "What's in the saddle bags, cousin?"

Frank unbuckled one side. "Well, well, looks like the stage coach money."

"All of it?"

He opened the other side. "Purtnear I'd say, 'ceptin' fer that hunderd dollars he give me and Jack fer walkin' 'round money."

"We split race money now," said Mankiller.

"Better wait on Story. He'll be pissed," responded Frank.

The Cherokee drew his Remington. "Mankiller no care. Want share money now. If say again, Mankiller take all." He eared back the hammer with an ominous click.

Frank nodded at Doe. "Give him his part."

Lee dumped the two sacks on the ground, cut approximately twenty-five percent out and put it in one of the flour sacks.

The Cherokee snatched it from his hand and looked over at Bennie.

"African, go saddle claybank…Mankiller watch these." He waved his pistol at Frank and Doe for them to move together and sit down.

"Gits so a feller cain't trust nobody these days," Doe mumbled to Frank.

"No talk." He glanced over his shoulder in the direction of the horses. "Bring horse to Mankiller." He turned back to Frank and Doe. "Throw guns in bushes."

"Aw, now Cal..." Lee stopped when Mankiller turned his cold obsidian eyes on his. "I'm doin' it, I'm doin' it."

He and Frank eased their shooters out of their holsters and pitched them into the brush ten feet away as Bennie led the horse into the firelight.

Mankiller swiftly mounted, never taking his eyes off the two men sitting on the ground.

"What's the deal, Cal? You don't trust us?" said Doe.

The Cherokee laughed. "You are *torwv hvtke*. That all need say...Sheeah, I go." He wheeled the dun around and spurred him off into the darkness.

EAST COOKE COUNTY

Story cinched up his saddle, checked the ties holding his saddlebags on, and then stabbed a toe into the stirrup and swung easily into the seat. "Shouldn't be anybody out this time of night, pard, so we'll take that ranch road up to Croesfield...Only a couple miles from there to Dripping Spring...Ought to be there before sunup." He nudged the red roan into an extended trot and headed toward the dirt road leading north.

DRIPPING SPRING

Frank and Doe didn't move for a long moment from where they sat. Finally, when they could no longer hear the hoof beats of the Cherokee killer's horse, they got to their feet.

"You know how close we come to gittin' shot?" queried Lee in a soft voice without looking at Frank.

Pierce slowly nodded. "Think I got a purty good idee."

"I heered he kilt a storekeep up to Tahlequah jest on account of him bein' a half-breed."

"Why don't that surprise me?" Frank glanced over at Bennie. "Put some coffee on, nigger." He turned to Doe. "You wouldn't happen to have any sweetener, would you?"

"Got most of a pint of Old Taylor in my saddle bags."

"That'll do."

NORTH COOKE COUNTY

Bass took a sip of his coffee, and then packed his pipe again. He reached forward and grabbed a twig that was sticking out of the fire, held it over the bowl and puffed a couple of times until the tobacco glowed. "Now, to my way of thinkin'...the three yahoos we been trailin' er headed north…Story headed south…My boy headed northeast."

He shook the fire from the end of the stick and began to draw in the dirt at his feet. Bass drew the path of the Red River, made a mark of their location near Brown's Crossing and another for Dexter. He then looped Story's path around Gainesville and back north, the three hardcases east and back south, completing the oblong circle.

"Bennie's route went north of Gainesville from the fair grounds an' cuts right through the middle," commented Fiona.

"Yep, Story and the others er goin' by way of Melviney, whilst Bennie is goin' straight to where they'll all be a meetin'."

"Where's Melviney?" asked Loss.

"Between Wanella and Penella," replied Bass.

"Huh?"

Bass shook his head and grinned. "Never mind…Wild goose chase."

"What?"

Fiona turned to Loss. "Wild goose chase is from Shakespeare's Romeo and Juliet…Romeo said, 'Swits and spurs, swits and spurs, or I'll cry a match.' To which Mercutio responded, 'Nay, if our wits run the wild goose chase, I am done; for thou hast more of the wild goose in one of thy wits than, I am sure, I have in my whole five'…See?"

"No, I'm more confused than ever, now."

"False trails, Loss, false trails," said Bill.

"By the Lord Jim, why the Sam Hill didn't you jest say skyhootin'?"

"I thought I did, Loss," replied Bass.

"You can't tell nobody nothing that ain't never been nowhere," quipped Selden.

"Aw, that ain't so…Have too been plenty of places."

Bass just shook his head. "Anyways, we'll jest move towards Dexter…it's near 'bouts ten mile er so…I make it. I'll scout ahead an' cut fer Bennie's trail, ya'll foller behind."

"I'll go with you."

"Not really necessary, Fiona."

"I wasn't asking." She looked at the big man with a grin. "And don't give me the gimlet eye."

"Wadn't about to…done learnt my lesson 'bout arguin' with you…Best git some sleep, we'll cut out couple hours 'fore dawn. Take us till daylight to git to where I think we kin cross his trail."

Fiona gave him another grin and a sharp nod.

Dawn was beginning to lighten the eastern horizon when Bass and Fiona rode out of camp. They had their morning coffee and a cold biscuit with hot bacon for breakfast.

"We'll take the old Mormon Trail east…should cross his tracks if'n he held true to the direction he went when he left the fairgrounds."

"Anything special about his horse's tracks?"

Bass nodded. "Front feets is kindly round, but the back is more mule-footed…Purty simple to spot."

"Easy for you to say."

They nudged their horses into a mile-eating amble gait.

An hour later with the sun throwing purple, crimson and gold streaks across the sky, Bass pulled rein on Flash—Fiona stopped beside him.

"See something?" she asked.

He pointed at the tracks just in front of them that crossed the dirt road, heading northeast. Fiona eased up a couple of feet and studied the ground.

"How on earth did you possibly see those tracks? We were making six or seven miles an hour."

Bass indicated the sides of the road. "Looky there…Now, in the middle, they's been a few riders an' a couple wagons goin' both directions that purty well wiped out 'ny cross traffic, but there an' over there, see the tracks come out of the grass and then go back on the other side?"

"Now that you pointed it out, yes."

"That be Bennie's geldin', still headin' direct toward Dexter. Step down an' help me gather some rocks."

Fiona had a puzzled expression on her face as she dismounted and started to search for stones. "How big?"

"'Bout the size of yer fist er so."

In a couple of minutes, she carried a double handful and set them on the ground beside where he knelt. She watched for a few seconds as he created a directional marker.

"Oh, a cairn."

He looked up at her. "A what?"

"Cairn. C-a-i-r-n...That's what you're building is called."

"Ah, the *ganidadv udowelv* in Cherokee."

She nodded. "Trail marker."

He had stacked the rocks about five inches high, starting with the larger ones and working up smaller. Then he placed three medium-sized on the northeast side of the stack.

"Selden er Bill an' probably Bodie too, will know we went in that direction an' should be able to foller our tracks. I'll leave plenty of sign."

"And if they can't?"

"Then it will be up to us to get it done."

***

CHAPTER FIFTEEN

DRIPPING SPRING

Bennie was stoking up the fire for the morning coffee when Story trotted up to the camp site. He looked up as Tom dismounted.

"Mornin', Mister Tom. You wants me to take care of Red Dawn? Coffee's jest 'bout ripe." He had set the pot on a flat rock close to the fire.

"Yeah." He held out the reins. "Give him a good groomin' and check his feet."

Bennie nodded and led the roan over to where the other horses were.

"Pierce, Lee, wake up!"

BASS AND THE LADY

The two men sat up in their soogans, rubbing their eyes and trying to focus on Story standing by the fire.

"Oh, hey, boss, just git here?" asked Frank.

"No, been here all night, fool...What'n hell do you think?" Pierce threw back his blanket, grabbed his boots, turned them upside down and shook them to make sure there weren't any scorpions or spiders inside. After pulling them on, he got to his feet as Doe was performing the same ritual.

"Coffee ready?" asked Frank.

"Yeah, bring me a cup."

Doe reached in his possibles bag and dug out an extra blue-speckled graniteware cup and pitched it to Story.

Tom took one of his black kidskin leather gloves, grabbed the handle and filled the cup, and then squatted down as the other two walked up with theirs in hand.

"Where's the Injun?"

Doe and Frank looked long at each other, finally Pierce's gaze went to the ground at his feet.

"Uh, he's gone, Boss."

"I can see that...Where's the money?"

Frank glanced back at Doe.

"Got it right here," Lee said as he picked up the flour sack from beside his bedroll.

"How much?"

"Uh...well, you see, Boss...uh, all but the Injun's share," stammered Frank.

"Excuse me, I don't think I heard you." He pitched his remaining coffee on the ground along with his cup.

"We had to give twenty-five percent to him."

"You made that decision all by yourself, did you?"

"He pulled down on us, Boss. It was either that or…"

"Or what?"

"Or he'd a plugged the three of us and taken all the money…You don't know that crazy Injun like I do, Boss. It wouldn't of bothered him one little bit, if we'd a given him any sass 'bout it," said Doe. "…an' he don't hoorah none."

"Did you give him twenty-five percent of the stage money too?"

"No, sir…He jest wanted what was his, I reckon…Is passin' strange though. He coulda taken it all," commented Frank.

"When did this happen?"

They glanced at one another again.

"Oh, not long after we got here," said Doe.

"Stupid sons of…"

Bennie walked back into camp. "Dawn is taken care of, Mister Tom…Had a bait of grain left an' I give it to 'im."

He looked hard at the colored man. "Where's my saddlebags?"

Bennie pointed over to the gear stacked under an oak tree. "Over yonder…with yer carpet bag."

He stepped over to the tree, knelt down and unbuckled both sides of the saddlebags, glanced inside, and then stood up.

BASS AND THE LADY

"All right, here's what we're goin' to do. I'm keeping Jack's share of the stage money...since he's disappeared. Frank, you'll get your third. I'll take half of what's left of the race money...You two nimrods can divi up the rest, and then we split...That suit you?"

He gazed coldly at Frank and Doe with his right hand loosely resting on the butt of his stag-handled Colt.

"Sure, Boss, whatever you say," said Frank.

"Fine by me," added Lee. "What about him?" He pointed at Bennie.

"I'll take care of the nigger. You two get your money and make tracks...Pronto. I hear tell New Mexico is nice this time of year."

NORTH COOKE COUNTY

Bass and Fiona tracked Bennie's gelding at an easy jog trot.

"Doesn't look like he's trying to hide his tracks at all," commented Fiona.

"Probably don't think they's no reason to. Bennie's not really a bad kid, he's never broke the law...before shootin' his wife...so his mind don't think like an outlaw's...Doubt it ever occurred to him to try." Bass abruptly pulled rein and stopped in the middle of the road.

She sidled up next to him and watched him pull out his pipe, pack and light it. He looked off straight to the northeast, and

311

then off more to the north and blew out a big cloud of blue aromatic smoke over his head.

Fiona had figured out some time ago that this was his way of pondering a problem, so she remained quiet, waiting for him to speak.

Finally, he took the pipe from his mouth, popped the bowl a couple of times in the palm of his hand and pitched the ashes to the road. "He's goin' to Dexter...But, he'not there now...Dime to a dollar Story sent him to get their gear...an' the Army money." He replaced the pipe in his coat pocket. "They goin' to meet somewhere else...Too chancy goin' to the Sugar Hill Saloon."

"Where are they going to meet then?"

"Don't know...yet."

OLD MORMAN TRAIL

"Hold up here." Selden raised his hand in the air for everyone to stop, and then pointed to the cairn of limestone rocks at the left side of the road. "They cut off here."

The four-man posse turned their mounts to the left and headed due northeast toward Dexter.

"Bass is leavin' a plain enough trail," said Bodie as they trotted along, cutting cross country.

Selden chuckled. "Didn't want us gittin' lost."

BASS AND THE LADY

"I kin see his and Fiona's tracks, but be danged if'n I can see anybody else's."

"That's the point, Loss. Uncle Jack has always said that Bass could track a fish up a river...or that he'll figger out where he's goin' and just meet 'im there," said Bodie.

"He's as good as I've ever seen...Ya'll know that's how he started out with the Judge...bein' a tracker?" said Selden.

"Really?" responded Bill.

"He was so good at it, plus bein' the best hand with a gun around that Parker give him a commission...That was over twenty years ago." Selden spit a stream of tobacco juice off to the side. "The Judge even personally give him a brand new .45 Peacemaker once. Believe Bass killed four er five with it, then went back to his .38-40s...Said he just liked 'em better."

NORTH COOKE COUNTY

"Are we going on into Dexter and then track Bennie from there?" asked Fiona.

Bass shook his head. "Gonna circle to the north right after we's cross Rock Creek and cut fer his sign comin' out of Dexter. Jest hope I'm right that they is meetin' somewheres up along the Red an' not over in the direction of Pottsboro."

They forded the thirty foot wide Rock Creek four miles north of Callisburg and headed on north, mostly paralleling the meandering creek—Bass never broke from a steady jog trot as he studied the ground they were passing.

A little over a mile after crossing the creek, Bass bumped the big gray down to a walk, and then a full stop.

"See something?" she asked.

He looked off to his right, and then back to the left. "Yep, the good Lord done bein' kind to us…There's his tracks." He pointed two feet in front of them.

"I can see the grass bent over that way, but how do you know that's Bennie's tracks?"

"Recognized the stride. Plus, his horse is done wore out. Short steps an' draggin' his toes." He nudged Blaze forward a step and looked straight down on his left side where he could see the ground through the grass. "See there? Mule-footed back feets…He come this way yesterdy."

Fiona grinned and shook her head. "Lead on, McDuff."

He looked over at her. "It's 'Lay on McDuff'…Jack done taught me some of that Shakespeare stuff."

"I knew that, I was just translating…won't happen again."

The trail led back across Rock Creek and headed in a westerly, northwest direction for almost two miles. Bass pulled rein again.

"Know where these be a leadin'."

"And?"

"Drippin Spring…Good clear water fer drinkin'…Whole lots better than the muddy Red." He dismounted, opened one side of his saddle bags and took out a pair of elk hide Apache style moccasins. He sat down on the ground, pulled his scalloped top cavalry boots off, donned the moccasins and laced them up to just below the knee.

Fiona had a puzzled look on her face. "What are you doing?"

He got to his feet, stuffed his boots in the saddlebags and handed her the reins to Blaze.

"Where did you get those?"

"Made 'em. Seen a pair on a Chiricahua Apache war chief one time, name of Shoz-Dijiji…meant Black Bear…Seen right off the advantage of his type moccasins fer slippin' 'round in the brush…Goin' in on foot so's if'n they's 'nybody there, cain't hear me come up. They horses would hear er smell ours an' they'd go to talkin' to one another…If'n the camp's empty, I'll whistle an' you kin come on up…If it ain't, I'll come back an' we wait on Selden an' them."

He disappeared into the thick woods like a wraith leaving Fiona to wait with the horses. *Sometimes that man makes me so mad…mostly because he's always right.*

Bass slipped silently through the woods up to the campsite on the downwind side. It only took a moment to discern that it was already abandoned. He stepped over to the ring of rocks where the fire had been built, put his hands over the ashes, and then on the rocks. He got to his feet and whistled twice.

Fiona snapped her head up and started to move toward his whistle when she heard the sound of hoof beats coming along their back trail. She quickly nudged Diablo behind a thick grove of wild plums—leading Blaze behind her—and positioned herself where she could see who was coming.

The other lawmen came around a large cedar at a jog, with Selden leading the way. She bumped her heel into the appy's side and stepped back out into the trail.

"Fiona, where's Bass?" asked Lindsey as they pulled to a stop.

"He snuck in on foot to where he thought their camp was..."

"Dripping Spring," interrupted Bodie.

"Right. He just whistled the all-clear right before ya'll rode up...I was heading that way."

"It's less than a half mile," said Bodie. "Been there many times, good water."

"That's what Bass said," responded Fiona.

"Let's go. You got the lead, Bodie," said Selden.

DRIPPING SPRING

Bodie and the others rode into the clearing next to the spring. Bass was sitting on a large rock near the fire ring, flipping a five dollar gold piece in the air. He held up his hand for them to not bring their horses into the camp area.

They dismounted and tied their mounts to some saplings near the edge and walked in, being careful not to step on any previous tracks.

"Hour late an' a dollar short, huh, Bass?"

"Most like two hours, Sel...Ashes is cold, but the rocks is still a bit warm.

"Which way did the ass-eyed hooligans go?...Oh, pardon the language, Fiona."

"Heard worse, Bill, heard worse."

"Well, that's just it. 'Pears they done split the money." He held up the gold coin. "Dropped this one in the dirt...an' then scattered to the winds."

"'Aye, that's the rub'," said Bill.

Fiona nodded. "Hamlet's soliloquy."

Bill grinned. "You don't miss a one, do you?"

"Not in my nature."

"Any idea who went where? Looks like we gotta split up too," asked Bodie.

Bass got to his feet. "Yep. The Cherokee went thataway...early." He pointed to the east.

"I got Mankiller." Fiona spun on her heels toward her horse.

Bass locked eyes with Bill, and then tilted his head in her direction.

"I'll go with you," Bill said as he fell in trail.

317

"Don't need help," Fiona said over her shoulder.

"Nobody goes alone…Not open to discussion…Believe I got seniority, don't I Selden?"

"I'd say…by near ten years er so."

Fiona reluctantly nodded her acquiescence. She and Bill cinched up their horses.

"We best water 'em before we take out, Mister Roberts."

"Good idea."

Bass watched them lead their mounts over to the pool and then continued, "Story and my son headed due south in the general direction of Mountain Springs and the other two, Pierce and Lee, went due west…Now, I gots to go after Story, 'specially since my boy's with him an' I still have paper on 'im…Reckon that leaves you and Loss to go west into the Nations. Bodie an' Walt ain't got no jurisdiction up there."

"We'll go with you, Bass," said Bodie.

Walt agreed. "Can pick up supplies or fresh horses if we need 'em at the ranch…It's that direction anyways."

CHICKASAW NATION

Selden and Loss crossed over into Pickens County—Love County after statehood. The trail of the two outlaws was easy to follow.

Lindsey pointed at the tracks. "These boys don't seem too concerned 'bout 'nybody followin' 'em."

"Meby they think they're home free. I've been thinkin' on what that Stephanie said about Tom Story's accomplices."

"What was that?"

"The one she named Doe Lee...'Member them lowlife brothers that wuz tied in with the crooked sheriff in Gainesville," said Loss.

"Pink, Jim and Tom Lee?"

"That's them. Two's in boot hill and the other is waitin' on Maledon's noose...'Pears as though there was a fourth."

Selden reined to a halt. "Oh yeah. We figured they stole horses in Texas and traded 'em for beeves in the Nations. Reckon that Doe Lee wuz the one that did the trading?"

Loss nodded. "Remember hearing of the Lee boys. Mind as Jim and Doe is married up to Chickasaw gals. Jim's place was up by Sorghum Flats, west of Ardmore, an' the other..."

"That'd be Doe."

"Yep...living smack dab in this county somewheres southeast of Marietta."

"Sounds 'bout right...You don't 'spose they might be headin' by Doe's homeplace, do ya?" asked Selden.

"Could be. Mayhaps since it don't look like they think they's 'nybody on their tail."

Selden squeezed his knees. "Come on Dan, we got work to do."

The spirited black horse willingly obliged.

Loss visually checked the tree lines ahead and along their flanks—looking carefully for the possible ambush.

DELAWARE BEND

Fiona and Bill set out following Mankiller's tracks almost due east from Dripping Spring at a slow jog trot over the rolling hills of mixed timber and grassy meadows.

"He's not being particularly careful to hide his tracks and he's in no real hurry...Notice that?"

"I'd say he thinks they gave us the slip back yonder at the railroad tracks and are home free," replied Bill.

"Well, I do notice one thing," commented Fiona.

"What's that?"

She chuckled. "We're not tracking nearly as fast as Bass."

"Yeah, he's only been doin' it for over twenty-five years...plus the Cherokee, Creeks and Seminole taught him."

"I believe it's not so much that he sees things we don't, but that he actually starts thinking like whomever he's following...Does that make sense?"

Bill pondered a few seconds. "I think you may be onto somethin' there...All right, you know this renegade a whole lot better than I do...Where's he goin'?"

"I would say he's going back to country he's more familiar with...the Nations. My feeling is that he's headed for the

Kiamichi Wilderness…A little over a hundred miles from here. He makes it there and I don't think even Bass could find him."

"I wouldn't make bet on that, but it behooves us to make sure he doesn't get that far…Look." He pointed at the ground. "He stopped."

"To roll a smoke…See that burnt Lucifer over there?" she said as she dismounted and picked up the matchstick. "He's in no hurry, that's a fact."

"I'm thinking his overconfidence is going to do him in."

Bill's hat suddenly flew from his head followed immediately by the boom of a long gun. "Son of a bitch! Spoke too soon."

He wheeled Tippy and spurred toward a nearby grove of persimmon trees, snapping off a couple of rounds from his Colt in the general direction of the shot to give Fiona cover while she mounted and followed.

They took refuge in a shallow coolie behind the copse of persimmons.

"Dropped something." She handed Bill his hat as she slid to a halt beside him.

"You stopped to get my hat?"

"Not really. I got it before I started…Hate for you to sunburn your forehead."

"Thanks." He stuck his finger through the hole in the crown and then jammed the hat back on his head. "Damn, brand new Homburg, too."

"Better your hat than your head."

"Yeah, but now I'm pissed." He stepped off his horse and pulled his '92 Winchester from its boot and headed off in a crouch down the coolie to the east.

"Wasting your time."

He stopped and turned back. "How do you mean?"

"He's gone. Mankiller's not one to sling lead from one position. He's a backshooter or a dry gulcher…He'll be waiting further down the road."

"So we just ride into his line of sight?"

"Not today."

Bill got a puzzled expression on his face. "How's that?"

"You know we were talking about Bass thinking like whomever he was tracking and I said I felt like he was heading to the Kiamichis…Well, he has to cross the Red and I think I know where…so we're going to work our way north and loop around in front of him…He's going to be traveling slower than we are."

"How do you know?"

"You didn't notice the right front shoe of his horse is loose?"

"Uh…guess not."

"It is…He's probably going to have to stop and pull it before it lames his horse…Give us time to get around in place."

322

BASS AND THE LADY

NORTH COOKE COUNTY

"Looks like Bennie's horse is a slowin' 'em down." Bass indicated the tracks. "Story gits ahead an' then stops an' waits."

"Where do you think he's tryin' to go?"

"I'd say Fort Worth, Bodie. I mind it's big enough he's figgerin' he could git lost in the shuffle."

"What about your boy?" asked Walt.

"Yeah...Reckon we'll find out...I'm gonna say they'll be a splittin' up soon."

FORT FITZHUGH

Story pulled rein beside a small branch with about a foot of clear water running in it. They were almost four miles south of Gainesville near the site of abandoned Fort Fitzhugh—the original location chosen by Cooke County for the county seat until the present site was picked north on the banks of the Elm. There wasn't much left of the old fort besides a dug water well and the caved-in remains of the ammunition dump.

"Let's water the horses and give 'em a bit of a blow," said Tom.

Bennie nodded, dismounted, loosened his girth and let his mount drink. "Where we goin', Mister Tom?"

"Been thinkin' on that some. I'm goin' down to Fort Worth for a while."

The young Reeves looked up. "What about me?"

"To be honest, Bennie, I really don't care…What with you bein' Bass Reeves own son and on the run, don't much think I want to be anywhere around when he catches up to you."

"You really think he's got papers on me?"

"I'm bettin' on it…Tell you what." He opened his saddle bags, pulled five twenties from one of the bundles of the Army payroll and handed them to Bennie. "Here, take this for some travelin' money and head east…maybe toward Shreveport."

He held up his hand and backed away from Tom a step. "Uh uh…That's stole money."

Story grinned. "So what? You're on the run for murder."

Bennie looked down at his feet. "I know…But I didn't go to do it…I mean it wadn't somethin' I aimed to do…You an' them other mens…ya'll planned on stealin' that moneys…Mind you kilt some folks gittin' it…didn'tcha?"

Tom stared at him for a long beat, and then stuffed the money back in his saddlebags. "Suit yourself." He cinched up, mounted and rode off southwest.

PICKINS COUNTY
CHICKASAW NATION

"What say we swing by Thackerville an' see if that Lighthorse, Cyrus Maytubbi is to home?…What'd he call the town…Nashoba?" asked Loss.

324

Selden nodded. *"Osí Hommá* or Red Eagle is his Chickasaw name…He'd know where Doe Lee's place is."

The two marshals stepped down and tied their horses to a hitching rail outside a white picket fence that surrounded a small, but well-kept whitewashed clapboard house. Selden opened the gate and was stepping into the yard when the small, but wiry full-blood Chickasaw walked out the front screen door to the wide porch.

"Marshal Lindsey, Marshal Hart…Good to see you."

"You too, Cyrus. Busy?" asked Selden.

After they filled Red Eagle in with the details, they mounted up and with the Lighthorse leading, rode off north.

"Not far to Lee place or really belong to Chickasaw wife, *Foshi' Lakna'* or Yellow Bird. She cousin to my wife."

"Is the Chickasaws all related?" asked Loss.

Cyrus almost smiled and nodded.

"See, now ain't this a whole bunch better'n trail rations?…Pass them butter beans," Doe commented.

"Got a point there, cousin," Frank agreed as he passed the bowl and took a big drink of ice tea from a mason jar.

"I don't think they's a way in hell 'ny lawdogs could track us to here an' they damn shore don't know who I am."

"Hello, the house!"

Both men snapped their heads toward the front of the house where the hail had come from.

"Who the hell?" exclaimed Frank.

"This is Marshal Lindsey, Doe…We know you an Frank are in there. Come out with yer hands up. No need fer 'nybody to git hurt!"

"Don't know who you are, my ass," exclaimed Frank.

Lee jumped to his feet, grabbed the single barrel Remington ten-gauge shotgun from over the door header and checked it was loaded. He pulled back the cheap white cotton damask curtain from one of the front windows and looked outside. "Only see two…Let's rush 'em. This scatter gun'll cut a wide swath."

Frank nodded and opened the door slightly. "We're comin' out. Don't shoot."

"What? What the hell you doin'?"

Pierce glanced at him and grinned. "Lyin'…We go on three. You out first blastin' with that widermaker, I'll foller with my Winchester. Catch 'em by surprise. One…two…three!"

He jerked the door open, Doe jumped out and pulled the trigger, firing from the hip. Frank followed, jacking a round into the chamber and bringing the carbine to his shoulder.

Selden dropped Doe with a round from his Marlin and Red Eagle shot Frank in the head from the side of the house before Pierce could pull the trigger—the outlaw never made it off the porch.

"I'm hit, I'm hit!" yelled Loss rolling around in the dirt next to Selden.

Lindsey dropped to a knee beside his partner. "Where?"

Hart sat up and pulled his knee to his chest. "My foot. He shot me in the foot."

Selden looked down at Loss's right boot. There were three buckshot holes in the top of his foot with blood starting to ooze out.

"Well, could have been a whole lots worse if'n he hadn't jerked the trigger so hard in his excitement and directed most of that double-ought into the ground."

"Somebody help me," came Doe's voice from the steps in front of the porch.

Selden got to his feet. "Stay put, be right back."

"Ain't goin' nowheres…This hurts like hell," said Loss as Lindsey walked over to Lee.

"You busted my hip, Marshal," moaned Doe.

"Yer woman inside?"

"Yeah."

"Cyrus, you want to get Yellow Bird and see if'n she's got some wrappin' we kin doctor Loss and Lee here with?"

"Me see," Red Eagle said as he went into the house.

"Where's the money, Lee?"

"Inside, on the table." He groaned. "Some in a flour sack an' more in Frank's saddlebags."

"Stagecoach money, too?"

"Yeah…Now, I didn't have nothin' to do with holdin' up that stage, killin' them folks an' stealin' that Army money."

"Don't matter much. You was involved in the race deal with Story. Ya'll killed three folks there…Killin' is killin'…Yer gonna git fitted fer a hemp necktie anyways."

"How did you know we wuz here?" Doe asked through gritted teeth.

"Story's saloon gal give us yer name…rest was easy."

He shook his head and flopped back in the dirt. "Damnation, gittin' to where a feller cain't trust nobody these days."

DELAWARE BEND

Fiona and Bill dismounted behind a thick stand of cottonwoods and scrub oak on a bluff just to the west of the confluence of Big Mineral Creek and the Red River.

"Now what?" asked Bill.

"We wait…That's a good ford down there. The Red gets a bit deeper after that creek empties into it." She pointed at the large creek on their right. "Hold! Speak of the devil…The perverse degenerate made better time than I thought."

Mankiller rode his claybank out of the tree line, stopped at the edge of the bluff over a hundred feet from the marshals and dismounted. He dropped the reins to the ground and checked the gelding's right front shoeless hoof and popped a pebble out of the grove between the frog and the sole.

Fiona handed her reins to Bill. "Watch Diablo, I'll be back."

"I think we both should go out and confront him."

Her steel-gray eyes flashed as her mouth tightened. "The obstreperous scum murdered my husband in cold blood...He belongs to me...and I don't need any help. He'll surrender or die where he stands."

"I hope you know what you're doing."

Fiona looked at him and winked. "I do." She removed her Peacemakers one at a time, inserted a sixth round in each cylinder and dropped them back into their hand-tooled holsters.

The fearless marshal stepped around the trees, out into the open and approached the Cherokee as he studied the path down the side of the bluff to the slow moving muddy red water.

"Calvin Mankiller...Deputy United States Marshal F. M. Miller...I have paper on you. You're under arrest...You coming peaceable?"

The big Indian spun around at the sound of her voice and a crooked smile crossed his scarred face. "Haw! Woman marshal? Mankiller go nowhere...You lawdog been houndin' Mankiller trail?"

"You killed my husband two years ago up in Tahlequah. I'm taking you in...alive or dead...You're choice."

He squinted his cold black eyes at her. "Tahlequah?...That half-breed?...Paugh!" He spat on the ground. "Needed killin'."

"Guess you didn't know I'm a half-breed."

"Then you die too." He reached for the Remington on his hip and just cleared his holster when both of Fiona's Colts roared simultaneously.

One slug went completely through the man just underneath his right clavicle and the other struck him below and to the right of his sternum. His pistol dropped from his limp fingers to the ground as he looked down at the blood stain slowly spreading across his once-white shirt from the hole in his barrel chest.

The renegade looked back up at Fiona with a puzzled expression on his face. "*Ageyv tsvsgina* kill Mankiller."

"I'd say so."

His knees sagged, he stumbled backward, disappeared over the edge of the bluff and splashed into the river thirty feet below.

She walked up to the edge and looked down at the receding ripples as the Red moved its inexorable way toward its rendezvous with the mighty Mississippi. Bill stepped up beside her and watched the water for a moment—Mankiller never came back up.

He turned to her. "He barely cleared his holster. How did you get so fast?"

"It's a gift."

Brushy Bill nodded. "Yeah...Didn't know you were part Indian."

"Not...Just told Mankiller that to piss him off...He hates half-breeds."

Bill grinned. "Yep, Big Casino used to say, 'Never let 'em get set'..."

"Who's Big Casino?"

He shook his head. "An old friend back in New Mexico...What was that he called you in Cherokee?"

"*Ageyv Tsvsgina.*"

"What does that mean?"

"She-Devil."

FORT FITZHUGH

Bass and the two Texas Rangers rode into the area that was once a military outpost built in 1847 to protect the settlers from the Indians—very little remained.

He glanced around at the tracks in the grass, trotted Blaze over near the branch and stepped down. "They split here. Story went thataway." Bass pointed to the southwest. "And Bennie went east...Less than an hour ago." He looked at Bodie and Walt. "Ya'll know I gots to go after Bennie."

The two rangers nodded.

"We'll go run down Story."

Bodie and Walt followed the roan's tracks for almost a half-mile until they reached the Elm Fork of the Trinity River. They crossed to the other side and scanned for his tracks.

"See anything?" asked Walt.

Hickman trotted Moon down the bank for ten or twelve yards. "Nope...Bet you anything he's still playin' it safe and stuck to the water for a while. He hadn't survived this long by bein' sloppy."

"What if Bass is wrong and he headed back north to maybe cut across over to Bowie or Decatur 'stead of goin' down to Fort Worth?"

"Well, I'll hang my hat on Bass' gut and check the bank down south. Why don't you go ahead an' foller north...just in case he does head west?"

Walt nodded and turned his blood bay gelding, Pepper, to the right and jogged north, cutting for Story's sign coming out of the creek.

Bodie watched his friend ride off and turned Lakota Moon the opposite direction and scanned the bank as they trotted south.

A little over half-mile south of where he and Walt crossed the creek, Hickman caught sight of one fresh hoof print on the edge of a shale outcrop along the west bank of the creek—he smiled.

"Nice try, pilgrim," he mumbled. "Come on Moon, that track's not over ten minutes old...Slowed him quite a bit goin' down the creek." He squeezed the faithful Mustang into an easy rocking chair lope out of the bottom and up into some scattered prairie grass.

The tracks led to a wagon-cut ranch road with eight inch deep ruts from the last big thunderstorm. There was some relatively new two barb wire strung along both sides of the road a little over twelve feet from the ruts. Sparse grass grew between the wagon tracks, but Story was keeping well to the side to prevent Red Dawn from possibly bowing a tendon from a misstep in the rough road. Bodie easily followed the roan's tracks.

He rounded a sharp turn in the road as it followed property lines and came face to face with Story squatted underneath a large bois d'arc tree just outside the fence. He was puffing on a long black cheroot while his roan cropped some of the blue-stem grass growing nearby.

"Howdy," he said as he blew a cloud of blue smoke over his head. "Step down and have a smoke."

Bodie nodded. "I'll step down, but I don't smoke."

He left his reins looped around the horn so Moon could wander over to the thicker grass near the fence line and graze with Story's horse.

"You followin' me?"

"Could say that..." the ranger replied. "...if you're Tom Story."

"And just who might you be?"

"Bodie Hickman, Texas Ranger."

"Got paper on me?"

"Nope...but been trailin' you from the race up in Gainesville...You're good, give you that." Bodie stepped out to the center of the road. "Gotta take you in for suspicion of conspiracy to commit larceny, murder and attempted murder...not to say nothin' 'bout the stage robbery and multiple murder charges the Federal marshals want you for up in the Nations."

Story reacted like he'd been hit in the face. He threw his smoke to the ground and crushed it with the toe of his boot. "I don't think so," he hissed as he slowly backed away from the ranger until they were almost fifty feet apart.

"I take it you ain't comin' peaceable?"

"I believe I said that."

Story snatched his stag-handled Colt from its holster and fanned off three quick shots. Two missed entirely and the third tugged at the side of Hickman's coat.

Bodie calmly drew, turned in the classic dueler's stance with his pistol extended at arm's length and squeezed off one round. The bullet impacted Story just below the second button of his shirt. He had a brief puzzled look on his face before all the strength left his legs and he collapsed to the ground in a heap.

"There's a difference between being fast and being accurate, sunshine. Like Wyatt Earp said, 'Draw slow, but shoot straight'." He dropped his Colt back into the holster.

Bodie walked over and knelt down beside the dying man. "Money in yer saddlebags?"

Story slowly blinked, nodded and coughed up blood that dribbled down his chin. "Would you...you do me a fa...favor, Ranger?"

"Sure thing."

"Make sure somebody good gets Red Dawn and takes...takes care of...him. He's a fine...horse...Kinda par...partial to him."

"Count on it...Got just the perfect folks in mind. He'll be well took care of."

Story never heard him.

WEST COOKE COUNTY

Bennie stopped at a small creek a little over a mile and a half west of the small community of Collinsville, just at the county line and dismounted. He loosened the girth so his horse could drink and graze a little. Throwing his slouch hat on the ground, he knelt down, cupped his hands and sipped some of the branch water.

"Bennie."

He jumped to his feet, grabbing his gun from his pants as he spun around to face his father standing twenty-five feet behind him. "Didn't hear you come up, papa."

"I know. You wadn't meant to."

"I ain't goin' back with you."

"Ain't no choice, son...I got's paper on you." He held up the folded warrant, and then put it back in his coat pocket.

Bennie shook his head. "I cain't, papa...I jest cain't go to jail."

"You danced, boy...You got's to pay the fiddler."

He slowly pulled back the hammer on his .38 and shook his head again and raised it up arm level, pointed straight at his father. "I ain't gonna go."

Bass just stood there, his arms hanging loosely at his sides and with a stoic expression on his face. "You broke the law...Now, drop the gun...I don't want to have to kill you, son......."

Bennie looked at the gun in his hand for a long moment, dropped it to the ground and sunk to his knees. Bass stepped over to him and helped him to his feet. The young man threw both arms around his father and burst into sobs.

"I'm sorry, daddy...I'm so sorry," he said through his tears.

"I know, boy. It's gonna be alright...Gonna be alright." A tear rolled down Bass' cheek, too.

***

EPILOGUE

SKEANS BOARDING HOUSE

Bass carried Baby Sarah in his left arm and reached out to help Jack work his way up the steps with his crutches with his right. McGann's leg was still in a white plaster cast up to his knee.

"I can do it...ain't a invalid, you know," grumbled Jack.

"Faith and me thinks he's gettin' more like a grouchy ald bear by the day," commented Angie from his other side.

"You would too, woman, if you were stuck in the house from mornin' to dark."

"I am stuck in the house from mornin' to dark...With ye!...Black-hearted blatherskite," she added under her breath.

"You want I should go down to the drug store and get him some Yagoda's Bitters?" said Bodie as he held the gingerbread screen door open.

"You'll be wearin' one of these crutches wrapped around yer head if'n you don't watch yer mouth...Dadburn kid."

"It's not constipated ye godfather is, Bodie Hickman...it's his sour disposition," replied Angie as she pinched her husband on the butt.

"Ow...watch it woman."

"How do you tell the difference?" asked Bodie.

"That was a lovely baptism," commented Fiona to Francis Ann as she and the rest followed inside. She carried little Bass and Fran had Cassie Ann.

"I'm going to cry again," said Annabel as she followed them into the parlor.

"Another five months or so, we'll get to do this all over again," said Francis, looking down at her bulging abdomen.

"Dinner will be ready in just a bit. Ya'll make yourselves comfortable. Angie, you mind givin' me a hand?"

She stuck out her tongue at Jack. "It would be me pleasure, Fayedarlin'."

"That was outstanding Miz Faye...don't know that I've ever had better peach cobbler."

"Why thank you, Marshal Lindsey."

"I'll have another helpin'...if it's alright, Ma'am?"

"Certainly, Loss, pass your bowl back down this way." Faye took the glass lid off the cobbler.

"How did Bennie's trial go, Bass?"

He pursed his lips for a second before he answered, "Judge give him twenty years in Leavenworth, after reducin' the charge to manslaughter, Selden...I tol' him if'n he kept his nose clean he might could git out in four er five years...I was proud of him...He took it like a man."

"What did Doe Lee git?"

"Date with Maledon."

There was a knock at the front door.

"Would you get that, dear?" Faye asked of her long time suitor and Francis Ann's father, Tom Sullivant.

"Of course." He laid his napkin down as he got to his feet at the opposite end of the table from Faye and headed through the foyer to the front door.

"More tea, Fiona?"

"Oh, I'll get it, Faye...You've done enough." She stood and took her glass into the kitchen as Tom escorted a Western Union messenger into the dining room.

"Telegram for Marshal Reeves," the young man said as he whisked his short-billed baseball cap from his head.

Bass rose. "Here, son...Give it to this feller here." He handed him a silver dollar and indicated Jack, sitting next to him.

"Wow! Yessir, Marshal! Thank you," he exclaimed as he handed the flimsey to Jack, took out his small notebook and a stubby pencil and waited for a reply.

McGann pulled his wire-rimmed glasses from a vest pocket and hung them on his ears as Fiona came back in with her fresh tea. He looked up briefly at Bass as he opened the envelope and took out the thin yellow piece of paper and read it.

He looked at the messenger and shook his head, indicating to the boy that he could leave.

"Who's it from?" asked Bass with some concern.

Jack removed his glasses, took a deep breath, and then looked back at his longtime partner. "From Governor Clarke…Judge Parker died this mornin'."

There were several gasps and sighs from around the long table.

Bass finally spoke, "I knowed he'd been to home sick fer the last few weeks." He paused to blow his nose. "Was hopin' he'd git over it."

"He was a great man," said Fiona. "Just sitting in his office was daunting…He had an aura of truth and justice about him and could look a hole right through you."

"He could that," commented Selden.

"A great man…Suspect there'll be some changes coming down the pike," added Brushy Bill.

There was a long awkward silence as all in the room who had met the Judge reflected. Then Selden took it upon himself to change the subject to relieve the maudlin atmosphere.

"Well, Bass, I still say we got to have a real race between Dan and Blaze...after all, they finished neck an' neck." Selden wiped his mouth with his napkin.

"Well, they's one problem, Selden...Wadn't nobody on Dan at the time," said Bass.

"Not my fault." Loss rubbed his neck. "Throat's still a mite sore."

"May have to include Story's roan, since he's out at the ranch now," added Tom. "He's a fine animal."

Loss took the clue from Lindsey and turned to Walt sitting on the other side of the table to keep the general conversation going. "Gonna have to git you a banner to pin all yer badges on, Marshal Durbin," joked Loss, looking at the silver shield pinned to his vest.

"Acting Marshal...till Farmer gets back on his feet...but mayor Hatcher is prodding me about runnin' fer Sheriff. Said they were havin' a special election in sixty days," commented Walt. "And I'm back to bein' inactive with the Rangers."

"I think you'd make a fine County Sheriff, Walt," said Faye. "What are your plans, Fiona?"

She glanced over at Bill, and then at Bass. "I don't know...Feel kind of...Well, I don't know what I feel. Relief maybe…Still trying to come to grips with the fact that I don't have to chase that evil man anymore…Just wish…"

"Yeah…shame we couldn't find the body. He still had that thousand dollar reward on him, didn't he?" asked Bill.

Fiona nodded. "That wasn't as important as seeing him get his due…I would have just preferred seeing Maledon's rope around his neck instead of a bullet in his chest."

SOLDIER CREEK
CHICKASAW NATION

A large dark man with long dirty black hair rose up from a makeshift rope bunk in an abandoned clapboard shack near the bank of Soldier Creek—just before it joined with the Red on the Nations side of the river. He lifted a leaf and mud poultice and looked at the angry red wound next to his shoulder, and then did the same with the one on the lower part of his chest.

He scratched the long white scar that ran from his chin to his left ear and laid back down on the filthy bed. His black soulless eyes stared at the mud and branch ceiling in the shadows above his head and seemed to burn with all the fires of hell…

****

TIMBER CREEK PRESS

PREVIEW

OF THE NEXT
EXCITING NOVEL FROM

TIMBER CREEK PRESS

LADY WITH A BADGE

By

Ken Farmer

Sequel to
BASS AND THE LADY

CHAPTER ONE

SOLDIER CREEK
CHICKASAW NATION

The hand reached up out of the water and grabbed an exposed root from a cottonwood tree sticking out of the creek bank. With intense effort, the weakened man at the other end pulled most of his bedraggled body up onto the clay slope bordering Soldier Creek at its confluence with the Red River.

He lay on the bank, half-in and half-out of the muddy water, trying to catch his breath for several long moments. It came in ragged, gurgling spurts as he coughed up dirty water tinged with blood. Finally, he managed to roll over on his back where he could breathe better—although the breaths were short and choppy.

With some degree of effort, he raised his head to look at the hole in his once white shirt. The profuse amount of blood that had leaked from his body had long since washed away after almost ten hours in the river. He managed to tear the shirt away from the ragged bullet hole with his left hand. It was no longer bleeding, but he still reached over and grabbed a handful of rotted leaves and red clay, pressed it over the hole and pulled the torn shirt back. He got another fistful, reached under the shirt and mashed it into the second hole just below his collarbone.

He finally regained enough strength after resting for several hours to crawl completely out of the water and up on to the dry, leaf-covered forest floor that bordered the creek. He rested for awhile again, and then managed to get to his feet with help from a piece of hickory limb lying beside his leg.

He reached up and pushed the long black matted hair from in front of his eyes and slowly looked around at his surroundings. "Mankiller lives."

SKEANS BOARDING HOUSE
THREE WEEKS LATER

The beautiful, statuesque brunette in a black fitted single button morning coat, set her carpet bag on the porch and went back inside the stately Victorian house. She came back out a few seconds later with her black pencil-roll brimmed, flat-topped John B., accompanied by a slightly-built shorter man—she turned to him.

"I got my telegram from the Marshals Service in Washington."

Marshal Brushy Bill Roberts looked deep into her steel-gray eyes. "And?"

"They gave me permission to go unattached for as long as I want...It's a new program and that actually allows a Deputy US Marshal to roam anywhere in the States they are needed—reporting directly to Washington...with Special Deputy Marshal status."

Bill grinned and pulled out a white envelope from his inside coat pocket and handed it to Fiona.

She glanced at him with a puzzled expression, removed an official-looking document and read it. "Well, congratulations Special Marshal Roberts and welcome to our exclusive club...I suppose we should partner up."

"My thoughts exactly...Special Marshal Miller...So now what?"

"Well, first, we go to Fort Smith and pay our respects at Judge Parker's funeral with Bass and the others."

A look of pain crossed Bill's face. "I think I'm getting a bit tired of going to funerals."

Fiona nodded. "I know." She paused to allow him to gather himself as she knew he was still feeling somewhat depressed over the loss of Millie. "After that, we'll see where the wind blows."

"What about home base? We need a regular location to receive our list of trouble spots."

"Don't see anything wrong with Gainesville. We have plenty of friends here to forward notices when we're out and about...There's train service east, west, north and south, plus we have the Rafter S ranch available to rest our horses...and ourselves as the need arises."

"Agreed." Bill pulled out his gold pocket watch, opened the case to see the time. "Train leaves in an hour."

Fiona nodded. "Unusual watch," she said, looking at the filigreed cover.

"Gift from John Chisum when I worked for him over fifteen years ago in New Mexico."

"Nice...You knew Chisum started his cattle empire just twenty miles south of here."

"Didn't know that."

"His 'Big White House'...as it was called...was located in Bolivar and his brand was 'The Long Rail'. His stock was referred to as 'Jinglebob Ear' because of the unique cut on their ears."

"Now, I didn't know that, either."

"I understand he moved his operation to New Mexico in '66."

"Knew that...Just didn't know where he came from."

She grinned. "Now you do…Shall we go?" Fiona bent over to grab her bag, but Bill beat her to it. "Uh, uh, uh…No need to get in the habit of that…Carrying my bag is in the same category as calling me 'Ma'am.'"

"Point taken." He picked up his own bag and they walked out to the street where their horses—his Morgan, Tippy, and her Appaloosa, Diablo—were tethered to upright iron posts with rings on the top.

PICKENS COUNTY
CHICKASAW NATIONS

The Cherokee renegade stirred around inside the tiny abandoned fisherman's shack he had been holding up in while his wounds healed. He picked up the hickory limb he had used to get to his feet when he crawled out of Soldier Creek four weeks ago—more dead than alive. He looked down at the almost healed holes in his chest and nodded. "Cherokee medicine strong."

He slapped the stick across his palm, and then pushed the rickety door open—it was only hanging by one piece of leather from an old shoe.

Mankiller eased down the creek bank and pulled a narrow leaf from a cat tail. He tied it around his head to keep his long nasty hair from his face, turned and headed off through the woods to the northwest.

The sun was setting as he squatted down in a grove of sweet gum trees and watched the farm house. It was located on a narrow dirt road a little more than two miles south of Oakland.

After two previous farms he had watched, this was the first that didn't have a dog. Only a man—half Chickasaw and half black—his Creek wife and a preteen boy lived there. Mankiller waited with the patience known only to the Indian.

Three hours past dark, a gibbous moon had risen just above the tops of the trees. When the last lamp went out inside the house, he got to his feet and stealthily crept toward the back. He could make out a two foot diameter stump with a single-bit ax stuck in the top—obviously used for splitting kindling for a wood burning kitchen stove.

He easily pulled the blade free, checked its edge and dropped the hickory stick to the ground in favor of the ax. Pausing for a moment to make sure there were no sounds coming from inside, he crept up to an open window and quietly crawled through.

There was enough light from the spectral half-moon streaming through the windows, that he could make his way around the dinner table and to an open door. The Cherokee could see a coal oil lamp with just a hint of a burning wick on a table near a bed. It didn't shed any appreciable light, but there was enough flame that the owners only had to turn the wick up.

He could make out two adult forms on the bed underneath a patchwork quilt. Stepping to the edge, he raised the ax high with both hands and brought it down forcefully on the nearest form, splitting the man's head like a ripe watermelon. The sound of the blade striking his skull was loud enough to wake his wife with a start.

She sat bolt upright, saw the outline of Mankiller standing over the bed, the quilt and sheets already covered in blood from her husband. Her piercing scream split the night for a brief moment and stopped abruptly when the sideways swing of the ax caught her across the throat, completely severing her head from her body. The grisly body part bounced off the headboard and then to the floor on the opposite side of the bed with a thud.

Mankiller saw a single-barrel shotgun leaning against the wall between the night stand and the bed. He turned up the wick on the lamp, picked up the old weapon and checked the chamber—it was loaded.

"Mama?"

He spun around at the sound of the voice and pulled the trigger on the ten gauge. The twelve-year old boy in the doorway was blasted completely back into the other room with most of his face and chest completely obliterated by the full load of double-ought shot at close range.

"Stinkin' half-breed." The renegade looked at the bloodied body nearest to him on the bed and spat on it.

Opening the drawer in the night stand, he found four shells for the shotgun and slipped them into his pants pocket. He paused, took them back out, placed them and the gun on the blood-soaked bed, and then looked down at his ragged, filthy pants and shirt.

There was an old three-drawer chifferobe against the near wall. In the top were two pair of blue bib overalls and several chambray, one boiled off-white shirt and a red union suit. Mankiller held the overalls first and then one of the shirts up in the air.

"These do."

Thirty minutes later, Cal Mankiller walked away from the clapboard farm house in clean clothes, a gray slouch hat, the shotgun, five dollars and sixty cents he found in a jar in the kitchen and a flour sack of food stuffs.

Behind him the tongues of flames licking out from under the eaves and hungrily consuming the cedar-shingle roof cast an eerie flickering light on the surrounding woods.

"Now, Mankiller find she-devil marshal."

***

TIMBER CREEK PRESS